HARRY L. FORSM

ABSENCE

ABOUT LIFE,

LOVE, SEX AND

THE ARTIST

JEFFREY SMART

AND PEOPLE

AROUND HIM DURING

HIS FIRST YEARS

IN EUROPE

HARRY L. FORSMAN

ISBN: 978-1-64669-598-0

www.forsmanabsence.com

Sanningen är alltid oförsynt. (*The truth is always offensive*).
August Strindberg (1849–1912)

CHAPTERS

PART ONE: GREECE, 1964

I Apollo and Dionysus

A Divine Revelation 11

Squeezed in Nature's Mighty Fist 17

Surrounded by Darkness 28

A Lonely Dog's Seemingly Causeless Barking 35

Mercy Was Not on the Menu 42

II An Assortment of Assaults

Exterminating the Unwanted 53

Beautiful Boy 59

For a Little Boy, No Start in Life Can Be Better
Than His Daddy's Love 68

Little Lads and Carnal Love 78

Love Works in Mysterious Ways 88

The Pleasures of Poverty 97

Learn from the Queen: Shut Up, Accept and Smile . 109

The Happy Prince 120

Presence 131

III Disappearing into the Darkness

The Love that Dare Not Speak Its Name 133

Pure Business 146

Fellini May Have Heard of You 151

Time Stood Still When You Left 158

PART TWO: ITALY, 1965 – 1974

V High Society

Dirty Old Queen Elizabeth 163

In Mother Mary's Bosom. 173

Mimosas in Bloom 182

Was Baba the Turk a He or a She?. 188

Having Gorgonzola for Breakfast 196

Sweet Love of Youth 201

Arse and Art in the Uffizi – Advice to a Young Man . 206

Wild Strawberries Are Frightfully Exclusive. 214

VI Arrivederci, Roma

I'm Sitting Here Writing a Letter to My Sister . . . 225

Taut as a Bow Her Body Was About to Burst 230

Adjusted to a Small Enclosure 237

Sounds of Happiness by Stazione Termini 247

A Friendly Chat About Jeffrey Smart 252

Last Letter from Italy 259

VII Via Della Conciliazione Leads the Faithful
to the Holy Father

to the Holy Father 261

PART ONE:
GREECE, 1964

I
Apollo and Dionysus

A Divine Revelation

High above the village, on a tall cliff, stood the local monastery church. It was whitewashed all over with lime and water. The village congregation had assembled on the Eve of Easter Sunday to celebrate that Jesus Christ returned to life. It was close to midnight.

"Why do you turn your head all the time?" Justin whispered.

Jeff shrugged. "I've had a divine revelation. There, look. From heaven, I'm sure. He's an angel."

Justin shook his head. "No, Jeffrey, please. Show some respect. Not here, not now."

The boy who'd caught Jeff's attention was a blond exception in the dark-haired crowd. He was surely not a native, although like everybody else, he held a red-painted egg in one hand and a smouldering candle in the other. His presence was bewildering. Jeff and Justin hadn't seen a single foreigner on the island since they arrived this morning. So how did a lone blond angel find himself in this house of worship in the middle of the night? And what could prompt him to land on this ignored and godforsaken spot on earth? A thin, blond beard struggled to grow on his chin. To Jeff this signalled an emotional involvement might cause more anguish than euphoria. And he looked young. Better stay away, or at least be careful if they ever met.

But Jeff's misgivings didn't bother Nature; it lured him with its promise of that overwhelming reward, central in the life of men. So, there he stood with his throat choked by longing and an erection he'd never asked for.

The church bell rang its twelve strokes and now the congregation knew for certain that Jesus Christ had resurrected. Christianity's holiest day of the year had begun. The crowd rushed out of church and ran jubilantly down the village's steep and narrow stone-clad footpaths shouting *"Christós anésti!"*[1] Men and women embraced each other as dearest brothers and sisters and congratulated each other for their salvation. *Christós anésti!* Jesus Christ himself had cared to save them and forgive them for their small and even dreadful deeds.

On the way down the cliff to the little cottage they were renting by the sea, sweat poured down Justin's wrinkled and unshaven face. "I'm pleased we walked all the way up to the monastery," he said. "Aren't you?"

"It was interesting," Jeff said. "As I see it, the poor sods celebrate a father's brutal killing of his son. But I'm sure they're happy in their primitive delusion."

"Yes, very happy, I'm sure," Justin said, and they continued their march downhill. As they approached the sea and their new little home for the summer, they saw the crust upon the waves twinkling in the starlight.

At home, Justin got a bottle of local Retsina wine in the kitchen and poured himself a large glass and lit a cigarette.

"A drink?" Justin asked,

"Give me a small glass, I'll go to bed soon," Jeff said.

---

1 Christ has risen!

They sat on their little terrace, looking over the Aegean Sea. The dark night was sparsely lit by millions of distant stars in a perfectly clear sky. A light and tepid breeze swept over the landscape. The sea was striking the sandy shore with long, slow waves.

"You're very quiet."

"Yes, I am." Justin lit another cigarette and emptied a second glass of wine. "In church, when I see these people, and even afterwards, see them trust without question …" He sighed. "I miss my old faith. It harmed me but it was also a blessing."

"There's no way back now, is there?" Jeff asked.

"No, I don't think so. I regret nothing. Yet I lack something— trust, commitment. And to be forgiven."

"Forgiven? What for?"

"I don't know," Justin said. "Everything? I remember as a child, I was always forgiven after Holy Confession. And this forgiveness gave me an inner peace."

"You still say holy?"

"That's what we called it. Confession was a sacrament. Nothing else."

"Do you harbour resentment towards me for this?" Jeff asked.

"No. I don't."

Jeff kept his gaze firmly fixed at where the black sky met the black sea. He could hardly discern the horizon. He slowly turned his head and looked in Justin's direction without meeting his gaze.

"Did you see the boy in church?" Jeff asked.

Justin coughed. "No."

"He seemed forlorn."

"Yes," Justin said after a while. "Maybe he was."

"He had a sunburn, so he must have been here for quite some time," Jeff said.

"Yes, maybe."

"If he's here alone, what kind of parents would let their child go alone to Greece and to this sordid place?"

Justin blew smoke into the night air.

"He didn't seem sure of himself," Jeff said, "despite his good looks."

"Yes, you're probably right."

"A boy of troubles, you think? A suffering soul in a beguiling body?"

"The kind you like," Justin said. "Be careful, Jeffrey, we're here to work."

"If he's alone on this miserable island," Jeff continued, "something must have brought him here. I saw pain in the young lad's eyes. I wonder if anybody else would notice, or was it only me?"

"Sorry, I didn't look."

Jeff stood up. "Don't drink too much, mate. Must be able to hold your brushes tomorrow, you know." He went into his room and shut the door.

"Christ, if he could mind only his own fucking business," Justin grumbled. He had another glass of wine and began to pass out on his chair. He staggered into his room and fell flat on his narrow bed. Within a second, he was asleep, still in his clothes. The burning cigarette in his hand fell to the tile floor and extinguished.

After dreaming, planning, and saving money for two decades, in December 1963 the two artists were ready to leave Australia. They boarded P&O's transatlantic ocean liner, the SS *Arcadia*, in

Sydney for a month-long voyage to London before continuing by land to Greece.

Before this decisive exit from their motherland, they could only afford to paint in their spare time. Justin worked as a teacher; Jeff wrote articles and made broadcasting and TV programs. Now they would dedicate their whole days to painting and hopefully make successful careers.

When Justin was in Greece as a young soldier during World War II, the barren, angular hills of the Greek islands mesmerised him. Now he was back on an island to paint those hills and mountains. He was pleased to be back and felt at home and comfortable in their whitewashed little cottage with its three small rooms and a terrace overlooking both the sea and the huge cliff that the houses of the nearby village were scattered across.

As for Jeff, living in a fisherman's cottage with no running water and no electricity was most definitely not to his taste. He landed on this backward island with Justin, his vocational brother for the past fifteen years, only because Justin wanted to stay in this place, and for no other reason. Jeff looked forward to autumn, when they would move to Rome.

Jeff had brought two comforting transitional objects from Australia. One was his own genuine duck down pillow, to give him a tiny bit of comfort at least at night. The other was T. S. Eliot's *Four Quartets* and also *The Waste Land*. He hoped Eliot would bring him the sophistication and relief he needed in this archaic, uncivilised world where they still lived with customs inherited from the Ottoman Empire. The *Four Quartets* awaited him every night on his bedside table as a necessary substitute for the inspiring human company whose scarcity he lamented.

Tonight, he read a long passage from *The Waste Land* and found lines he could relate to his present condition, painting "the primitive" in a more esoteric form:

The road winding above among the mountains
Which are mountains of rock without water
If there were water, we should stop and drink
Amongst the rock one cannot stop or think
Sweat is dry and feet are in the sand
If there were only water amongst the rock
Dead mount in mouth of carious teeth that cannot spit
Here one can neither stand nor lie nor sit
There is not even silence in the mountains
But dry sterile thunder without rain

Lying on his bed, he read the lines and then read them once again with tears in his eyes. Would he see him again? The vision of that boy up in the church lingered in his mind. He had a strange feeling, as if he needed him, just to go on, a person he had never seen before, just a stranger in the night. Nature's bloody whims were trying to make him a victim again. But he needed to stay firm and not be shaken by emotions. *Come scoglio immoto resta,*[2] the aria by Mozart and da Ponte, was a major beacon in his life, which encouraged him not to let feelings unstable him.

He decided to get up and take a walk on the waterfront and take in the night's breezes. Instead he breathed in and out deeply and slowly and fell asleep with Eliot's thin little book still in his hand.

---

2 As a rock stands solid

Squeezed in Nature's Mighty Fist

At daybreak, the crows from a neighbour's rooster woke up the new inhabitants. The sun was shining, the sea was blue and calm. The peaceful washing of the waves against the sandy shore welcomed them to a calm and gentle world.

Justin came out on the terrace on unsteady legs, coughing and red eyed, with a burning cigarette in his mouth. He placed two crude and chipped cups on a wobbly table in the middle of the terrace and heated water in a dented metal pot on the gas stove. They had no bread so the two shortbread cookies they had tucked away at the hotel yesterday served as breakfast this first morning in their new home.

Jeff had woken up two or three times in the night after a both enticing and forbidding vision from a dream. There was a boy, alone in the crowd that filled a room dedicated to pagan worship. He was an angel who could take the role of either a delightful ornament or a ball and chain for whoever dared to attach him to his life. His hair was blond and silky, washed each day by the salty Aegean Sea, then bleached by the same golden sun that shone equally on Apollo and Dionysus, one the god of order and reason, the other of chaos and emotion. His skin was soft and light brown, his lips filled with a desire to kiss and be kissed. His slim teenage body longed for affectionate and lecherous hands to feel delight in it.

Should he get up, or linger in this fantasy of corporal elation? His body yearned to linger but in reality, there was only one choice. Too much pleasure leads to destruction, while work and order are a more secure road to future victories. He rose, pleased to have triumphed over Nature.

The artists sat in silence on the terrace and looked over the blue sea in front of them. Justin coughed and rubbed his eyes. There was only a single tea bag, which they shared. They nibbled on their tiny pieces of shortbread.

A young boy approached on a small donkey shouting *"Psomí!"* He jumped down and led the animal to the edge of their terrace. *"Psomí!"* he shouted again and took out a piece of bread from a big bag. Fresh bread, still warm and fragrant from the oven.

"What a heavenly smell. What's he saying? Piss on me?"

"He looks so sweet," Justin said. "I think he wants to sell bread."

They bought two lumps of bread and managed to communicate to the boy he should come back the next day. The boy repeated the word *psomí* several times, and they assumed this was Greek for bread.

"He was indeed pretty," Jeff said, "this piss-on-me boy, and I saw you fancied him. I would suggest we are very careful how we behave towards the natives."

"What the bloody hell are you saying this for?"

"Oh, please, don't have an Irish fit. I only suggest we should be careful. Especially with the very young ones. A reasonable stance, isn't it?"

Justin got up from the table. With shaky hands he managed to pull a strong Turkish cigarette out of the package. Still shaking, he put the cig in his mouth, lit it and inhaled.

Jeff took his teacup to the washing basin. He checked the small water tank above the bowl. There was no water.

"They should fill the water containers every morning, didn't we agree on this?"

"Yes, I think so," Justin said.

"So why is there no water? I have to tell them. What a nuisance."

"It's early, Jeffrey. Have a little patience. As soon as they see we're up the girls will come and make our beds and sweep the floor."

"We've been up for over half an hour."

"It's still early."

"I hate when people don't do what they're supposed to do."

Jeff walked over to their landlord, who had moved out of their home to let it to the foreigners and now lived with his wife and three teenage daughters in a nearby one-room shack. Jeff clarified what he expected from them: fresh water every morning as soon as they got up and both their rooms cleaned. He was strict but respectful. To have positive relations with the natives was essential.

In the late afternoon, the artists walked the long and steep way up to the village to try the local cuisine in what was the village's only restaurant at this early time of the year. An unadorned room with eight rough wooden tables greeted them, as did heaps of dead flies in the cobwebbed windowsills.

A young lad put a pottery jug of local red wine on their table and mumbled something in Greek.

"*Kalispéra*,"[3] Justin said, exhausting his Greek vocabulary. The young boy responded with a smirk and Justin stuck out his tongue at him.

3 Good evening

"There's no menu!" Jeff exclaimed. "And they understand nothing but bloody Greek. Should we leave?"

"There's no other place to go to, Jeffrey. Be patient. We'll get something." Justin lit a cigarette and kept an eye on the young lad, busy with minor duties at the tables while repeatedly scratching his behind.

"I don't have patience to wait for all eternity. And for what?"

The restaurant door swung open and the boy from church walked in. He was alone. Maybe he saw them but did not look their way. Jeff forgot about ordering. He was sure he had never seen him before last night, yet there was something familiar about him. Watching him turned Jeff's body into uproar. Quickened heartbeat. Shortness of breath. Parched mouth. Agitated private parts and stomach.

The boy was smiling as he talked to a pair of men having a drink at a table near the door. How beautiful he was. Last night Jeff saw a glimpse of sorrow in his eyes. Pain and beauty, young and innocent and in need for love. Appetising, for sure, but not now and not here.

Jeff looked out of the window and took a deep breath to clear his head. He had a sip of wine. Nature had returned to play its usual tricks and spoofs, and then leave him stranded with an intolerable agony if he wasn't careful. He could let this pass. Love was overestimated. One could live one's life well enough without.

But then Jeff's bold determination to remain solid as a rock was shattered. The necessary cautions in courting he adopted from his studies of Freud and German philosophers were reduced to dust by just a second look at the face of this captivating adolescent boy. Pleasure flooded in and promised more if he were smart enough. His underpants were sticky. In love, for sure, but horny too. Was there a difference? He could not be bothered. One thing was clear—his need for another was stronger than he had assumed in his preparations for a safe and decent life. Now he was squeezed in Nature's mighty fist. And it was such a pleasure.

His body had chosen for him; there was no more need to fret. He was alive. What more was there to ask for? He wanted him; he had to have him. But this route could do him harm and he would need to take precautions.

He cleared his throat and took a sip of wine, prepared to act.

"Justin, please. Tell the foreign youngster down by the door we don't know how to order. We need his help."

"Why not go yourself? Are you all right? You look peaked."

"Please, Justin dear. I beg you."

"I hate when you get bloody weak."

Justin took a huge gulp of the warm Retsina wine, wiped his mouth and plodded over to the rye-blond lad by the door.

"I'm sorry to trouble you," Justin said. "Do you by any means speak English and do you know how to order here?"

"Yes, I do," the boy said with a slight foreign accent.

Justin did not recognise the boy from church; he had not cared to look. Now the boy's light-blue eyes looked at him as if there were no filter between them. At once he realised, he never looked at people in this way or they at him. Was this boy fearless? Too young and immature to know the perils of the strangers of this world or how to make himself protected?

Justin returned to their table, emptied his glass of wine, lit a cigarette, and inhaled deeply.

The boy waved at him to follow into the kitchen. At a large

stove, the cook opened his pots one by one. Letting the customer have a look at his cooking served as the menu for non-locals. Arbitrarily chopped-up chunks of flesh of uncertain origin bobbed in greasy sauces of various hues. Justin was not tempted.

"You learn to get used to many things here," the boy commented when he noticed Justin's grim frown.

"Would you give us some good advice? My friend and I have just arrived. Would you care to join us?"

"I'd love to. I've been alone for quite some time; my Greek is poor, you see."

"Excuse my friend for having bothered you," Jeff said when Justin and the boy sat down. "I'm Jeffrey." He let out a nervous laugh.

"Here in Greece they know me as Léon, easier to say than Lennart," the boy said.

"What do we call you?" Jeff asked.

"Call me Simon. I don't like my name."

"Why not Léon, closer to your real name?"

"As you wish, but I prefer Simon. Lennart is only for official papers. Simon I like and I have chosen it myself."

"Ok, Simon then, unofficially."

"Will you stay for long?" Simon said.

"Half a year, if nothing happens," Jeff said.

"Oh, so long! Foreigners usually stay only a day or two; I'm pleased to have met you. Why are you here?"

"We're artists and we're here to work," Jeff said.

"I do a little painting myself, but only watercolour. Abstracts. I splash water and colour on things. Can I have a little of your wine?"

"Sure, here." Jeff poured Simon a glass, which he swallowed in one swig.

"Are you an art student?" Jeff asked.

"No, painting is only for pleasure. I read a lot. And scribble when my spirit moves."

Jeff had to restrain himself not to laugh out loud. "What do you scribble when your spirit moves?"

"Whatever comes to mind. No real plan. A poem yesterday, I think. Not in English, so I can't show you."

There was a long pause.

"Do you know T. S. Eliot?" Jeff asked. He did not think that fate could be so gracious. But if the boy said yes then Jeff would know that he had met his destiny. The fever burnt his cheeks.

"No, sorry. I know his name, but I don't read English poetry. But my French is quite good, so I can recite a poem in French if you like?"

"A poem you've written?" Jeff said.

"No, please. Don't think too much of me." He laughed, refilled his glass of wine, and helped himself to one of Justin's cigarettes.

Jeff smiled. "My French has become rusty in recent years."

"Doesn't matter. It's nice even if you don't understand. This poem is by Verlaine, what he sees and thinks in jail, after having tried to shoot the one he loved." The boy stood up and recited slowly, with his arms and hands underlining the words:

Le ciel est, par-dessus le toit,
Si bleu, si calme!
Un arbre, par-dessus le toit,
Berce sa palme.

La cloche, dans le ciel qu'on voit,
Doucement tinte.
Un oiseau sur l'arbre qu'on voit,
Chante sa plainte.
Mon Dieu, mon Dieu, la vie est là,
Simple et tranquille.
Cette paisible rumeur-là
Vient de la ville.

- Qu'as-tu fait, ô toi que voilà
Pleurant sans cesse,
Dis, qu'as-tu fait, toi que voilà,
De ta jeunesse?

Jeff watched the youngster's mouth as he recited, his full lips, his pink tongue, and brilliant white teeth. Oh dear, what a sweet angel. Those light-blue eyes mesmerised him. This was no ordinary boy, he seemed not to be afraid of anything—and what's more, he cared about poetry. And he was gorgeous. Jeff wanted him. Would he love Eliot?

The artists applauded as did one or two of the local guests. Outside, a gang of younger boys watched them, their faces pressed against the windows.

"Look at all the kids," Justin said. "What are they looking at? Us?"

"To look at foreigners," Simon said, "is entertainment for the kids and then to get something out of them if they're lucky."

"Interesting," Justin said. "Many faces there for me to paint."

"What was this poem about?" Jeff asked.

"Passion, and where passion may take you if things go wrong," Simon said.

Jeff was silent.

"I want to ask for more wine." Simon looked at Justin. "You?"

"Yes, do that, please," Justin said.

"Can you pay for another jug? I didn't take enough drachma with me."

Justin smiled. "Sure, no problem."

They had their meal—a bony stew supposedly of lamb, but more likely goat. The artists invited the youngster to be their guest.

"Why alone on a Greek island, this early in the year, citing poetry of passion in French?" Jeff said with a cheeky smile.

"I needed to be free and get away from things at home and be myself."

"Things at home, I see. Isn't it dangerous here? If you live alone? You look so young."

"Sometimes you must pay a high price for being yourself and not like others. Any artist would know this, yes?"

"That's wise, coming from such a young man."

Simon chuckled.

"What does your father want you to do in life?" Jeff asked. "Be different and read French poetry of passion alone on a Greek island?"

"My father?" Simon looked taken aback. "He doesn't give a shit." He shook his head. "Can I have one of your cigarettes, Justin? I left mine at home."

"Of course, dear boy," Justin said. "They're all yours if you like them."

"Doesn't he have ambitions for his son, your father?" Jeff persisted. "Most fathers do, don't they?"

"Do they? I don't know. But why do you ask about him? No, he doesn't care what I do." Simon lit one of Justin's Turkish cigarettes. "Not a fucking bit, if you want to know." He frowned and looked away.

Jeff was excited. His prey had received his bullet in the centre of the most tender part of his chest. Simon would be so much easier to handle now that he had located the wound.

"But your mother cares, I'm sure. Very proud of you, isn't she?"

"That's an entirely different story. If she could guess where I am, and if she could command them, she would send the whole army to bring me back to her." Simon coughed; the Turkish cigarette was strong. "They call this maternal love, I think, or some bloody fucking shit like that."

Their conversation fell silent. Each fought alone with thoughts and emotions he was not able to express off hand. They lit their cigarettes and began to smoke before they had finished their meal.

"This place is charming," Jeff said. "And the food was excellent. What a joy to be here. I'm sure we will return soon. Don't you agree, Justy?"

Justin smirked. "Oh, you liked it? I'm happy to hear."

"We'd like to see you in our place," Jeff said. "Why not come down and join us for dinner tomorrow night?"

"I can't promise," Simon said, "but if nothing keeps me in the village, I would be glad to come. When?"

"We stop working at six o'clock sharp and have drinks. If a little aperitif would please you, you're welcome to be there at six. Or any other time that would please you."

In the early evening of next day, excited and with mixed

expectations, Simon hurried down the steep and winding road to the little rented cottage where the Aussies lived, near the white windmill on a small isthmus of the Molos, as that part of the seashore was called.

More than one or two drinks for the road sloshed about in his empty stomach. He hoped they would eat soon and that these ancient men would not want to be too friendly with him. You could never be sure about single men coming to these islands.

Surrounded by Darkness

When Simon arrived at ten minutes to seven Jeff was newly shaved, and an unmistakable whiff of cologne impregnated the air on the terrace. He came out on the sand and kissed Simon on both cheeks. He was dressed in his best evening leisurewear and was all smiles and pleasant words.

The youngster was late, but they still had time for a drink before dinner.

"How did you end up on this miserable dump?" Jeff asked.

"By accident," Simon said. "And now I haven't got the money I would need to leave. Wouldn't know where to go anyway, so I stay, and I wait."

"Waiting for what?"

"For someone to come along and bring order into my life."

"On this backward island?"

"Not necessarily. It's a starting point. Next week I may be living with an oil prince in Arabia, who comes here and discovers I'm the one he wants as a companion." Simon smiled when he saw Jeff believed his ironic words.

"Good luck," Jeff said and thought about his wealthy friend Mic in Rome, the president of British Petroleum in Italy. Not a prince and not in Arabia, but petrol ticked the box.

Justin, who had been silent since their young guest arrived, also thought of Mic and hoped for God's sake the boy would not end up with him and become a brat.

They enjoyed a lavish meal together, chicken flambéed in brandy, Jeff's own speciality. Time moved towards nightfall and the sun set behind the hilltops.

The rustic scene on the little terrace was dimly lit by their only kerosene lamp. The rusty lantern hung from one of the slender rods put up over the terrace to allow the hops to grow freely and form a leafy roof. Toads were belching. An aroused donkey was hee-hawing nearby. A string orchestra made up by thousands of cicadas was howling and filling the dark air with its love sound. Here they got to know each other, surrounded by fierce sounds and strong odours from the sea.

"Why this island?" Justin asked. "Nobody has heard of it, and it's awkward to get here."

"I was sent by the police."

Jeff seemed amused. "Oh dear. Deported? For bad behaviour?"

Simon laughed. "I lived in Chalkida and had to leave fast as lightning. So I rushed into nearest police station and asked if they could recommend an island, and I had to leave at once. The constable in charge wrote me a letter of introduction to his friend the chief of police on this island, so I went here. I saw he liked me, so I trusted him. Men like each other here, and they're not afraid to show it. They're close to each other compared to men in our countries. Sometimes too close."

There was a pause before Simon continued.

"There's always someone who's friendly in ways you never see at home. A young soldier even gave me money for food and a cheap hotel room for the night when I was stranded in Athens. And soldiers are not well paid."

"And he wanted in return …?"

"Nothing. We saw each other in the railway station. He was on his way to his family in Thessaloniki. He liked me, I guess. He saw I was in distress and asked me if I had a problem. I told him I had no money and knew nobody in Athens, and he helped me."

"He saw you, blond and beautiful, and he was smitten, poor chap."

"Poor chap? I don't think he was poor. He made me happy, both for the money and for his care. And I saw that he was also happy to make me happy. Is that to be poor? I thought it was a kind of sweet and innocent love, the kind I need."

They laughed, each for his own reason and stared into the darkness that surrounded them, drinking and smoking. A constant roaring from the waves that washed up on the beach and crushed on distant cliffs echoed through the darkness.

"Did you like this brandy?" Jeff asked.

"I appreciate when drinks are for free," Simon said.

"Yes, but take it easy. It's a steep walk back to the village."

"I know my limits, except when I go out and dance."

"Well, there's no dancing here."

"Oh, yes. Every Sunday evening every café is crowded with guys dancing. No women. Only guys."

"You dance with men?" Jeff said. "That's unusual, to say the least. I've never seen men dance with each other in all my life. Where I come from, in Sidney, Australia, men are forbidden to dance with each other, even in bars where there are only men."

"It's common here. It's not exactly foxtrot cheek to cheek, more male bonding. We form a line of guys together, arms around each other's shoulders. The guys who sit and watch buy drinks for dancers they like. A waiter comes up to you with the glass on a tray. You must drink all at once to show gratitude to the person who paid and put the empty glass back on the tray. They buy me drinks till I almost can't keep standing on my feet."

"Sounds vile."

"They want me to be so drunk I can't resist them." Simon sipped on his brandy.

"Resist them? In what sense?"

"They want to fuck me."

"Didn't you like my attempt to make Turkish coffee?" Justin asked. "I don't think either of you even tried it."

"It was fine," Jeff said. "So, you were dancing and drinking, or what? And then they want to fuck you?"

"Don't you know about this?" Simon asked. "Greeks fuck young boys as much as in ancient times, at least here in the countryside. And young boys fuck each other. They form couples in their early teens. *Masí*, together, they say and make a sign by putting left and right index fingers close to each other. The sign shows they're together as a couple, and everybody knows one is buggering the other."

"And after dancing, when you're smashed, you get raped, is this what you say?"

"Not exactly raped, I guess … but … I don't know."

"You *guess* you don't get raped? Oh, my dear."

"If I don't want to, I kick their legs and try to run away. Most times I succeed getting them off of me."

"And sometimes you want to? Is that what you say?"

"Well, want … that's rare. I let it happen. But only sometimes."
They were silent.

Justin stood up. "I'll go to bed now." He shook hands with

Simon then bent down and gave him a gentle kiss on the cheek.

"Let's go to my room," Jeff said, "so we can talk without disturbing Justin."

The youngster took another sip and went around the corner on wobbly legs to have a pee. Jeff heard him urinating on the sand for a long time. They went into Jeff's room and he shut the door behind them, then filled Simon's empty glass.

They talked for an hour or two, mostly about Simon's life at home and here in Greece.

"It's getting late," Jeff said. "It would be … inconvenient for you to walk all the long and dark way up to the village now, wouldn't it? Would you be safe?"

"As long as I don't meet someone who knows me."

Jeff lay down on his bed and patted the space beside him. "Come, you can lie here beside me. We're both getting tired, aren't we?"

"Yes, I'm tired." Simon sipped his brandy. "Can I test one of your cigarettes?" He lay down on the bed and Jeff shifted to give him room.

"Sure, here."

As Simon smoked, Jeff moved closer and put a hand on the boy's chest.

"You'll be better off with me than with a stranger out there in the dark. How old are you? I haven't asked. I'm sure you must be older than you look."

"I'm old enough, I guess. I need to blow my nose, you have a paper or something?"

"Here, take this. You can sleep here, son. Perhaps you may even let me embrace you a little?"

"If you wish. But don't call me son and don't kiss my mouth. I don't want that."

"I'll make it pleasant for you. You're such a sweet kid, I like you so much."

"I need that." Simon sighed and took another sip of his brandy. "Hunger for love is my problem."

"As for everyone, I suppose," Jeff said. "The demand exceeds supply, and economics is a dismal science."

"What?"

"When the demand exceeds supply the seller can name his price. Like with diamonds or emeralds, rubies and sapphires."

"I'm too tired to think, sorry."

"Let me take off your shirt." Jeff's voice cracked. "Are you still comfortable?" Half of Jeff's mind urged him to be prudent with his young guest. He was in love after all, whatever being in love meant. The other half of his mind burned with pure lust.

"I will kiss you with a lot of … affection." His voice cracked again. "My gentle boy, how compelling you are."

He kissed Simon on his cheek, then on his neck, then on his chest, then on his naked stomach, breathing in the fragrance of the boy's half-erect cock. He had not touched it yet.

But kissing the boy was not enough. Jeff's love asked for more. Tethered between the wild stallions of prudence in one of his legs and of pure carnal urge in the other, a barbarous death stared him in the face. Both stallions galloped furiously in opposite directions. He had to untie at least one chain, or he would be torn into bloody shreds of human flesh.

But he even so wavered. Prudence saw the boy as vulnerable and so alone, a trinity of an adult mind in a young man's body with the emotions of a child, but his dazed mind no longer cared. Nature was strong and promised a magnificent gratification if only he would follow its demands and not care too much about his conscience.

The slow and soft physical intimacy of his host's approach aroused the boy and eventually, he was properly sodomised. Not that Jeff needed to insist. The boy was drunk and tired and half asleep. Jeff's lovemaking manifested itself with the same urgency as coughing when you have an irritation in your throat. There was no sign of an overwhelming emotional experience, only relief of sexual tension, nothing more.

And so on the third day after Nature, or was it a god, presented the boy to him, Jeff consumed the love he had wanted since Easter Saturday, the only day of the liturgical year when Christ is dead.

Simon turned his back to Jeff, pleased the act had not been painful and long-lasting, so he could go to sleep. If only there had been another bed to sleep in.

A Lonely Dog's Seemingly Causeless Barking

After a few hours' sleep, Jeff was awakened by a dog's seemingly causeless barking. He passed over the terrace as the sun sneaked up over the horizon and noticed how the many little rises in the sand threw shadows over the ground and coloured it pink. He went into the kitchen and prepared breakfast for the three of them.

"Did he go home?" Justin asked when he came out of his room.

"I've made us a proper feast," Jeff said, sweeping his hand toward the lavish breakfast table he had just laid. There was shredded orange marmalade, strawberry jam, cheddar cheese from England, black Greek olives, slices of fresh tomatoes, soft-boiled eggs, fresh figs, a big jar of cold orange juice, a tin of Dutch pasteurised milk, cold butter and toasted piss-on-me.

"Think of it," Jeff said. "Just yesterday we had nothing. Today is another day, and we have everything a man could want. Not because of luck, not because of some godly grace, but due to my decision to give us something, and my efforts to do so. You can see this table, Justy, as a manifestation of my belief and conviction. The same as with our work here: on our canvases there is nothing until we create something of value with resolution and boldness."

"All credit to you, Jeffrey, with my undivided appreciation. Did you hear my question?"

"Eh?"

"Did he go home?" Justin repeated.

"No. He's still here. Asleep, I think."

"In the guest room?"

"In my bed."

"Oh, is that how it is?" Justin reached for one of his Turkish cigarettes, lit it and inhaled. "Very well."

"I feel like I'm newly reborn, Justy! Everything looks different. The colours, the trees, the sky!" He took a few steps in a dance. "Oh, what a won-der-ful moooorning, oh what a beau-ti-ful daaaay," he sang.

"I know the feeling," Justin sighed.

"I feel like a teenager again."

"Shouldn't you wake him up, so he can have his breakfast with us?"

"Let the poor boy sleep. He's had a rough time." Jeff went into the kitchen to get the teapot.

"I bet he has," Justin mumbled.

They sat down at the table.

"He's a wonderful chap. But strange, he's like an old man and a young child in one." Jeff sliced himself a big chunk of cheddar. "But I'm so happy."

Justin coughed. "It's gone that far? Oh, dear."

"There's something wild about him, or desperate. He travelled three days and three nights from his home in the icy north and arrived in Athens late at night. He had no hotel booking and he didn't know anybody. Imagine a beautiful blond young teenager, alone at night in a tough city where he doesn't know the language. He had awful experiences, he was robbed and abused, and they cheated him."

"Oh, dear."

"He's a lovely human being, not like those boys, you know, self-obsessed, mannered, haughty and God knows what. He's not like them; he's different and a pleasure to be with."

"And he loves you?"

"Justin, please! How can you ask such a question? I'll tell you what I think: my Easter vision in the monastery church was a real angel."

"Be careful, Jeffrey. Losses in matters of the heart—or dick, if you don't mind—can be bloody hurtful and damaging, as you well know." Justin stubbed his cigarette on the plate, and it sizzled as its glow was extinguished in the grease.

"I know, I know. I'm careful. I won't end up in deep water that's for sure." Jeff went into the kitchen to make more fresh tea.

"See you 'n' teeeea," he shouted when Simon came out on the terrace.

"Why do you shout like that?" Simon asked.

"C-U-N-T—cunt—like we used to say as kids."

"And you still do?"

"Yes, just for a bit of fun. Justin loves it. Shout see you 'n' tea and he will smile and be invigorated. He's a bit simple minded, poor Justy." Jeff served the boy a nice cup of tea and toasted him two pieces of piss-on-me.

"Would you like anything else?" Jeff asked. "I can boil an egg for you if you want?"

"No, it's fine. You've given me the best breakfast I've had for months, even years."

"Glad to hear that. How are you feeling?"

"I'm fine, just a bit of a hangover. How wonderful to live in a place like this! "

"Why thank you, Simon."

"Jeff, last night, I don't remember so well, did you say you would buy me rubies or sapphires or something?"

"No!" Jeff laughed. "I mentioned them only as examples of the wealth people can acquire if they possess something others may want to have. I don't have such resources. You'll have to wait for your Arab prince."

"Brian got a job in Rome!" Justin came out to the terrace with a letter in his hand. "Listen, Jeffrey. Isn't this lovely! We can live together in Rome! All three of us."

"Who's Brian?" Simon asked.

"Brian was my boyfriend for ten happy years," Justin said. "I was kind of a daddy for him, I suppose, and gave him at least a little stability in life, which he lacked as a child. And a lot of love, I hope. I still love the boy, even if he's a grown-up young man by now."

"How old is he?"

"Twenty-four, twenty-five something. I don't remember exactly? Jeffrey, how old is Brian?"

"He'll be twenty-six in October. The tenth."

"Last December," Justin said, "just before we left Australia, he told me he's straight. So no more sex. But he had never fucked a girl! So how the bloody hell can he say he's fucking straight? After ten years with me. Don't you think that's strange?"

"Not really," Simon said. "He didn't change in a day, I suppose, but went through a process. I know how it can be."

"You know? How can you know that?"

Simon reached for Justin's package of cigarettes. "You're happy to have had a love relationship for ten years. I haven't managed for a single day."

"You're young, there's time enough for you. I was still a fucking virgin when I was thirty-four. I didn't even masturbate, mind you." Justin laughed and lit a cigarette.

"And now?"

"Twelve years ago, Jeffrey gave me a book about Darwin. Then we had many long talks, Jeffrey and I. Eventually, I renounced the Church, left God and Jesus, and replaced them with booze and promiscuity."

"At times you must act as a broom," Jeff said, "and sweep the dross out of your friends' minds."

Justin smirked. "Yes, thanks to Jeffrey's heart-warming intervention I'm clean now, as everybody can see."

"From what I've seen of the sketches in your room, you still paint pictures of events in the Bible."

"I paint from my past, when these stories were a reality. *The Presentation of the Virgin in the Temple*, or *The Entombment of Jesus*. Even if I've lost my faith, I've kept my feelings for that faith, which the young man had, whom I was. And the child."

Justin sighed and was silent. "Do you understand anything of this?"

"Yes, I do," Simon said. "I think I do. You still live with something you believed in despite you found everything was a lie. Poor Justin."

"You're so sweet, Simon. I wish you all the good in life. Fifteen bloody years ago, I would have said I would pray for you. Now I can offer nothing more than a fucking impotent good wish."

"To me there's no difference, so that's okay." They laughed.

"Have a cig." Justin pushed the pack across the table.

After lunch the three of them went to a little beach behind dunes some hundred yards away, where the artists had begun to take regular rest after lunch. They would sunbathe on the fine sand and swim behind the reef or in the little lagoon created between the reef and the shore. At four they gathered on the terrace and had a nice cup of tea. Then Simon strolled the beach while the artists worked.

At six o'clock sharp they all had drinks and then visited the little outdoor restaurant, Kokalénia, two hundred yards down the beach with six tables in the sand. They had a lot of Retsina wine and a delicious moussaka.

"I'm dizzy," Jeff said when they got home. "I'll rest for five minutes, no more, back soon. Make us a cup of coffee, Justy, and let's have some biscuits. I bought a package. It's on the worktop behind you, Simon."

He shut the door to his room and lay down on his bed and belched. Had he eaten too much or too hastily, or wasn't the Retsina good? He fell asleep.

The white windmill by the waterfront looked eerie in the light cast by a waxing crescent moon. Legends said that nymphs and satyrs from the ancient days returned to earth on nights like these to regain power over hearts and minds that they had lost so many thousand nights ago. A lonely wanderer would hunger for a human bosom where he could find solace in creepy nights like this.

Jeff woke up still dizzy. He looked at his watch—he'd slept for almost a whole hour! He sat up and listened. No sound from the terrace. Had Simon left?

He got up and carefully opened his door a crack and looked out through the narrow opening. Nobody at the table. He opened the door a little more. Nobody on the terrace. He took off his slippers and tiptoed barefoot across the terrace to Justin's window. The room was dark, but he thought he could discern movements in the bed. He thought he heard whispering.

Jeff was about to faint. But the other person in the room, if there was one, was surely just one the locals who always seemed to be lurking in the darkness. Justin took a drunken chance and went to bed with him. That must be it.

Jeff returned to his room, still unsteady on his legs. He closed the door behind him and sat down on the bed. *It's impossible, it's impossible.*

He heard a door open. He got up. Somebody was pissing on the sand. He opened his door a crack. And he saw what he had feared.

He closed the door and lay down on the bed. He tried to breathe. His hands were ice-cold. There was a pressure around his head. He mustn't cry. He must not be upset. He would not get angry. He would not accuse anybody of anything. He would not punish anybody for anything. He couldn't be sure. He still didn't know what. It could be innocent. He was tired. He was not well. He sat and stared in front of him for quite some time. He was immensely tired. Eventually he fell asleep.

Mercy Was Not on the Menu

When Jeff woke up, well after sunrise, he first noticed the violent bashing of the waves against the shore, much more forcefully than on any other morning. Then he heard Justin making tea in the kitchen. He got up and slowly prepared himself for what could be an unpleasant conversation. He took a couple of deep breaths and wet his lips with his tongue.

Justin was walking between the kitchen and the terrace table, laying the table for breakfast.

"Did he go home?" Jeff asked.

The three tea cups on the table answered his question.

"No," Justin said and continued to set the table. "He's still here. Asleep, I think."

"In our guest room?" Jeffrey asked, almost pleading.

"In my bed." Justin let his words fall with the merciless thud of an axe.

They were silent. Justin finished setting the table and returned to the boiling kettle in the kitchen.

Jeff stood immobile, looking out over the sea and considering how to respond to this grossly offensive insult.

"Please, Jeffrey, forgive me," Justin said while putting the teapot in the middle of the table. "I'm so sorry. I never wanted to hurt you. It just happened. I was … fucking drunk. It was a moment of weakness."

"You're selfish," Jeff hissed. "Careless!" He shook his fist in the air.

Justin lit a cigarette. "What the bloody hell can I say? I'm sorry." He shuffled around on the terrace like a hunchback. "Forgive me. Please, Jeffrey."

"Without me you wouldn't even be here!" Jeff shouted. "What the fuck do you think you're doing? You're a parasite!"

"Jeffrey, please. I have failed, I know that. Show me the leniency becoming of a great man. Please. Remember *La Clemenza di Tito*, Jeffrey. Powerful men have suffered more pain and still been merciful."

"Shut up! In another time and culture, I would have killed you by now." Jeff banged his fist on the table. "And that. Would have been. A proper. Response." He calmed himself and continued: "But now we shall behave as if nothing has happened. No mention of who spent these nights here or there or anywhere. Not a word. We shall bury this. Do you understand?"

"Yes, Jeffrey. Bury."

Jeff took a swift jump up the two steps to Justin's room. "Goo-o-od morning!" he sang as if performing a *recitativo secco* from a favourite opera. "Time to wake a-a-up! Sun is shi-i-i-ining!"

"Oh, my god," Simon grumbled, turning around in Justin's bed. "I have such a hangover."

"Rise and shi-i-ine," Jeff continued with his *recitativo*. "A lovely breakfast … is waiting for Simon … on the terrace."

"Oh, how sweet you are, both of you," Simon said after he had emptied a glass of fresh orange juice and spread cold butter on the piss-on-me, still warm from the oven.

Justin lit another cigarette from the one he was smoking. Jeff poured Simon a nice cup of newly brewed tea.

"It's been lovely to be here," Simon said. "But I must return to the village. My landlady is worried, I'm sure."

"So what?" Jeff said. "She's not your mother."

"I'm her only income. She's keen to have me stay. She's a lonely widow."

"Selfish," Jeff said. "Typical of women. Will we see you again?"

"I hope so. If you want to." Simon scratched his eyes and looked away.

"Of course we do," Jeff said. "Come back this evening."

"I'll see what I can do. If not, perhaps tomorrow, or next day."

"Don't wait too long. We may forget you," Jeff said. No one looked at any of the others.

Justin was silent. He withdrew to his room, to his cigarettes and to his work.

Simon returned to the village. It was past ten in the morning, and Jeff and Justin should have begun to work more than an hour ago. Precious time wasted. A cool wind swept over the landscape and one or two raindrops were in the air.

Jeff was unable to concentrate on his canvas. He gave up and took a walk along the shoreline.

The barren mountains on the other side of the wide bay seemed almost proud of how long they had endured the wear and tear of nature. Clouds were rushing in and the sea began to roar, but the coming storm would mean nothing to these mountains. Jeff shrunk from an unwelcome comparison with the mighty powers of nature confronting him.

He was confused by the lack of anger and grief he would have expected to feel. He had been betrayed—or had he? No one had made any promises. Everyone was free. If he was free and they were free, and he accepted that, well, he was aware the cost of freedom could be high. He had to pay, it was as simple as that.

Still, he wavered. Should he let his infatuation die away? As he strolled along the shore his bare feet sank into the wet, soft sand, and the inevitable waves from the mighty sea erased his footprints one by one.

Surrounded by mighty manifestations of nature he stood on a tiny little solid rock, *scoglio immoto*, with water splashing all around. It dawned on him: Simon did not want him. Not now. And not the other night. He had misused the boy, and so had Justin, no doubt. A sense of guilt came over him, and anger at the boy; anxiety arrived in faithful company. A pressure in his chest and throat. How he despised these debilitating introspections. He needed company. And work. Had to get home. He quickened his pace.

Back at the cottage, he lay down on his bed with a throbbing headache. He took an aspirin, and then one more. What a fool he had been. But he had only followed Nature's laws. He was a man who found an object to use for what a man was made to do. There wouldn't be a single species in this world if males had not lived up to what Nature had commanded them to do. Jeffrey Smart, as he lay there today, was the end result of chains of events that stretched for billions of years. Could he reverse that remorseless evolution? What was his personal responsibility in this great plan of Nature? He was not the architect but just one screw in Nature's great monument to itself.

He got up and went over to Justin's window. "Justy! We must talk. Things can't go on like this. You've been a bloody fool. What the hell were you thinking?"

"Thinking? Nothing. I was drunk." Justin kept on painting. "Trust me, I never wanted to do you any harm." He put down his brush, took his burning cigarette from the ashtray, and inhaled. Jeff turned away and left him as he coughed.

The sky above their cottage was leaden by low grey clouds. The rain had begun to fall and muddy sand around their home splashed onto the whitewashed walls.

For lunch Jeff made a vegetable salad, topped with one tinned sardine for each of them. A piece of piss-on-me was left from breakfast and half a small bottle of tepid water. The luncheon he prepared looked frugal, and it certainly was. Jeff would readily prescribe hair shirts for both.

"Justy, we've pissed in our pants. Warm and pleasant for a brief moment, then wet, cold, and stinking for a long time unless we clean up the mess." Jeff cut the head off his sardine and threw it away for the cats. "I invited this dear angel to have dinner with us. Then he finds himself being taken advantage of when drunk!"

"Don't be angry. Please, Jeffrey, I can't stand if you're angry with me. I know I have failed. Please, forgive me! Show mercy." Drops of sweat rolled down Justin's wrinkled forehead.

"Forgive you? Look, mate, I have a perfect piece of advice for you about forgiveness." Jeff knocked on the table. "Think! Think before you rush off and do things you cannot defend. This would considerably reduce your need for forgiveness. And that's a straight fact."

"Oh, Jeffrey, you don't understand. If I would think first, I would do nothing and have no life." Justin lit another cigarette; it nauseated him and he threw it away.

"Whatever choice we make," Jeff declared, "it comes with a price we have to pay. So don't try to run away, because it isn't possible."

They were silent. Thunder cracked in the distance, and the sky was turning black; the rain would soon be heavy. The wind was lashing the hops on the roof above them, and leaves fell down on the terrace.

"I want Simon to come and live with us," Jeff said.

For the first time since they got up this morning, they looked at each other.

Justin smirked. "Jeffrey, please. We're here to work, to make a living, not to play an ancient Greek drama and end up killing each other."

"Exactly. Work. During our six months on this island, I will have to create paintings of the highest quality, so people will pay enough for me to live a decent life. But this island gives me no inspiration. I don't see this place with your eyes. I need something to stimulate me. Simon fits the bill."

"If he lives here, this home will turn into a circus ... or worse."

"Listen. I have made this decision: as long as we are castaways on this wretched island, I will live in celibacy. What I tell you is a vow, a solemn vow."

"For Christ's sake! This arrangement would drive you mad."

"I will be inspired. He affects my perception; as an artist you should understand this, Justy. He intoxicates me in the right way."

"It's madness," Justin repeated.

"If things go wrong, we deal with it."

"But what's he going to do all day?"

"He will read, he can write, we will talk?"

"Talk?" Justin wondered.

"Look, he's still a teenager, but he has read more than you could ever dream of reading. With him I'll be able to talk about anything. I need that stimulation."

Justin shook his head. "He's just a boy."

"Look, Justy, I need him here, and I want him here. Well?"

The thunder was right above them and heavy drops of rain beat like pistons into the sand. The fierce wind flung swirling pieces of hops down on the terrace. The sea boomed against the shore and threw flotsam far onto the land.

"He could be fun to have around," Justin said. "He seems a jolly boy, and I like him."

"Fantastic! And neither of us ever makes a pass at him. Do you understand?"

"No problem. Neither of us?"

"Neither of us."

They agreed to remunerate the boy with free lodging, free food, and free drinks. Their spare room would be his bedroom. He could spend his days in any way he wished while they were painting. No obligations but to be a model if and when requested.

For the remainder of the day, the artists hid from the stormy weather in their small bedrooms. That evening, Simon did not come to see them. Jeff blamed the weather.

The next day was warm and sunny, but still no Simon. Despite the pleasant weather, Jeff spent most of his time fretting in his room.

On the third day Jeff arose from the hard seat in front of his easel and decided to act. He had become too involved to let events run their own course. He would challenge Nature if it was trying to keep him from the youngster he seemed to need so unconditionally.

"I'm going up to the village," Jeff said when he passed the door to Justin's room. "I can't let him return to that barbaric Arctic Circle."

"Do you think it's worthwhile losing half a day's work? If he's interested, for whatever reason, he'll come and see us."

"For whatever reason? What do you mean by that?"

"A poor young lad could be driven by any sort of motivation. You know this much better than I do, Jeffrey. Don't pretend."

"I noticed a malicious tone in your voice."

"No. Relax, I wish you the best of luck on your mission."

"Mission? There's no mission. I'm only going up to the village to find the lad and talk to him, that's all. Nothing to fuss about. You talk too much."

"Oh, I can shut up, if that's what you want," Justin said. "No problem. If you think there's nothing to worry about, there's nothing to worry about. You know best, Jeffrey. I'll shut up and say nothing. That's what I'll do. Just so that you're pleased. Yes, I will fucking well shut up, if you pardon my bloody French."

The ground had not yet dried up. Jeff strolled along the still damp path by the seaside, steadying himself when he slipped on the gooey mud. He was far from light-hearted by the time he had struggled up the steep footpaths with muddy feet on wet sandals.

In the village, a police constable on patrol seemed to understand when Jeff said the name Léon. He took Jeff to a little whitewashed house with blue doors and window frames. The house stood at a cliff-edge and overlooked the valley deep below, with the brook they always crossed on their way down to the Molos. The view was staggering.

An old, bent widow dressed in black opened the door. She exchanged words with the police constable, nodded, smiled and returned into her house. Jeff noticed the colourful combination of a black figure, clear-blue door and window frames and a flowerbed with pink roses and sparkling red geraniums, all along the whitewashed front of the house. The colour combination appealed to him. Sometimes Jeff used those clear and simple colours as if he still were painting in the colour-book he got from his grandmother for his third birthday down in Adelaide in South Australia over forty years ago.

"As you can see," Jeff said when Simon soon appeared at the door, "I come here to talk to you escorted by the forces of the law. Do you mind?"

"No. I'm delighted. This constable is Panagiotis. Good chap and loyal to my dear friend, his boss, as far as I know."

"Oh, nice. Hello, Pana... what was it? Glot, something?"

"Don't bother, it's not important."

"Can we go to a café and sit down and talk?"

"Sure. Can you pay? My money hasn't arrived yet. I haven't eaten since I had breakfast yesterday morning."

"Poor boy, why didn't you come down to us? I could have cooked for you and been happy to do so."

"I didn't want to come as a simple freeloader. My money should've been here days ago. The fucking bank system in this country is from the Stone Age. Do you have a cig? I haven't smoked since yesterday."

They had a cup of Turkish coffee and Jeff presented his and Justin's offer. Simon accepted at once. The boy's immediate consent excited Jeff and he wondered if his vow of celibacy was somewhat premature, perhaps.

"So he swallowed your bloody bait," Justin said.

"If at all a bait, it was a pure lump of sugar, with no hidden hook," Jeff said, "which you know very well, so I don't understand what you mean."

"Yeah, sure," Justin said with a twisted smile. "Why has he not come down to see us?"

"He didn't say anything, and I didn't ask. Perhaps he wanted to think. In certain matters he's a wise boy. And that's a straight fact."

"I'm sure. But when you called, he came running?"

"No, it wasn't like that. Not at all. He's not a puppy."

"I see." Justin lit one of his Turkish cigarettes and inhaled.

"I don't want to exaggerate," Jeff said, "but this may be a turning point in my life." He got up, took his teacup to the sink, and turned around. "It's not a fling, you know. I want this boy for life."

"I hope with all my heart that you are right in this and things will turn out the way you want and deserve."

The next day Simon said goodbye to his landlady and paid her what he owed, and a little more. Once again, he walked down the steep hill, this time with his suitcase in one hand and his typewriter in the other. Even if the men were old, already in their mid-forties, he was thrilled to have got a pair of companions to talk to, and who seemed to like him a lot. He needed that.

And he'd love to live by the seaside and sit on their lovely little terrace and read and write and have free food and free booze. And little was expected from him and they had agreed to leave him alone. He didn't want to exaggerate, but he thought this might be a turning point in his young life.

II
An Assortment
of Assaults

Exterminating the Unwanted

"Oh, bloody hell," Simon shouted. "Unless something is done about these … I don't know what to call them … life here will be intolerable."

Simon was upset by beings that carried out their dreadful deeds in darkness. The mere mention of them appalled every sensible mortal being the way undesirable creatures always evoked disgust in ordinary people. Every normal person was sickened by the sight of them even though these bastards feared the normal light of day and fled as soon as anyone discovered them.

"Can't they be done away with?" he continued. "Why not eradicate them for good? Who wants them around, anyway?"

Justin laughed. "If you knew how to get rid of them, you'd be the most celebrated man in the world, and then be knighted by the Queen. Wouldn't he, Jeffrey?"

"Could be. But if he were successful, he would disrupt the ecological balance, for sure. Even if we don't like them, all existing kinds are necessary. Faggots, bureaucrats, and cockroaches alike are all indispensable to make up the world as it runs today."

"Sure," Simon said. "But beliefs or scientific knowledge

won't solve this problem. Do something, Jeff. You're a practical man. Get us a final solution to this invasion. They're far too many. Where I come from, they don't even exist."

"Ha. That sounds familiar," Jeff said.

In the evenings, when they arrived home and lit their rusty kerosene lamp in the kitchen, hundreds of cockroaches swamped the floor, the stove, the sink, and the worktop, and more of them every night.

Jeff bought a small cage to hang from the ceiling by a rope, so the roaches could not reach it. The one who was in charge of the kitchen that day put everything in the cage that a roach might desire before they left the cottage to go out for dinner.

After a few days there were no cockroaches in the kitchen when they came home. Simon was contented and lavished praise on Jeff, who sucked it up, purring like a kitten lapping cream.

"Sometimes, having a handyman around could be profitable for you, dear Simon," Jeff said. "I take it, getting rid of these un-wanted creatures is to my credit?"

"Sure, but considering your great debt," Simon replied, "your balance is still negative. So no profit for you to cash in. Sorry, Jeff."

"Not yet, that is."

"'Hope fully in the grace that is coming to you,'" Simon cited. "Peter 1:13, if you may have forgotten."

"Ha, ha, you're so funny. But learn from this, both of you: there are always practical solutions to problems if you believe in your capacity and have the required resoluteness. Being able to solve problems defines a man. Don't you agree with me, Auntie?"

"I don't know," Justin said. "For me, such things are not important."

Then one night Justin was in charge of the kitchen. When they returned home and lit their kerosene lamp, bread, food remains, and used glasses were on the worktop, the stove, and in the sink. He had forgotten to put things into the cage. The roaches had returned and enjoyed a feast. Jeff had a fit.

"This is how life may turn out when you live with somebody who is Irish." Jeff turned to Simon. "I could stay up all night and tell you how much I have suffered from having lived with or travelled with your old Auntie. If you share a bathroom with her, she'll use your toothpaste, and when it's finished, she'll have the audacity to point out it's time for you to buy a new toothpaste."

Justin, who was laying down an alkaline germicide, hopefully working as a strong enough deterrent, did not answer.

"When I was so very gracious, in Sydney," Jeff continued, "to lend her my *extremely* expensive crystal Orrefors so she could serve drinks to her dubious friends, she didn't bring back the glasses the next day. After a *week*, and only after I had pointed out *every* day that I needed the glasses in my own life—that's why I bought them, not to lend to her, but to use them myself—she brought them back on a tray. After a week. And guess what. Guess what! She had not washed them. She brought back my expensive and exclusive crystal Orrefors *dirty*! And when I pointed this out to her, what did she say? Oh, I'm sorry, I didn't think you would be so frightfully fussy. *Fussy*! That's how you may be treated when you have to suffer life together with someone who's Irish."

Jeff had worked himself up into a frenzy. Justin, finished fighting the roaches, lit a cigarette and leaned against the worktop, waiting for Jeff to continue.

"Besides being Irish," Jeff went on, "Justin's family were also

Catholic—what a combination! This had many downsides. For example, when the Irish-Catholic mother urgently needed to shit, but her young child Justin occupied the loo, she put herself on top of her child and shat between his naked legs. That's Irish, and that's being Catholic, and that's what your old Auntie's family was like. No wonder she's turned into this drinking, agzy, belligerent, and impossible person to be with. Look at her face. It's Irish and she was born to be angry and impossible for other human beings to live with."

Justin smirked. Simon looked embarrassed. Nothing in life had prepared him to discuss the defecation habits of a friend's mother.

They threw away the damaged food, killed as many roaches as possible, brushed them onto a shovel, and showed them down the rubbish bucket.

"Rubbish where rubbish belongs, and may they never return to disturb our peaceful life here," Jeff declared.

"Agree wholeheartedly," Simon said. "We'll get rid of them for good now. Nasty types."

"For good is the word," Jeff chimed in.

"Nasty?" Justin said. "A strong word for innocent animals, only because you don't like them. Show some compassion for the poor creatures everybody seems to hate."

"No. I hate them. They disgust me," Simon said.

"You're so gorgeous when you're angry," Jeff said. Simon grunted. "I only want to tell you what a wonderful person I think you are."

"You know how it is, Jeff. Please don't."

"I could make you so frightfully happy. If only you would give me the chance."

"Oh, Jeffrey, please, you've promised."

"I could *really* make you happy."

"Yes, I'm sure. Good night, Jeff, sleep well."

Simon took the two steps into Justin's room, which he had to pass to get into his own room from the terrace.

Jeff retreated to his monastic cell, shut the door, and turned the key around twice.

"Ha!" Justin exclaimed when Simon passed. "Jeffrey locked his door. Do you know what that means?"

"No."

"He locks it when he's tossing off."

"Oh, please, I don't want to know."

"You will soon find Jeffrey sometimes seem to reject things and talk ill of people. Don't take this seriously; see it as a kind of perverse banter with no harm intended."

"He hits you hard," Simon observed.

"Yes, he does. I'm not tired enough to go to sleep yet. Do you want to share a glass of wine with me? It would be nice."

"No, thanks. I need to sleep. I've already had too much to drink."

"Perhaps another time—you're always welcome."

"I know. Good night, Justin."

"Sleep well, my prince, and may a lovely angel make you happy in your dreams."

Simon shut the door between their rooms before he could see Justin blowing him a kiss. He collapsed onto his bed and immediately fell asleep.

Emerged into the world of dreams, each in his own room and his own bed, as it had been decided and agreed upon, they travelled through the night shepherded by dreamy incidents that harboured their longings, their needs, and their fears.

As on every night, the stars and the moon provided the only light on the Molos. In the darkness of their kitchen floor, a thin, spooky moonbeam glared on two single roaches, survivors from the recent repulse. If lucky they would find a minute piece of food to sustain them for another day and make them fit to copulate once more, before they went to rest, maybe tonight for good. To impregnate the other with your seed, no other thing was more important when you were threatened by deaths in a large number, by misery, misfortune, or disaster. This action of survival at red alert was central for each surviving specimen of cockroaches in the world.

Beautiful Boy

On a Sunday morning after breakfast, Simon and Jeff cleared the table. Justin continued working on a painting, which he called *The Presentation of Young Jesus in the Temple*. At his first visit to the learned old men in the Temple, who upheld the eternal truths of the period, young Jesus made a deep impression on those who heard him speak.

In the kitchen, Jeff gave Simon one of his many lectures about the prerequisite for a successful career in the arts.

"Many components comprise talent. If you're an artist within the figurative arts, one essential skill is the capacity to draw. As necessary for the artist as a rich and diversified vocabulary for the serious writer and a never-failing sensitivity for each word's emotional charge, like Proust, whose language I admire more than that of any other."

Jeff went over to Justin's window. "Did you bring a photograph of *Harlequin*?"

"No, I didn't. Why?"

"I want to show Simon an example of failure caused by inadequate drawing technique."

"Don't use *me* for that, for fuck's sake," Justin mumbled.

"Don't be so angry, Auntie dear. I am trying to explain to Simon how difficult painting can be if you don't have the proper talent for drawing. Your *Harlequin* would be a perfect illustration. That's all, and nothing to fuss about." He turned to Simon. "Gosh, she's Irish."

"Whatever, I don't have it," Justin muttered.

"Now, listen, Simon, and I'll explain. Your Auntie painted a clown lying in a bed, it's called *Harlequin* and Brian was his model. I say *in* a bed, but I should say *on* a bed, because this harlequin is floating about half an inch above the bed. He even scraped Brian off, and made a second attempt, and even a third, but never got the body to rest properly in the bed. This disastrous failure was a consequence of your Auntie's bad drawing techniques. Practise may help to improve your skill if you're not sufficiently talented. Therefore, many artists practice drawing regularly. Preferably this should be done every morning. Don't you think we should draw for an hour every morning, Justy?"

"Sure, why not? And now we have a model in the house."

"No, I don't think this would be a suitable job for Simon. He's one of us now and cannot stand there naked in front of both of us."

"What a fuss. But okay, if you say so."

Simon was asked to find a suitable model who could remain immobile in every single position for at least two minutes and without scratching his behind. He hurried up to the village and returned with a boy named Georgios.

Jeff examined the young boy with unashamed prurience. "Is he one of your ... bedfellows?"

"Not exactly bed, but yes. Why?"

"May not be so good if he thinks somebody may want him. After all, we will draw him in the nude. He may get the wrong ideas."

"You can't control this guy's mind," Simon said. "I'm sure his head is already full of ideas."

"We'll see. He may be good as a model."

"He'll be delightful to check out in the nude, I can assure you of this," Simon said.

"Oh, can you? You must understand this, Simon. To enjoy peeking at naked bodies is not why we're drawing nudes. Anybody will do; an old wizened lady would be perfect. Much more demanding to draw, and they can usually stay still longer in a given position. There are more important things to a human being than a young, fresh body. If you haven't yet understood this? Have you?"

"I'll have a piss. Excuse me," Simon said and went around the corner.

"Justy!" Jeff cried. "Come out and have a look at Georgy here. Do we want this one for our drawing exercises?"

Justin came out with a beaming smile. "Oh, he's young! And beautiful. And naughty, I can see that. Look at his eyes; they're like baits, charming and glistening in the water, come and swallow me and be caught. Hmm."

"You sound very jolly. Anything I don't know of?"

"To tell you the truth, Jeffrey, I'm in a hilarious mood. Do you know something?"

"No." Jeff sounded as if he expected unpleasant news.

"I will be happy again. Got a letter from Brian this morning and do you know what?"

"The glass of water wants you to drink him again?"

"He's coming here! The filming in Rome hasn't started yet, so he wants to come and stay for at least three weeks. Isn't that jolly news?"

"Perhaps. Will there be orchids for Miss Blandish again?"

"I suppose not. Brian is straight now, so … But I love him." Justin sighed. "It's as simple as all that. To have him with me again will be lovely."

"You don't know how much *with you* it will be, do you?"

"It doesn't matter, Jeffrey. I love him, and just to have him here makes me happy, whatever."

"Let's hope so." Jeff laughed. "Love is a popular word. It can be used for many purposes."

"Georgios is no blushing flower." Simon returned to the terrace while buttoning his fly. "He's young and attractive, but he's no baby doll or toy. Even if his priorities differ from ours, and they do, he deserves normal human respect."

Jeff frowned. "Of course, he does. Why would you even say that?"

"Forget it." Simon waved his hand in front of him as if brushing away his words.

Young Georgios appeared to be convinced he could do more for the foreigners in the little cottage by the sea than pose for them. When Simon and the artists returned slightly inebriated from Kokalenia after the evening meal, their beautiful young model was sitting by their terrace waiting.

Barefooted, half-short trousers, with no buttons in his fly. Buttons had to be bought in Athens—too expensive for the young, so their flies were always open. A short-sleeved and mainly unbuttoned wrinkled and slightly dirty white shirt exposed most of his chest. His thick, curly hair surrounded his face like an ebony picture frame. Even from this distance they saw the sparkle in his dark eyes and his impeccable white teeth behind his thick pink lips, drawn apart by an inviting smile.

The way his body was displayed made his intentions easy to read. They quivered in the air like birdsong aimed at attracting an available mate to the foliage of a nearby shrubbery.

Here I am, Milord, come and taste me, devour me or enjoy me as it pleases you. I will be your devoted servant in everything you would want from me, my highly regarded gentlemen. Want to fuck my tight little firm arse? You're welcome, dear sir. You want to lick and suck my lush and heavy dick? You're more than welcome, sir. My tongue, my dear gentlemen, is good at everything and everywhere. You're welcome, Milord.

Justin beamed at their young model. "Doesn't he look as if he came out of a painting by Caravaggio?"

"There will be problems," Jeff said, "if this impertinent little boy thinks he can invite himself to be here morning, noon, and night. We have to put a stop to this. Tell him he's welcome here *exclusively* on the hours we have informed him. No other time. You understand?"

"He's here now," Simon said. "And he will stay with me. I want what I want, and I want it now."

"How old is he?" Jeff asked.

"I have no idea."

"Ask him."

"He doesn't know how old he is," Simon said. "Shepherds and goat-boys on this island don't carry identity papers around with their herds. They never know when you ask them. How old you are has no relevance in their lives."

"They should know at what age they begin school?"

"Yes, that's when they're mature enough to sit still for thirty minutes saying nothing."

"Gosh, they're primitive," Jeff said.

"I don't think so. They are closer to nature than we are, and view matters in a different way."

"It's not my business," Jeff said, "but what on earth do you think a boy like him may give you? Eh? Just raw sex. And it wouldn't be good sex. But fuck him, for God's sake, if that's what you want. As I said, this is none of my business."

Simon grabbed the boy by the arm and took him into his room. The door between Simon's room and Justin's was left ajar, and the window blinds were not properly drawn. If anybody would choose to be tactless, Simon and Georgios were as on a stage. Justin made that choice, and so did Jeff.

"Something isn't right," Jeff said to Justin and frowned. "I watched them for several minutes. He seems so uncomfortable with the young chap. He doesn't know what to do. To be blunt, they're not making love."

Justin lit a cigarette. "Do you remember when I told Simon about Brian claiming he was straight? Simon said he was familiar with the issue."

"So?"

Justin kept his gaze fixed on Jeff. "Simon is straight—that's what I think."

Jeff laughed. "No, you're mad, Justy. Of course, he isn't. If so why would he be in this country having sex with guys?"

"To find out? Didn't he say he was here to … what? Be different or something, be himself or whatever?"

"Too farfetched, Justy. Keep to the facts. That's a good rule in life."

Justin returned to his work. Jeff smoked a cigarette and sipped on his wine. He got up and went over to the window to Simon's room. The two naked young boys clung to each other, kissing, touching, and cuddling. He could hear Simon's voice, both in English and in Greek.

"Love me. Don't make love to me. Love me." Georgios was lying unmoving on top of him. "*Agápa me. Min kánete érota. Agápa me.*" Simon pressed Georgios's body to his own with his arms around the boy's shoulders and his legs around his butt. "Love me. Don't make love. Love me."

Jeff sighed and turned away. He retreated to his cell and turned his key around. After an hour he came out for his usual break from painting. He looked into Simon's window. The youngster was taking a nap. Alone.

Georgios returned at eight o'clock the next morning. Simon invited him to share breakfast with the gentlemen before the much-anticipated drawing exercise began.

At nine o'clock sharp the four of them assembled in Jeff's bedroom to start working. Simon explained in his poor Greek that he should take off all his clothes and stay still in the position any of them showed him.

"*Ta panta?*"[4] He hesitated to pull down his underpants.

"*Nai. Ta panta.*"

The self-assured cockiness they saw yesterday faded. He blushed and licked his lips. When he pulled down his not quite clean and threadbare underpants, his dick swelled and the pink and sticky glans crept out of his dark and thick foreskin.

Jeff's room was small. The naked model was close to the three men who drew him. He kept fidgeting, and they told him again to stay still. His dick rose and sank and rose again. Up and down like

---

4 Everything?

a dumbwaiter in a mansion. Full of hot food and heavy on the way up from the kitchen, light on the way down from the dining room with empty plates and cups. At the highlight of its impressive rise, the young boy's magnificent male organ pointed stiff to his belly button.

"It seems he finds his work exciting," Justin said.

"He may come without touching it," Simon said. "I think it would embarrass him to ejaculate in front of us."

"If he would get a visit from the reverend Father Up," Justin said, "I'm sure he would shoot at once." Father Up was an acquaintance Justin had met several times as a highly regarded Catholic altar boy performing his duties to the church.

Georgios soon relaxed. Lying down with his back turned to the artists, he fell asleep. Justin got up and smacked his butt. Not hard, more like a caress.

Awake and modelling, the boy found it difficult to stay still even for half a minute. The artists needed at least one whole minute, preferably two for every new position. Still, they used the full hour, and both artists were pleased with their training session.

Simon invited Georgios to stay for lunch. Then Georgios followed them to their usual after-lunch swim by the small beach behind the dunes. There the gorgeous boy presented them with a show: naked, he splashed around brazenly in the water and up on the little reef and jumped and dabbled and ran around as if he were a well-trained penguin in a zoo.

Simon and Justin enjoyed watching his perfect body and his joy of life and his pleasure at being the object of their admiration. What they were offered was a sight for gods to watch. So rarely life showed its most endearing side. Jeff paid no attention.

In the early evening, Georgios came back to the terrace again with a big, black lobster he had caught in the sea and put the lively animal on the terrace table, urging them to buy it. He refused to go away until they would buy the squirming and squirting animal.

Jeff dug in his heels. No lobster and no more drawing exercises. And that was that.

"Get away from here," he shouted and pointed in the direction of the village cliff. "Out!"

Georgios grabbed his black merchandise and trotted off towards the path up to the village.

"One must get rid of unnecessary disturbances, that's a fact." Jeff returned into his monk cell and closed the door behind him. Simon and Justin had come out on the terrace when they heard the shouting

"So you see what may happen," Justin said to Simon. "I think you were too close to the beautiful boy to suit Mr Smart. Wonder whom he will separate you from next time."

"It doesn't matter. I never invest enough to be seriously hurt. Jeff can never harm me."

"I hope you're right in this."

"Don't worry, I manage."

"I hope so."

For a Little Boy,
No Start in Life Can Be Better
than His Daddy's Love

Simon had made the acquaintance of a young German man who had been staying on the island for only two or three days. Now he was going back to Athens and invited Simon to dinner up in the village the evening before he left.

After dinner, they had coffee and drinks at the outdoor café on the Platía, the only great square in the village. At the other end of the square, native young men were singing and dancing in the evening sunset. Their bodies cast long shadows on the white walls of surrounding buildings. The wind in the large mulberry trees hummed with the songs they were singing to the plucking of a single bouzouki guitar.

When the two foreigners sat down at the café, the local boys performed their dances like dizzy peacocks. Proud of their cocks, dizzy by cheap ouzo or an occasional expensive beer, and whipped up by powerful passions. They beckoned to the foreign boys with their arms and legs and with cheerful smiles and laughter.

Two young muscular roughnecks ventured to approach and offered a sip of ouzo from their own cups. One pushed his hot and hard lower abdomen smelling of raw and dirty sweat against Simon's shoulder.

"They want us to get drunk," Simon said. "Don't drink."

They could see a rebuff of their offer as a stinging rejection—or even worse, an insult. But Simon took the risk: "*Ochi, apópse den thélo*."[5] Too late he regretted the word *apópse*, tonight.

The bigger lad grabbed hold of Simon's neck. Not hard, but nevertheless. Simon looked up at him. The guy winked and said something with a mushy voice, possibly a threat. To be on the safe side, Simon added, "*Alli mía méra*."[6] The same implication again. He should have kept it shut.

The guy stroked Simon's cheek and smiled. He scratched his behind with his other hand and called out to his dancing mates, "*Masí!*"

With a smile, he paced back to his dancing and singing mates and made the sign, putting his index fingers together and raising up his hands for everyone to see. "*Masí*," he called out again, and promenaded proud across the square with his companion.

Their mates applauded them and continued to sing and dance. The menacing mood lightened, at least for the moment.

Ill at ease, the German chap turned anxiously in his chair. "What was that all about?"

"They're always sexually aroused and want to fuck. A Westerner is especially prized, and the more so if he's young and blond and nice to look at. They think I am."

"So they're bisexual?"

"I don't think so. They're just exceptionally horny in this part of the world and they fuck anything. They're not choosy. They'll even—you wouldn't believe me if I told you."

"Tell me."

5 No, tonight I don't want to.
6 Another day.

"They fuck dead animals. Chickens."

"You're joking."

"I haven't seen it, mind you. Only hearsay."

They were left alone for the rest of the evening. The dinner's host went to his room in the local pension, to return to Athens next morning.

Simon was alone. The sky was getting dusky. He was getting worried. He should have left the village well before the sun began to set. Leaving now was risky.

As twilight fell, he hurried down the steep and narrow stone-clad footpaths. When he had left the major pathway, there was no other light than what the moon and stars provided.

Soon he heard a heavy breathing close behind. He didn't turn his head for risk of losing balance. His heart beat faster. He could hear its strokes.

The guy behind came up beside and in a husky voice he said, "*Kalispéra, file mou, pou pas?*"[7]

"*Sto spíti mou!*"[8] he fizzled without looking at his follower.

The guy said words that Simon didn't understand in a mild, seductive tone and smiled at him. When Simon looked into this young man's eyes, he knew at once that this guy wanted him and got excited just by looking at him. But no *masí*! The thought of being fucked disgusted him. And this night it was out of question and never on the road.

"*Ochi, apópse den thélo,*" he said again, the phrase he used before tonight and knew so well from several times before.

He put his arms 'round Simon's chest, and Simon tried to twist

---

7 Good evening, my friend, where are you going?
8 Home!

70

out of his grip. They mildly wrestled with each other, and in the dusky night they stumbled down the hill. Simon threw a punch but missed, then swung and missed again. He tried to kick the guy who jumped away with ease. He hit him with his elbow, but this had no effect.

Then out of the dimness came another guy, dark and unshaven, muscular and stinking of sweat and God knows what—the one who offered him a drink before.

With a relentless grip he wrapped his arm around young Simon's chest. The young guy grabbed him from the other side and Simon was secured as in a giant vice of tendons, ligaments, and muscles. He thrashed and struggled while they laughed, as if his fight for freedom were nothing but a tease.

Their stumble downhill slowed. They kissed and sucked and licked him with moist and ardent lips, wherever he was bare and grabbed under his clothes. Their hot breaths blew over his face, both panting loud and heavily. A part of him was scared; a part of him was not indifferent to the embryo of lust awoken in his body by their eager courtship. His kicking and his wriggling to get out of their grip diminished.

When they reached the outskirts of the village, night had fallen. It was dark. The boy lost contact with the ground and hang between his two assailants, who squeezed him in between them with their heated bodies, urging to get even closer to him. Ultimately, he was overpowered by his inner enemy of a compelling need to be possessed and savoured, by eager lips and hands of any human he perceived to be a proper male.

Give me some loving, he heard in his bewildered head, *give me some loving,* in the singsong cadence of a lullaby that might have calmed him when still a little toddler. Who sang for him this moment in the night? He did not know what happened to him anymore; he gave himself away completely to strange young men and had no thoughts about the danger lurking in the all-embracing darkness.

The young men realised at once when their prey had fallen, that he was theirs, and flung themselves with ardent yearning over his lone and longing heart. God help him now, devoted disbeliever. What was he getting into here? God help him now.

They hauled their loot upwards a slope into a spacious cave. The Greek boys soon were naked, and Simon was undressed while kissed and sucked on every surface of his body.

The Greeks had arms and chests and buttocks that were granite hard. They fucked him brutally and coldly. Their pleasure rose with rapid penetrations in and out as deep as their hardened dicks had length. To satisfy their white-hot lust was all that mattered. They sucked and bit the neck and tender cheeks of their victim.

One fucked him first, and then the other and then they changed position once again, and he was fucked not once, not twice, not three or four or five but many times. There was no pleasure for him, just pain and fear that they would harm an inner part of him.

As brutal as it was, one fact was clear: the stiffness of their dicks evinced the fancy he evoked in them and their restless quest for him revived a sleeping memory from the bottom of his mind in this horrendous moment of pain and fear and of exposure. These two young men, the same age as his father when he was celebrated in the sport arenas, showed their recognition of at least his body. An interested gaze, a gentle touch, a smile, a simple word that showed a sign of love he longed for as a child, but nothing. What these guys gave him now was nothing close to what he needed as a little kid, but still. When close to death from dehydration, you wouldn't ask if what they offered you to drink was clean enough. You took it, maybe even with a sense of gratitude.

But now he sold the domination of his body to get a kiss by men who found him worthy of that recognising kiss, he never got at home, when as a little kid he shrieked his silent howl for Dad to show he liked his little boy at least a little if nothing else.

They paid a cut-price for a feast on his young body but what the fuck, he did accept the bargain and so did they. He could have kissed them just for that, for touching him the way they did, with lust. For all the pain, he could have screamed with fear and agony. But he did not. Instead he sought to gather this pittance of an un-intended alm that life was willing to bestow him with.

When needed they let water pass just where they stood. Hot urine squirted from erected organs as from a Roman fountain built with sculptures of goddesses and fauns. Their brutal pagan cele-bration of youth and body and sexual excitement went on until they were exhausted and saturated for the night. They dressed and left, each to his own little cottage in the village or down by the sea.

Hungry and thirsty, Simon woke up in the early morning and made breakfast, bedevilled by an aching arse that preferred not to be sat on. When Jeff came out from his monastic cell, he stopped and stared at the youngster's face with an alarmed expression.

"What? What are you gawping at?" Simon asked.

"Go and have a look." Jeff retreated into his room in haste, slammed the door, and turned his key around twice.

Simon stared at his face in the mirror. A red-bluish-purple-pinkish-green-brownish bruise reached from his right ear down to his neck and up over his cheek to his eye, around his mouth, under his chin and over most of his throat, ending at his larynx, which was almost black.

He smiled; this huge hedonic hickey would serve him as a testimony when he made visits to the village or to the Kokalenia restaurant. Everyone would see that men had wanted him. You were not kissed and sucked like this unless they wanted you; he had a proof he was a person worthy of a passionate desire by men.

Justin came out on the terrace. "I hope you enjoyed that, whatever it was." He lit his first cigarette of the day and sat down to have a nice cup of hot tea.

"No, I didn't."

Justin shrugged. "What a pity."

Jeff returned from his room. "What have they done to you, my son?"

"They raped me, more or less. I fought, I hit, I kicked, but they were two and they were stronger, and they forced themselves upon me."

"More or less? What's that? Did you want them to fuck you? Yes or no."

"I did *not*. I hated it."

"So why did you let it happen? Did you scream for help or try to run away?"

"Who would have heard? So late at night. And it was dark. They could have hit me. And I wasn't dressed."

"Meaningless excuses. Where were you, anyway? And how did you get naked?"

"In a cave. I wanted part of it! That's true, I can't deny … But not the way that things turned out."

"Oh, I see. You wanted to choose from a smorgasbord? Only get what suited Little-number-one but nothing for the other part. We've been selfish again, haven't we? Let me explain this narrow little slice of life. If you're married to a meek and feeble fellow in a common Anglo-Saxon middle-class marriage you may indulge in sexual cherry-picking, but not if you're in a cave with strong and horny peasant boys in Greece. You've lived here long enough to know. One involves oneself with these people or one doesn't. I don't. You do. So pay the cost. Simple. That's how life works. Everything you choose to do or not to do has a price that you must pay, popularly called consequences."

"All I wanted was a piece of tenderness and affection," Simon whimpered.

"I know, poor little thing. But you won't find that celestial treasure in this garbage heap and not from these guys. They only use you to empty their seminal vesicles in a pleasant way."

"Gosh, you're cynical."

"Straight facts, my dear. Pure, straight facts."

"I'm sure it was a rape. They forced themselves upon me and they were strong. I had no say."

"Tell me every detail of what happened." Jeff got up from the table to heat more water for tea. When he returned, he said, "Have a nice cup of tea, and share everything with me, and I will decide if they raped you or not."

Simon told him, from the moment at the village square until they left the cave.

"As you tell it, son, I would say they raped you. You made

abundantly clear you wanted to be left alone."

"Yes, but. And this is a big but. It's also true that when I realised, that I could not resist them any longer, I adapted to the situation. Is this a strange expression? Can you adapt to a rape, and if you do, does this reverse the verdict?"

"Absolutely not. You did what you could to manage."

"But I must admit again their lust for me awoke a frustrated longing to be close and to be loved, no matter how." Simon took a deep breath. "One could say I tried to enjoy as much as possible, to ease the pain with something there to get for me."

"The initial strong element of violence and coercion still makes this a rape. What and how we eat and drink while stranded for weeks after a plane crash in the Andes is different compared to when we're at a gala dinner in the Palace with the Queen. How we act should in all cases be judged according to the circumstances."

"How do you think a court would see this?" Simon said

"From what I've experienced, the law is one thing, the judges see things their own ways."

"What if this happened to a girl of my age? Don't go out alone in the darkness, lassie? And don't dance provocatively with men who give you drinks and want to shove it in between your legs?"

"A situation like this would never occur with a girl," Jeff said.

"Why? Should occur even more often."

"Every girl and every woman learn that whatever happens is only atrocious and terrifying, and nothing else. A woman would never be sensible and adapt to the situation, the way you did, clever boy. And if she did, her sisters would condemn her, and this would be a worse experience for her than the rape."

"To shut up afterwards would be the best strategy for a woman, I guess."

"No woman would be mad enough to enjoy any part of a rape, as you did, clever boy, but if they did, they would be excommunicated by their raving sisters."

"To me it seems you were seduced," Justin said. "But I don't know, maybe you weren't, if you see what I mean."

"Oh, rubbish," Jeff said. "What Irish utter nonsense."

Simon had lost his sunglasses during the night. On their way home after shopping in the village, he left Jeff and Justin and hurried to the cave and wasn't he lucky! There lay his sunglasses among fresh and stale goat-droppings he hadn't noticed the night before. He picked up his glasses and hurried home.

At the cottage he found Justin smoking in front of his easel. Jeff was locked in his room. Simon made himself comfortable with a fresh nice cup of tea and snuggled up in a chair to begin his study of texts by writers who wrote in a language that was not their own. He began with Conrad's *Heart of Darkness* and found it surprisingly boring.

And so life went on. Today very much the same as yesterday, and nothing seemed to change. Like most other days, it was calm and pleasant, a day of peace. A light breeze swept in under the roof of the leafy hops; the air was warm but fresh. Their shining, life-giving Helios up in the sky faithfully spread life and warmth to every living organism, to ancient gods and humans, to animals and plants alike. Waves caressing the sandy shore had the effect of a lullaby on a sleepy mind. Simon dozed off with Conrad's dark heart resting on his aching lap.

Little Lads and Carnal Love

On lucky days, their jovial postman, Hippolytos, who owned one of the few bicycles on the island, delivered their mail. When he did not, if they cared to check their mail, they had to waste half a day's work by walking the long and tiresome path up to the post office in the village. So they always saluted Hippolytos's arrival with joyful greetings.

Still sitting on his bike, the postal worker slowly picked out one letter at a time from his bag and ceremoniously announced, "Mr Jeffrey Smart!" and handed over Jeff's letter. Then the next letter was handed over in the same flamboyant way to whoever was the addressee. It took a little time before all three of them had received their allocation for the day.

When somebody thought the content of his letter could interest either of the others, he read out loud for them to share.

"Here's from old Gosse again, he's in Athens now." Jeff had opened and read his first letter of the day. "The old sod writes he'll be coming here a week later than planned. Listen to what he says: 'My dearest friends Jeffrey and Justin. Five days ago love found its way again, as always. This time thanks to my new gorgeous friends, beautiful Kostas and lovely Nikos. I was sitting on a pleasant bench in lovely Zyntagma Square when two absolutely wonderful kids passed by. And believe it or not, I didn't need to do more than smile at them, and they came up to me with their gorgeous smiles and wanted to be my very dearest best friends. So beautiful, with lovely black curly hair, and the most delicious little bodies for this old man to enjoy so much. Sometimes God is gracious beyond belief! I thank God every day for what he gives me. They say they're fifteen; I think they're younger. Kostas has just developed a sweet little black bush above his already thick and dark little love-stick. They are my most lovely company and visit me at Hotel Grande Bretagne every day. They're always ready for the most wonderful and lovely play with their "Big Daddy." I'm so happy, and I don't want to leave. My visit to you two, my dearest friends, will have to wait at least a week. I am sure you understand. These two little angels, with a touch of devil behind their ears, have captured me. I haven't been as happy since sweet little Jose in Barcelona, if you remember lovely Jose.'" Jeff stopped reading and looked up. "And so it goes on. Gosse has been hit by Cupid's arrows again."

"Gosse is so welcome whenever he wants, there's no hurry," Justin said.

"Who is he and what's he going to do here?" Simon asked.

"He is a dear friend of both of us and will be nice company as a paying guest, nothing else. Gosse is a retired medical doctor; he was a surgeon commander in the Australian navy during the war. Now he cruises around schools in London, where he lives. He's got this special gift for gaining the trust of those poor little things who yearn for a big and well-meaning daddy. And who could be a kinder dad than Gosse? He adores them! He's probably had hundreds, mostly thirteen, fourteen years, I think. Several of them have stayed his friends for years. The sweetest of his many stories is when he was the guest of honour at the wedding of one of his former boys. The boy and his new wife invited Gosse to cut the wedding cake together with the newly wedded couple! Fantastic, isn't it? Totally unbelievable! As far as I know, Gosse asks only for what they are prepared to offer. I think taking part in their pleasure is what pleases the old sod the most, which is why they remain friends."

"How old is he?" Simon asked.

"Seventy-four. But in reality, Gosse is a little boy himself, superficial, accepts only what is easy and uncomplicated in life. His favourite film is *South Pacific*, which he has seen over fifty times, he says. He's a big, fat, smiling old sunbeam. The boys seem to adore him, and so do we, don't we, Auntie?"

"Yes, Gosse is a real darling to have around, couldn't disturb a fucking fly," Justin said. "Every time he came to Sydney, we had a lot of fun together, dear old Gosse and I."

When Dr Lane arrived, he engaged Jeff and Justin to "book" one or more boys for a special day and hour. There was no lack of ardent volunteers, and for a cheap price too. The equivalent of twelve shillings sixpence was the requested fee out on the island, considerably cheaper than in Athens. This price cut suited Dr Lane well, since he was living on "only a little pension, pet."

Young Riccy soon became the surgeon commander's focus of interest. Riccy was a thirteen-year-old boy, soon to be fourteen, living on the island during the summer holidays with his mother, Mavy, from the United States of America. He had seen his father, a Greek artist who lived in Paris, only a few couples of times when he was still a little child, too young to remember.

"Poor lad," Simon said, "to live alone with this emotional woman. I feel sorry for him. She squanders all her feelings on him. And no father there to put a stop to it."

"She's not only emotional," Jeff said, "she's also good looking, and quite possessive and demanding. To be perfectly honest, I like her. Not sure I would have liked her as a mother. Too much cuddling and too many kisses. And her female friends, they only smile and think it's cute."

"He's a nice kid," Justin said.

"Too nice. A bit screwed up, I would say," Jeff concluded dryly.

"His mum and his dad have prepared him for this old goof's attention," Simon said. "Gosse plucks Riccy as a ripe fruit on the tree his parents planted years ago."

"You may be right," Jeff agreed. "The kid has been muddled into a suitable prey for a predator in the shape of dear old Gosse, a true specialist on lads who need a good daddy in their lives."

"Why do you call him a predator?" Justin said. "The boys adore him, and don't see themselves as prey, as you call it. Then I'm a predator as well and Brian was my prey when we met? Is this how you see it?"

"No, Justy dear, of course not. I only expressed a commonly held view. Brian, he's as bland as a glass of water and could never be compared to something as exciting as a prey."

"How do you know all this you say?" Justin asked Simon. "That Riccy will join Gosse because he has no father and his mother kisses and cuddles him? When I was your age, we didn't know anything about anything. That masturbation was an offence to God constituted our entire knowledge of sex."

"Study! Read books!" Simon said. "How do you get to know anything in a serious way? By talking to Annie and John next door? Or by reading a sensationalist articles in a daily newspaper? If you want to know anything you have to be serious about it and go to the sources. To gain the superior state of being knowledgeable costs time and effort. Knowledge is not a porridge somebody else has chewed for you ready to glide down your throat for free."

"Now you sound like Jeffrey ..." Justin said with a skewed smile.

"I cite my university professor."

"You've been to a university?"

"Only for a month."

"You must have looked like a baby only a year ago."

"University admittance is not determined by your looks, Justin. Bu let me tell you how it is with kids and kisses. Some kids live with a mum and a dad who love their children and who also love each other. Hopefully these parents also know how to express their love without infringing on their kid's right to a living space of their own and the right to have full control of their own bodies. These lucky kids will rarely be open to invitations from other grown-ups who want to play with them and overhaul them with kisses and intimate touches."

"What's wrong with kisses and touches?" Justin said.

"It's wrong if you don't want, but you let it happen only because you can't say no, or your parent has forced you to obey her."

"Is this what you learned during a month at the university?"

"Don't try to invalidate what I say by shifting focus to some irrelevant detail."

"Sorry, sir," Justin said. He smiled and inhaled deeply. "Do all kids with parents like Mavy get picked up by older men?"

"No, we're different. Some of us are born with a sensitivity which can make us more responsive to certain emotional influences, for example being without a father or living with a possessive mother."

"Oh, I see," Justin said. "That could explain a lot."

"Yes, it could. And it does."

A few days later when they sat down for a nice cup of after-noon tea at four o'clock, Jeff declared, "We've got the latest news on the Riccy front! He and Gosse were out swimming together. The old bugger suggested they should take off their swimming trunks when they were a long way out. The dear old sod began to caress the poor boy, who got horny by being touched. When Gosse was a little naughty, the boy got uneasy, so Gosse let his finger glide out. Their play in the water resumed for another ten minutes. Riccy was happy as a clam, Gosse says."

"That old bugger is a goof," Simon declared. "I wish he weren't here."

Jeff soon revealed that Gosse had made "considerable prog-ress" with the kid, who followed Gosse around most of the days and spent time in his new mate's rented room.

Jeff shook his head. "The world is full of mysteries."

"That's a kind way to put it," Simon said.

"It's evident the boy likes him, and that is what matters. Nothing else."

"If you say so. He won't harm him as much as his mother, I'm sure."

Later in the evening, the artists visited their neighbours, an American couple, Bob and Silvia Wehrheim, who lived with their young daughters five hundred yards away and farther inland. Bob was an artist who painted huge abstracts and Silvia was a physicist on leave from her university.

Alone at home, Simon sat down on the terrace to continue his investigation of how well a writer managed in a language that was not his own. Now he read *Lolita* by Nabokov.

In the warm night, the dim half-light of the full moon created an uncanny atmosphere on the Molos. No breeze moved the hops above the terrace and no soft splashing from the indolent waves moved Simon's lonely soul to sleep. In a nearby cottage young men were laughing and arguing. Simon heard the sounds from primordial times resound from deep inside their chests.

After an hour or two he stopped reading and was dozing when a young boy trotted by on a lively colt. The young horse bubbled over with a life-affirming spirit and his little master was shaken up and down. The boy rode bareback, squeezing his bare knees into the horse's flanks and used only the horse's bushy mane as reins. The magnificent horse was a chestnut stallion with a white blaze as a facial marking and white socks.

The colt neighed and lifted its forelegs up in the air. The lad shouted commands and the animal seemed to calm down. The boy laughed and waved at Simon and sent him a big smile. With confident ease he kicked the horse into a canter, and they rode away.

The scene brought Simon back to ancient times when centaurs roamed this part of earth and Socrates and Plato were their friends. He sighed, got up, and turned off the lamp above him.

Then as it often happened in ancient times the horse and rider reappeared. The lad slowed his prancing colt. Its hooves clapped against the stone as it trotted onto the terrace. They went right up to Simon, who was struck by the couple's mighty appearance. Young but still a stallion after all.

The creature whinnied and shook its mane. In practice, free

to walk away yet chained by the boy's stronger will and superi-
or mind. The youthful cavalier bent down beside the submissive
brute's muscular neck.

"*Kalispéra sas, phile mou.*"[9]

"*Evkaristó.*"[10]

"You want to enjoy my company," he said in Greek and
jumped down from the horse.

"You're a big boy on this lively horse. How old are you?"

"Fifteen, my mother says, but I don't think she remembers well."

"I'm impressed to see you manage such a huge beast."

"We live with sheep and goats and horses since we learn
to walk. I don't remember the last day when I didn't ride a
horse. To sit on him is as natural for me as it is for you to sit in
that chair."

"How different life can be for different people."

"You want to be *masí* with me? I'm a good boy."

Simon giggled. "I have no drachma for you."

"It doesn't matter. I like you. I've seen you dance, and
rumours say you like to be *masí*." He said and put a hand on
Simon's shoulder. "I'll be quick. I am a Greek, you know."

He took Simon's hand and put it to his open fly. It was hard
and throbbing. He pressed Simon's hand closer and took it out.
It was warm, hard and soft on its surface and had a familiar
scent, as if not washed for several days and tossed off many
times since then.

"No, please. I really don't want to," Simon said. "I am so tired.
And I have a headache, dear. I'm sure you understand."

---

9 Good evening, my friend.
10 Thank you.

Now was the proper time to use that phrase, to show to mankind and to all the gods that he was part of a respectable community and knew the proper things to do and say. Although he spoke in English, he knew this boy would grasp the meaning of his words. "I'm tired, dear, and I have a headache—I'm sure you understand" was a familiar phrase in every bedroom on this earth and in every language known to man. Many times, these words resulted in a brutal beating, all around the world. "Shut up, old hag, and suck my dick, and I will fuck you in your ass" was also spoken in every bedroom and every language known to man in every little corner of the world.

"I like you so much." The boy stroked his cock and kissed Simon on his mouth. Simon returned the boy's kiss. The boy ejaculated right away, and his spunk squirted over Simon's bare legs.

"I'm sorry." The boy took off his shirt. He squatted in front of Simon and wiped his spunk off Simon's thighs.

"Is that okay? Are you all right?"

"Sure."

"I hope to meet you soon again, when you don't have a headache. Then I can be a better friend for you. *Masi.*" He smiled and scratched his behind, then jumped up on the colt, bound to stay in place and wait as taught.

When the young horse trotted away, his master put both his hands up in the air with his index fingers close to each other. "*Masi!*" he shouted again.

Simon leaned against the wall around the corner as he tossed off, pleased to have avoided to be *masi* this time. He returned to his chair and had a glass of wine before he went to bed.

The savoury smell of the boy's body followed Simon into his

dreams, one where nothing seemed to have a meaning you could understand with ease and ancient gods were dancing 'round with humans, animals, and plants.

Love Works in Mysterious Ways

The Greek nights always shivered with lust, even more so in the heat of summer. Luscious sounds and sensuous odours from beasts and humans permeated the air. The congenital craving to touch and be touched close to another human being's body was omnipresent.

For the native youths, eager to come off well in their first sexual experiences with another human being, goats, sheep, or dogs served as their introductory partners. At times, a lucky opportunity presented itself as a single man from England.

In the middle of the summer, a few foreigners arrived on the island, and the little terrace on the Molos became the place to visit in the late evenings. Guests were offered an assortment of cheap drinks, titillating gossip, and the opportunity to find a friend, at least for the night.

From a distance one could hear the repetitious sound of the most popular Greek tune of the day as it found its way from Kokalenia's kitchen. *"Sagapó se ponó os allós kanís"*[11] howled all night long like a mare in oestrus. The singers' wails pierced the listener's mind and body and prepared him or her for the night's pleasures.

Among the summer guests was the wife of the poet who was Henry Miller's Colossus of Maroussi—and she was a friend of Henry Miller, no less! Jeff had a friend in Australia by the name

---

11 "I Love You in Pain Like No One Else"

of Germaine Greer, an aspiring young writer who introduced him to Miller. So Jeff was extra excited by this woman's addition to their little salon.

And there was Mavy, the dipsomaniac mother of Dr Lane's latest conquest, thirteen-year-old Riccy. She praised her home country's national conviction that sexual relations must be sanctioned by God Himself in Holy Matrimony to be acceptable. "'Love and marriage go together like a horse and carriage'—that's what we sing, and that's how we live," she proclaimed in her strong American accent.

It was a topic of discussion as to how well Mavy could uphold her principle when she was so often stumbling more than half-drunk along the waterfront late at night unsure of where she was headed. She might be offered the guiding support of a burning soul in a steaming hot body who'd waited patiently out in the night's darkness for a single woman on the terrace to become available.

Lonely women from any part of the world were intensely worshipped by every boy, young man, and adult, each of them mentally and physically prepared to give every pleasure he could master with a prepared organ always sticky with pre-cum, which signalled a readiness to unload, here or there, now or later. Thus, by coincidence, he might contribute to the Christian injunction to populate the Earth, with the benevolent aid of a not-too-old woman on her unsteady stumble home in the seductive half-darkness of the early dawn.

These were the hours in life when a feeling of unbearable loneliness defeated every sensible thought that might still linger in the desolate mind of a drunk and solitary woman.

There were also "Dear Old Gosse" and little Riccy, Mavy's thin, well-behaved, obedient, and always smiling little son. Mommy's best friend, whose soft boy-hands Mommy found comfort in holding when she could not go back to sleep at night or early in the seductive half-darkness of the morning hours. Since Dr Lane arrived, Mommy still got her share of the lad mainly at night. Dr Lane's enjoyment of the youngster was mostly limited to the daytime, but nobody complained.

"That boy needs a father to protect him from the selfish claims his mother makes all the time," muttered their neighbour Silvia Wehrheim. "A father creates balance in a family. If one parent is missing, requests for comfort and solace from the other parent may burden children not mature enough either to deliver or to reject what is requested of them. A teenage boy doesn't gain self-confidence by sleeping next to his mother at night."

Jeff nodded, trying to look interested. He thought Silva was a clever woman, but sometimes expressed slightly too complicated views.

"I don't like her," Simon said. "When she looks at me her eyes see something that makes me feel belittled. And she never says a word. But I don't give a shit for what she thinks. I only wish she wasn't here. Mothers I've fucking well had enough of, thank you."

If he was not the Terrace Court's Queen, Jeffrey Smart was at least its First Lord Chamberlain. He used his office to ventilate several of his most cherished opinions.

"You may not think I look much like an artist, but more like an accountant at some prestigious bank? That's the thinking in lovely Australia at least, where people expect an artist to have flamboyant dress, exuberant hairstyles, or startling facial hair, and to flounce around as if he were on the stage in a cabaret."

"Oh, we get this again," Justin grumbled.

Jeff turned to Simon. "Sing out, Strindberg! Does your old Auntie look more like an artist than I do? I hope you're not as superficial as the common ignorant flock of sheep?"

"You're both mad enough to qualify to be seen as artists, if that is something to aspire to? As a devoted European, I'm not yet aware of attitudes in extremely far-off places."

"I'll tell you something you may not know about far-off places," Jeff said. "And why would you know anything? Who in this world would care a shit about Down Under?"

"Easy, Jeff," Gosse said. "We're two sons of our dear Australian soil here, and I'm sure we will protect our beloved motherland from malicious slander, won't we, Justin?"

"Eh. What?"

"We'll see if there's anybody here who will challenge me," Jeff said. "Listen to what I have to say about Australia and the people who chose to go there or to stay there for incomprehensible reasons." He turned an empty wooden box upside down and climbed up.

"The people of Australia," Jeff declared with a strong and convincing voice, "have nothing a decent person can value: no culture, no sophistication, no natural beauty or style and no elegance inherited over the centuries, precious qualities you find in well-selected parts of Europe. The so-called 'common man' in Oz—and common he is—lacks an ounce of interest or capacity to appreciate anything but beer and Sheilas. He's culturally backward, ignorant, uneducated, and has a narrow and limited perspective on everything, including beer and Sheilas."

There was a light murmur in the surrounding group as Jeff climbed down from the box.

"Well, well, well, my dearest Jeffrey," Dr Lane said. "You'd still want to come down and see us now and then, wouldn't you? I can tell you one thing we're bloody good at in lovely Australia, mate, and that is making money. And money—never forget this, Jeffrey dear—can be used for buying paintings, even paintings by Australian-born artists who have deserted their home country and may find their products difficult to sell for an acceptable price elsewhere."

A few people in the congregation laughed carefully.

"Even if my dear Irish friend may appear more of an artist than yours truly," Jeff said, "it is an undisputable fact that in some respects he is less of an artist than me and lacks the technical skills of a proper artist."

These words introduced an attack on Justin's glazing techniques, one that occurred out of the blue at irregular intervals.

"First you must decide," Jeff said and talked as if he held a lecture in front of the congregation, "if you're only going to highlight a certain part or varnish the whole painting to preserve it. This you don't seem to understand. I have seen how you mistreat your paintings with too much turpentine in the vanish. If varnishing is what you want to do? Is it?"

"I don't want to hear you crank up this same old hurdy-gurdy again and again. I'm sick of it," Justin grumbled. Affected by a mixture of various drinks he did not speak with ease. "I knew everything about glazing and varnishing before you knew how to clean your own ass. So don't fucking pretend you know better than me, how to treat my own oil paintings, because you bloody well don't."

"He's so drunk he wouldn't even recognise his own mother," Jeff said.

"Don't fucking talk about my mum. Your mother, she fed you with sour vinegar. That's what you've got in your arteries, Jeffrey, vinegar, vinegar in your heart."

"Now he's got to the stage when he prattles about his mother."

"My mum, she loved me. That's the difference, like milk and honey. That's the point I want to make if you see what I mean." He dropped his glass, and it sent out a spray of wine as it shattered. He bent down to pick up the pieces and toppled forward, impaling his hand on a shard when he braced his fall.

"And now he's bleeding. So typically Irish. They drink too much and leave others to take care of whatever they wreck." Jeff laughed at his joke, and some guests followed him.

Justin straightened up and bellowed as if out of his senses: "SHUT UP!" He stumbled toward Jeff with his bleeding fist.

The chatter on the terrace died out as people watched the scene.

"I WILL KILL YOU!" He managed to focus his dimmed eyes on Jeff and lashed out at him with his bleeding fist. He lost his balance and was down on his knees in front of his adversary.

"Kill you, I will fucking well kill you!" he whimpered. He grabbed hold of Jeff's bare legs, smearing them with blood as he tried to pull himself up.

"Oh, leave me. Back off!" Jeff pushed himself free and stepped back, and Justin fell back down to his hands and knees.

"I will kill you, I will kill you," he repeated between sobs and coughs.

Simon helped Justin up, and the drunken artist stumbled out on the sand and went around the corner.

On unsteady legs Mavy turned her glass upside down. The wine splashed on the terrace stone. "I'm not wanted, so I call this a square. Nobody cares if I'm here." She shuffled out onto the sand. A young fisherman, less than half her age, rushed out of the darkness and helped her with his strong arms not to fall.

"Aren't you taking Riccy with you?" Silvia shouted.

"Riccy, come with me." His mother stretched out her hand. Her son was standing next to the voluminous Dr Lane, who rested his hand with a light touch on the boy's shoulder.

"I want to stay," Riccy said.

"You *want*?" Mavy shouted and looked at her son with eyes as fierce as those of Mozart's *Die Königin der Nacht*. "That's not how a good boy should talk! What has Mommy told you to say?"

"Dear Mommy, may I stay?"

"*May I*, you say, not *I want*," she shouted and wagged a menacing finger at him. "How many thousand times have I told you?"

"Sorry, Mom. May I stay?"

"No. You may not. You come with me. Always listen to what Mommy tells you to do."

She turned around and was on the point of falling. Her cavalier from the darkness held her. She gave him a faint smile. He scratched his behind and returned her smile.

"The boy is big enough," Dr Lane said. "He doesn't need his mother all the time, and it's not so late. I'll bring him home to you later if you want. With us, he's in good company."

"And better than with his mother, in her state," Jeff said.

"Shut the fuck up, Mickey Mouse," Mavy shouted. "None of

your danged business." She twisted free of the young fisherman and threw up on the sand. Jeff laughed.

Mavy wiped her mouth and took one unsteady step after the other out into the darkness. Maybe the young fisherman continued to aid her in her delicate incapacity. He may even have helped her to lie down and have a short rest in an empty fishing boat pulled up for the night on the sand. Dr Lane took care of her young son, and nobody knows for certain whether his mom returned to her bed before dawn.

"Where is Justin?" Jeff asked Simon.

"I don't know; he went out after your quarrel."

"There was no quarrel. I told him a straight fact which he could not tolerate so he threatened me. Do you think he meant what he said?"

"I think he wants to kill you, but not do it. Now I want to know where he is. I don't want him to drown in the water and go meet his maker."

Simon found Justin on his knees in the surf a couple of hundred yards away. Simon helped him up and slung Justin's arm around his neck.

Jeff met them close to home. "Oh, bugger!" he shouted over the waves crashing against the rocks. "How ghastly! She's fucking throwing up again! Cast her into the water! That will make her sober up! So Irish, throwing up on other people."

By the time they had finally carried Justin home, the guests had left the terrace. Simon threw Justin on his bed and went down to the sea to rinse Justin's puke out of his shirt.

They fell asleep at once and slept till half past seven in the morning, when they were awakened by the strong spotlight of their always wonderful and beloved life-giver, the Mediterranean sun—with the assistance of the rooster next door, of course. Another day to create art and to live their lives. Drunk to bed. Early to work. The same routine as every day.

It was generally assumed that nobody recalled what was said at night when they were drunk. But Simon remembered Justin's outburst and so did Jeff. Could his artist friend harbour a doggedness to carry out his hidden aim or were his threats just empty words? You never knew about the Irish.

At noon on the following day, Riccy and Mavy were seen swimming and sunbathing together on the little beach behind the dunes. As usual, Riccy was naked to his butt and his mother lay beside him topless, which was off-beat at the time and certainly illegal in their home country, the United States of America.

In the evening after dinner Mommy and her son were back on the terrace. Mavy was charming, and Riccy was entertained by a jovial and constantly cheerful Dr Gosse Lane. The same routine as every night.

Dr Lane left the island after two weeks of unexpected amorous pleasures. He was accompanied to the bus by Jeff, Justin, Simon, and young Riccy, who wept heartbreakingly at Dr Lane's departure and was inconsolable for the whole morning.

"Love works in mysterious ways," Jeff said.

"Now he's back in his mother's care," Simon added, "and she can have him all for herself. So what's he crying for?"

The Pleasures of Poverty

At noon in the middle of the hot summer, the sun was at its zenith and frying every organic object exposed to its gaze. Jeff was alone at home on the terrace, reading letters and enjoying a light breeze under the protection of their roof of thick green hops.

"Does anybody know Lennart?" someone shouted down by the beach. A young Nordic-looking man came strolling up the soft sand, headed toward their cottage. He resembled a young gentleman from the early part of the century, with an aristocratic stature dressed in semi-long khaki pants and a matching shirt. A dark-skinned, sweaty servant carrying his large and heavy luggage would have completed the picture.

"Why are you shouting?" Jeff shouted back.

"I'm looking for him. Isn't that obvious?" the young man said, dropping a single suitcase on the terrace. "Do you know him?"

"Yes, I do," Jeff said.

"Good. May I sit down?" The young man nodded toward the chairs, then sat without waiting for Jeff's consent. "It's tiring to walk in this soft sand."

"Did you come all the way from the Arctic Circle to see Lennart?"

"Arctic Circle? Hah! Funny. No. I live in Paris. Do you know where I can find him?"

"Yes, I do." They measured each other up. "He'll be here soon."

"Ah! Good. So, at last I found his hideaway."

Jeff shook his head. "He is our friend and he's not hiding from anything."

"Hmm. A friend? I see. I call it a hiding place since he ran away from everybody, without even leaving a note."

"Not the same as hiding."

"He could have said where he was," the young man pressed.

"Obviously he did, since you are here." Jeff smiled, having gotten the best of their quick repartee.

"Could you be so kind as to offer me something to drink? It's hot."

"Sure. Mineral water?"

The young man wrinkled his nose.

"Whiskey?" Jeff suggested.

"No." The young man frowned. "Not at this hour. Do you drink whiskey before lunch?" He looked at Jeff with a smile that could be interpreted as condescending.

Jeff did not answer. He stood between the kitchen and the terrace table and waited while the young man stretched out his legs and unbuttoned his khaki shirt.

"Water, please. If it's cold and bottled." The young man smiled. "Do you have that, sir?"

"Everything is primitive here, but we have a small icebox."

"As long as it's cold, I don't care how you store it."

"Making small talk, nothing else. Don't you make small talk in Paris?"

"I haven't got the slightest idea." Both seemed to decide small talk in Paris was not a matter worth a fight. "No offence intended."

"None taken." Jeff went into the kitchen and returned with a glass. He'd put two ice cubes in the water.

"This is not in a bottle!" the young man protested.

"Look, the water was in a bottle before I put it in the glass. Do you want to *see* the bottle?"

"Yes, please. One can't be careful enough. And the ice cubes? Where does that water come from?"

Jeff said nothing, grabbed the glass and threw out the contents on the sand. He went back into the kitchen and returned with the half-full bottle and put it on the table with an empty glass.

"Thank you," the young man said. "Very kind. Even if this bottle is open. But never mind."

"Before I go back to my work, is there anything else I can serve you?" And he added, "Monsieur."

"No thanks. I'm fine. Pleasant breeze on this terrace. Vital in this awful heat."

"Feel free to enjoy yourself." Jeff picked up his letters from the table, went into his room, and firmly shut the door.

"And thank you for the water, sir!" the young man shouted. He put on a pair of round Lindberg eyeglasses, took out a notebook from his chest pocket, and began to write with his Waterman pen. According to people who knew him, he was no stunner, but he still attracted attention from those young women who responded amorously more to mind than to physique.

When Simon returned with Justin from a morning swim by the dunes, he introduced his old schoolmate to his patrons.

"Max's father is a famous county vicar in our country who has written several of the nation's most popular church hymns. His parents live in a culture-protected mansion close to the old royal couple's baroque summer palace, built as a small Versailles. You would adore it, Jeff."

"Oh, I see," Jeff said and there was a sudden sparkle in his eyes. "Do they know the royal couple?"

"No, but they greet each other politely when they meet in the royal English garden. It's open to the local people, so my parents usually take a walk there."

Simon took a sip of his tea. "On Max's mother's side there is another famous man," he continued. "Max's maternal grandfather is a distinguished author and also head of the most significant revival movement in the country. Max now studies in Paris at L'Institut des Hautes Études Cinématographiques, the world's most prestigious cinematography school."

"Interesting," Jeff said as he stood up. "I once was a student in Paris myself, you see. Fernand Léger was my teacher. He made a film you may have seen?"

"No, I don't think so," Max said.

"You have productive families to inherit from," Jeff said, "both from your mother and your father. A combination of good ancestry, determination, and the stamina to work hard are good signs for a young artist striving to make his mark on the world. Perhaps we can expect an avant-garde cinematographic work? Like Buñuel?"

"I'm not a careerist," Max said. "I rather detest success. I will use my knowledge to promote social progress, not to enhance and enrich myself, which I find a deplorable and heartless ambition in a world with so much suffering."

"When you say cinematographic work," Justin said, "do you mean a movie?"

Max was invited to share lunch with them. Jeff took time and effort to prepare his favourite meal, a big, Greek chook flambéed in local brandy.

"Flambéed chicken for lunch?" Simon looked puzzled. "Are you all right, Jeffrey? When I see you prepare a banquet dinner for a lunch, I fear some of your central neural connections may suddenly have become miswired."

"He's so funny, this boy," Jeff said and turned to Max. "What do you prefer—white or dark?"

"I'm sure Max doesn't know what this means," Simon said. "In the small and insignificant place on earth where we live, we call things by their names. A chest we call a chest, a thigh we call a thigh, and the toilet, the place you refer to with the ridiculous euphemism 'bathroom,' we call the shit house. Different customs in different cultures exposing the collective mind of its citizens."

"If you're talking about the chicken," Max said. "I prefer a juicy thigh."

"In polite society," Jeff said, "we do not serve juicy thighs but dark meat. I will now serve you dark meat. Hand me your plate."

"I certainly don't belong to a polite society," Max said, "or share the customs of any polite society. I'm not a snob because I study in Paris or my parents go for walks in a royal garden."

"Hand me your plate. You'll get your juicy thigh if that is more to your taste."

"Yes, sir, it really is. And I have no regrets saying so."

Max and Simon looked at each other and smirked.

"What is your impression of Greece so far?" Jeff asked as he plated Max's chicken thigh.

"I'm surprised how poor people are. As if they haven't yet recovered from the war."

"I came to Europe in '49, four years after the war," Jeff said in a lecturing tone. "Then people were *really* poor,"

"Wasn't it difficult to enjoy life living among people who were so extremely poor?"

"No, not at all. Why should it be difficult?" Jeff said as he carved the chicken. "Nowadays there's too little poverty."

"I don't understand what you mean," Max said. "Too little? You mean too much?"

"I'm not sure what you don't understand. Nowadays people aren't poor enough. And there's not enough poor people. Poverty is good, I think. Keeps people in place. Who would do all the dirty work if everyone had enough money?"

Max scowled. "You must be joking. And it's a bad joke."

"I'm sorry you think so. Still, I'm convinced there's a basic law of nature which keeps poor people poor under all circumstances. Poverty depends on people's stupidity, you see, and there's no shortage of that. People who are not stupid, don't subject themselves to a life of poverty; they do something about it."

"Now, wait a minute," Max said. "This opinion is … extreme. Not just extreme, it's … based on ill will and a sick view of fellow humans and totally unacceptable."

Jeff chuckled. "It's not an opinion, dear boy. It's a simple straight fact. No political ideology in the world can rescue a person from his own stupidity. Though there are ideologies which make stupid people even more stupid, if possible. But I suppose you're just too young to have understood this yet."

Max's face turned red. "Everything you say is pure fascist drivel! How can you, who sit here in comfort on a sunny island, talk like this while poor people slave in dark and smoky factories? You should be ashamed of yourself, old man."

"Please," Simon complained. "Both of you, please."

"The elite of humanity," Jeff continued with a smile on his face while he served himself a slice of brandy-drenched chicken breast. "Despite threats and prosecutions and even executions, the elite of humanity has provided mankind with knowledge and offered emancipation. Most people chose to ignore these hard-earned gifts from the elite. Instead they cling to ancient fantasy stories. And they care mainly to satisfy their more basic instincts without interest in art and beauty and science and knowledge. On top of this, they form political parties with the exclusive purpose to steal money from the talented and hardworking few and encourage ignorance and loitering amongst the many."

"No, Jeffrey, please," Simon protested. "Show some restraint."

"I am not going to argue with you," Max said, "because I can see that you're a prisoner of your foul political creed. But even if the reality were as you say, which I disagree with, you should use your superiority, as you see it, to give support to the less fortunate. This is a humanist and non-fascist stance. But now I've had enough of this." He dropped his cutlery on the plate and turned around in his chair.

"From the very first second I saw you," Max said, "I was convinced you were a full-blown fascist through and through."

"Take it easy, young man. I'm just an ordinary, well-informed citizen who see things the way they are, the simple straight facts staring us in the face."

Max stood up. "I thought people with these views were uneducated thugs or depraved over-class brats with no brains."

"Don't leave, Max, please," Simon said. "Please, both of you!"

"I can't stay here and pretend I wouldn't hear those words ringing in my ears," Max said. "I didn't like this man when I got here, and

I like him even less now. How can you live here with this full-blown fascist?"

"He likes me."

"Really? What happened to you? Leave this place. Come home and make yourself a decent life. Barbara still loves you."

"My life here is fine."

"Is it? *J'en doute.* Why don't you leave with me? I'm on my way to Turkey and then to Persia."

"Persia? I don't like Persians; they cut their children's dicks. Can't be human."

"I hope you don't wake up too late." Max said. He shook Justin's hand and left without saying goodbye to Jeff.

"Not so well done, Jeff," Simon said. "Max is a deeply devoted left-wing Social Democrat, and he's famous for being temperamental. He hasn't been kicked out of two or three private schools for nothing."

"With his background he should have learned to behave better. You don't rush away when invited to a meal simply because you can't accept somebody's opinion. What kind of behaviour is that?"

"You may have a point, but you express your views as deliberate provocations. Be nice, Jeff, be British, you're supposed to be more accommodating."

They finished their lunch in silence. Jeff threw Max's half-eaten chicken thigh out on the sand for the dogs.

"What Jeff said may have sounded worse than it is?" Simon said to Justin when they were alone. "About poverty, I mean."

"No, my dear child, it's the other way around." Justin sighed while working on the background of one of his portraits of local peasant boys. "Way bloody worse than what it sounds." He smiled. "But I don't want to tattle."

"Yes, you have to!" Simon grabbed Justin's shoulders from behind and shook them. "Now you've made me curious, tell me. What?"

"Oh, don't shake me! Look what you did!"

"Sorry, you spoilt only the background. You can repaint that. Now tell me."

"I don't want to make it difficult for you and Jeffrey to be good friends. I would rather have my tongue cut out than say anything that would cause a rift in the relationship between you two."

Simon laughed. "Hilarious. Now, tell me something nasty about him."

"Okay," Justin sighed. "But purely on one important condition, that you never, ever tell anybody, and in particular Jeffrey. I don't want to plant a seed in his bloody mind that could make him misunderstand my dear appreciation of him, irrespective of fucking whatever, if you pardon my French. Do you understand?"

"Mouth shut. If questioned, I know nothing."

"Good. Take a chair and sit here beside me, so I can talk to you *sotto voce*."

Simon brought a chair and Justin handed him his package of Turkish cigarettes. Simon lit one for Justin and passed it over, then lit one for himself. Justin kept working on the portrait.

"Four years after the war," Justin began, "in 1949, Jeffrey came to Europe and on a small island off the Italian west coast he hired a summer home, the same as here. Only four years earlier, battles between the Nazis and the invading British and American troops had impoverished the land. People still had nothing. They survived on fish they could get from the sea. They dealt with illnesses and hunger and malnutrition in children by praying to the saints. They had no money. Up by the main road with almost no traffic, they tried to sell belongings of doubtful value. Any little penny they could earn they spent on candles in the church and lit them for the Virgin, hoping for her benefaction."

Justin paused. "Please, Simon, can you get me something to drink? To speak for so long dries out my mouth."

Simon brought him a glass of cold white wine. Justin took a gulp and continued.

"Anyway, Jeffrey settled with a group of Australian and British friends. Attractive young local men, the ones Mr Smart likes, soon learned how to get a small share of Jeffrey's wealth, as it was to them. These lads were rotten poor. They crawled for him. They were obedient in everything. Never have so many handsome and strong young men been fucked up their tight virgin asses as on that island during Jeffrey's stay."

"Gosh! Sounds like a heaven for him."

"He became king of the island. As you well know, my dear Simon, nature equipped Mr Smart with a mighty tool. When this tool gets steel hard and works like an oiled piston, you'd better have a virgin in heaven for holy intervention." Justin emptied his glass and filled it with more white wine. "The pain you have to suffer for your poverty, a bleeding arse."

"Jeff seems to have an inclination for islands," Simon remarked.

"I don't know about that." Justin put down his brush. "Don't tell him I've told you. Promise."

"Yes, yes." Simon laughed. "Oiled piston was it?"

"That term just came to my mind. You know what I mean."

"Isn't this how people behave who have a little more towards those who have a little less? They buy or corrupt others to gain sexual pleasure, but with discretion. I thought paying for the other was normal standard in courtship? Invite someone you fancy for a meal. Or you gladly pay for the movie tickets. Don't people buy and sell sex all the time? At least they hope to get their pleasures granted with gifts. Not to mention the motives by those who willingly receive what they are being offered? Usually girls and women, isn't that so?"

"No idea," Justin said. "I don't know about these things. Will we see Max again?"

"We'll find out tomorrow. I can't go up to the village and see him now. It's too dark. I always run into someone who can't resist me."

"Jeffrey often says everything has a cost. To be attacked by horny men is what you must pay for being so gorgeous."

"I wish they would leave me alone."

"We do, Jeffrey and I."

"That's why I like to be here even if Jeff makes a pass every day. Discretely but still. And his declarations about how wonderful I am, make me irritated."

"Jeffrey is fond of you," Justin said.

"I guess he is. Why do you talk as his advocate?"

"I don't know. But I feel guilty that I told you about Italy."

"Don't bother. I've already forgotten."

"You're such a kind person, Simon. I wish you all the best."

"I know you do."

"Didn't I tell you Jeff would separate you from anybody you lined up with?"

Simon laughed. "Is that what you think he did?"

"He made Georgios rush away, and now this chap."

"Maybe you're right. We'll see."

"You never know, except that Jeffrey is always planning and scheming to get what he wants from other people."

Learn from the Queen:
Shut Up, Accept and Smile

The following week, Jeff was sitting alone on the terrace in the early morning.

"Are you Jeffrey Smart?" someone behind him asked with a Scandinavian accent.

Jeff turned and saw a fair-haired young man. In an instant he saw the boy lacked Max's aristocratic arrogance, thank God.

"I'm Erik. I was L-L-L-Lennart's schoolmate." He reached out and they shook hands.

"Oh, another one. How do you know my name?"

"He-he-he writes ab-b-b-bout you."

"Oh, does he? What happens here isn't much to write about. We work most of the time. A book about us would be boring."

Jeff studied the young man with the professional interest of someone who has spent hundreds of hours drawing nude bodies of different shapes and sizes. Erik's proportions were anatomically abnormal. He was not a midget, but well below average height. His head was too large for his body and his arms were too short, barely reaching below his hips. A prominent bulge suggested a well-developed organ between his bandy legs. His hair was white and thin, and his face was chalky with a sharply undershot chin and no growth of beard.

When Simon and Justin returned from their morning swim, they sat around the table to have a cup of tea together.

"Erik's father is also an artist," Simon said, "and most people in the country have enjoyed his paintings. One can't say this about yours, Jeff. Your paintings are stuffed into a small museum in a local town Down Under, isn't there where they are?"

"They're not at Guggenheim. Yet."

"They print his father's paintings on postcards and send them out to every household in the country for free at Christmas, with a choice to pay for them."

"I see. And he paints with his mouth?" Jeff asked.

"Yes, my f-f-f-father was b-b-b-born without arms," Erik said.

"Must be difficult," Jeff said.

"I don't think you would gi-gi-give much fo-fo-for my f-f-f-father's p-p-p-p-paintings. They're rather conv-v-v-ventional."

"Yes, they usually are," Jeff said. After a long silence he added, "There are well-regarded scholars who believe the sombre mood of Sibelius's work was due to the fact the composer was so richly endowed by nature he could hardly get it up. Or in, if up."

Simon looked abashed. "You're not serious?"

"Which implies not only our inner but also outer constitution may affect the character of our artistic products."

"Wonder what you will be known for, Jeff," Simon said. "When you're dead and have become famous. It won't be for your dick."

Jeff chuckled. "Is this what you sit here and scribble in that impossible Arctic Circle language? Perhaps I should burn your papers to save my reputation?"

"I may do as Gide. He met Wilde and Lord Alfred Douglas in the desert in Algeria. Thirty years later he wrote about their meeting in *Si le grain ne muert* and showed the world that bastard Bosie was a bitch. Maybe you and I have a similar meeting? Simon meets Jeffrey Smart on an isolated Greek island? How about that, Jeff? But you must be famous first and interesting enough. I don't want to waste my time and effort on somebody nobody cares to read about."

"Oh, you're so funny, my pretty little thing."

Later in the day, native neighbours with a fishing boat invited Simon and Erik to follow them to the other side of the island, where no blonde man had set his foot in living memory. Simon filled a basket with piss-on-me, cheese, salad, and olives for a small lunch.

In this remote place far from the village, the two Nordic young men attracted attention, so they left the place where the local people gathered and found a half-secluded spot on the beach between the cliffs. They sat down to share their light picnic.

A young boy, a child, came and joined them. He carefully sat down behind Simon and leaned against his back. Simon continued to eat and talk to Erik. After a while, the lad began to suck Simon's earlobe. First lightly, then more intensely.

"Why is he doing this? Retarded?" Erik asked.

Simon shrugged. "There's always inbreeding on islands, you know. A slight mental retardation may be common. And sucking is deeply rooted among us. Remember from our biology lessons? The name of our scientific class, *Mammalia*, derives from the breast we suck as infants. We are suckers by nature." They laughed.

"Just be careful what you suck and in what part of the globe you are when you do so. You know that cunnilingus and fellatio are illegal in several of the United States."

"It's unbelievable how some people find no limit to their hate when it comes to hunting down every little form of the pleasure we may give each other as human beings."

"Yes, and it seems that everywhere the haters rule," Erik said.

"Now he's touching my back," Simon said. "This is more like an invitation. Does he look at you?"

"His eyes are closed most of the time. But he's checking me out now and then. How does it feel?"

"It's erotic. I can't deny that. I can sense his craving in how he touches me. He's under my shirt now. He would try to fuck me if we were alone."

"He's young!" Erik exclaimed. "Eleven, twelve, no more, I'm sure."

"That's when they begin."

"How do you know?"

"More than once, I've been chased by a whole group of kids like this one. One night they got me down on the ground. On my way home. I wasn't sober. They were all over me and tried to pull off my trousers before I saved myself. Most of them had their dicks out and they were not hanging down."

"And now? With this one?"

"I do nothing. I sit here and try to eat. I don't even see him. He's touching me gently. It feels pleasant."

"He's smiling at me now," Erik said.

"One could say he's molesting me."

"Yeah, sure."

"I don't feel molested though," Simon said. "It's surprisingly sweet."

"What're you gonna do?"

"Nothing. I hope he stops soon and leaves."

"Well, then make him leave. And what if someone sees us?"

"*Óchi, den thélo*,"[12] Simon said. The kid got up and ran away.

"Life is different here," Simon said. "But it may give us an insight into the human mind and our condition. We might even get a glimpse of our progenitors. Who knows?" They laughed.

"Deep down, we're still more like animals, you mean?" Erik asked.

"Why not? Don't forget their brain is still unchanged in ours. Parts have been added, nothing removed. We still lodge the snake's brain in the centre of our own. I feel the animal in me is chained and wants to get out and be free."

"Don't let your snake brain take command over you," Erik laughed.

They returned home in time to share a nice cup of tea with the artists at four o'clock.

"See you 'n' tea!" Simon shouted, as he always did when tea was being served.

Afterward, Simon and Erik chatted with each other in their native language. Jeff and Justin were in their rooms painting. As always, Jeff shut his door to the terrace while Justin's door and window were wide open. Erik left after an hour or two.

"Why were you so unfriendly?" Simon asked when Jeff returned to the terrace. "Why bring up physical abnormalities, like Sibelius's dick?"

"I *was* friendly! I served him a nice cup of tea. Twice. I even passed him the sugar when he tried to reach for it with his short

12 No, I don't want to.

arms. But you can't deny the chap is a bit awkward."

"So what? He's well educated, he's kind and humble, and he's my friend! And who isn't awkward or queer for that matter?"

"The chap disgusts me. He's repulsive and cheesy. You think so too, I'm sure. You're just too kind-hearted to admit it."

Justin came out from his room and sat down by the table. "I bloody well can't stand him."

"What?" Simon asked. "Who? Why?"

"This Charlie Blumenthal, or whatever his bloody name is, he drives me up the fucking wall. He's awful, I can't work when I see the bastard and hear his stammer."

"Justin!" Simon exclaimed. "How can you be so inconsiderate? You disappoint me."

"Hate me if you need to, but I don't want to see him here again."

"If you don't want to see him, I will tell him to not come here," Simon said.

"A most unpleasant person," Jeff said. "I feel so sorry for him. Life must be terrible when you look and sound like him. And he's got no manners. I agree with your Auntie. He doesn't belong here; we're a different sort of people. He's not our kind."

"I know I should be more charitable," Justin said. "Since he's your friend, I must ask you to forgive me, but I have no other choice. If he is here, I can't work."

"No, Justin," Jeff said. "There's no reason to ask for forgiveness."

"Aren't we meant to be more charitable to each other?" Justin said.

"Meant?" Jeff exclaimed, affecting outraged shock. "Nothing is meant to be in any way, Justy dear. You talk as if you still believe somebody thought this world out and intended to make happy people love."

"Maybe ... how else could we explain things? Why do we love if love was not put in our hearts?"

"First, the heart has got nothing to do with love. Love might quicken its pace, but it beats the same when you're attacked by an ill-tempered kangaroo. Second, we 'love,' as you call it, because those who automatically took care of their offspring helped them survive to a greater extent than those who did not. When this selection had gone on for hundreds of millions of years the capacity to take care of the offspring was part of their heritage, and let's assume some rudimentary affection was connected, and was well established in the vertebrate long before we emerged as *Homo sapiens*. This was an embryo of love which later was refined by other selection mechanisms, but the basic capacity to care with affection is far, far older than we as a human species."

"If that is true, wouldn't it be better for us if we loved everybody?" Justin asked.

"No, it would be worse," Jeff said. "The same as most of us are born with an affection for our offspring, we're also born with a dislike for those who deviate from our clear perception of a normal standard in our group. We see this in our children, who turn against those who they perceive as too different, when free from curtailing parental influences. And in ancient times, in parts of our world, a new-born child who did not match required standards was placed alone out in the woods to be returned to nature through the system of digestion of predators and their defecation on the fertile ground. We learn from this we must get rid of that which we dislike and clean our living space of its negative influences in our groups, in our families and neighbourhoods and in our nation. This is what you just have done, Auntie. Now we can live in peace and unity in our little group without the disturbing and work-in-hibiting influences of Charlie Blumenthal. And may he live in peace in some other place, not here."

"Not much peace for the poor sods you punch out," Simon said.

"You're too emotional, my boy. Look at things with reason. We should learn from the children, who discriminate with no qualms. They kick out those they don't like. It may not be 'nice' but it promotes life in the long run and nurtures peace and harmony in the group."

"That sounds ridiculous. How can discrimination support life?"

"Listen, if hostility towards those who are annoyingly different is a good, as I claim, one may ask why we teach our children not to mistreat those who are strange. We do this because we fail to see how we make our offspring as hypocritical and false as we ourselves. This will eventually make them neurotic and incapable of love. The choice we face is to be true to nature and become loving bastards or be civilised hypocrites who can be nice but don't love. And then make people mistake nicety for love."

"No. Too complicated for me," Justin said. He lit another Turkish cigarette on the one he was smoking and went into the kitchen to pour himself a large glass of Retsina.

"You've said before it takes all kinds to make a world," Simon objected.

"Yes, but the world has many facets," Jeff said. "Where you're accepted, you can stay. If not, better luck on another island where you don't need a sharp beak to survive. Move to where nature welcomes you. If there is no such place for you, down the drain you'll go."

"Society is not nature. If I live in a bad environment and if the people I live with are bad, what then?"

"There's nothing good or bad for nature, only survival or extermination, as you well know, Simon, so I don't understand why you argue. You find a niche in your environment, no matter how it is, and survive, or you don't. This principle has created everything organic you can see around you, humans, animals and plants, yourself included."

"I can see another 'principle' that makes us survive. Think of a loving parent overwhelmed by an infant's first smile. That is the love that makes us survive. Or a patient and praising father helping his son to ride on his first bike. These fathers exist, you know, even if none of us have ever met them. There you can find fragments of love if you have the proper eyes to see with."

"My dear, what a sweet angel you are," Jeff exclaimed. "When you talk the way you do, I get tears in my eyes. It's true. How can anybody who is so impossible to live with and looks so gorgeous say such sweet things?"

"Please, Jeff. Don't."

Jeff sighed. "You don't like him much either, this Charlie Blumenthal. He's not your kind of chap, to put it mildly. You didn't talk to him like you did to Max. With Max you smiled twice as much as you did with poor Charlie. Discrimination, my dear boy, takes many subtle forms. Don't shake your head. It's always at work, even in devoted hypocrites who claim they don't discriminate. Without exception, whenever a hypocrite declares his approval for something, there's always something else he hates even more. But the worst is not their hatred but their total unawareness. And so they blindly roam the world and call the deeds of their hatred liberation."

"You have no common sense," Simon said. "Why fight against everything and everybody? Learn from your Queen: shut up, accept and smile."

"I fight because I believe in reason, while the common people prefer to be slaves to their emotions. To go with the crowd and have the correct view—or what you call 'common sense'—serves as a survival kit for those who are afraid of life. They need to shrink life to a pinhead small enough for their minute capacities to manage, the way head-hunters shrink heads to make themselves feel mighty and important. Then they hang their reduced little correct views like shrunk heads in their dwarfed minds. And notice that these are the same people who gladly submitted to the commands of ruthless men to march mentally blind-folded to be slaughtered by the millions on the battle fields in what they now call the Great War."

Justin lit yet another cigarette. "Whatever you say and no matter how much you think you know, for me this is simple. There are those I love, and they are not many, and the rest I don't love. Most of my life I lived with a creed where loving everybody was mandatory. That was ludicrous, and when I realised, I left that creed, and I will not return."

With that they retired to their individual artistic pursuits. Simon composed a poem about a headhunting dwarf slaughtered by his giant mother. Jeff sketched the outlines of a new painting with endless apartment buildings, homes for the common man in a charmless suburb. Justin began to paint *The Forgiveness of Judas in the Temple*. The temple rested on a cliff high above the sea, and Judas Iscariot looked more like a middle-aged man of Irish descent than a young Jew from two thousand years ago.

Simon invited Erik to a last supper up in the village to convey the message of rejection from his patrons.

"The d-d-day we're b-b-born we ent-t-t-er into-to-to-to he-he-hell or into-to-to he-he-heaven." Erik was forced to stop and gasp for breath. "And we're d-d-d-doomed t-t-to st-st-stay there fo-fo-fo-fo-for life." was Erik's philosophical comment to the Aussies' verdict.

At school, Erik had soon accepted nobody was attracted to him. He took a deep liking to Barbara; she found him repulsive and refused to allow him in her presence. Then Greek prostitutes came as a rescue. And he plunged into lovemaking.

On his first visit to the women in Piraeus, Athens's sleazy harbour town, Erik spent every penny his parents had given him when he graduated. The best-spent money in his whole life, he claimed.

He was a popular and well-liked customer among the prostitutes. The women perceived his white hair as blond and hence attractive. His small size and lack of facial hair appealed to women with a paedophilic inclination. They welcomed him with warm and soft human holes where he could dip his proportionally too-large dick and they nourished his soul with comfort and friendly appreciation.

Erik died after a short period of severe illness caused by a genetic abnormality.

The Happy Prince

Jeff was convinced he was worth more happiness than the poor crumbs life bestowed him at the present. Two major obstacles prevented his contentment: his vow of celibacy, for which Justin served as the custodian, and young Simon's lack of interest.

Jeff wanted the boy with an even greater fervour than he had felt the first time he caught sight of him in the monastery church on the eve of Holy Sunday. That purely physical attraction was now threaded with his admiration for Simon's wide-open mind and the special attraction of his erratic behaviour. Nothing but a close union with the boy would ease Jeff's painful urge.

Two considerations gave Jeff hope that he might mitigate his pain, and perhaps even open the door to a more gratifying cohabitation with the boy. First, his vow of celibacy was undoubtedly limited to his time on this island, not for the whole of universe or for times eternal. This straight fact would allow Jeff latitude should he and Simon be together at another place and another time.

Second, Jeff was familiar with learning theory and was convinced that every person could be encouraged to change his behaviour with suitable persuasion in the form of a tangible or intellectual gift—often called a token in scientific learning experiments with rats. The reward could be an invitation to a splendid feast, or an extravagant trip abroad. The promise of lifelong support, for better or for worse, in sickness and in health, was one of the more popular awards.

The social stigma in civilised countries of using money as a reward in intimate relationships could be surprisingly costly, and result in headlines in serious newspapers and magazines when a public figure was involved. Sophisticated people had to buy and sell each other by more subtle means.

Following these simple premises, Jeff concluded a trip to Athens, he and his Easter vision alone together, would give him a welcome opportunity to enter into a more fruitful relationship with the boy. There could be orchids for Miss Blandish again, in Jeff's parlance; they could be *masí*, as the Greeks would say. They could fuck, as the proper Anglo-Saxon buddies would put it or make love which would be the female equivalent.

Jeff was acquainted with a minor Athenian hotel, Xenia Melathron, behind the mighty Grande Bretagne at Syntagma Square. They would have their own shower, important for proper lovemaking. He had measured the size of the bed: *cinque, dieci, venti* … a king-size bed offering ample stalking grounds to hunt his prey.

To Jeff's delight, Simon consented to the excursion, and Jeff practically skipped as they went to the beach hotel, where the island's only taxi waited to take them to the small port on the other side of the island. There they boarded the little skiff that took them to the ferry moored at anchor in the roadstead. Such a complex itinerary for getting in and out of the island had protected this island from penetration by unwanted outsiders. As a young man Peleus's son Achilles profited from the impenetrability of the island, hiding in a girl's clothing on the island's tall cliff, where the monastery church now served the locals.

On the mainland Jeff had parked his old Simca, which he had

bought in France and driven himself and Justin through Europe. They picked up the car in the garage and drove down to Athens. Jeff was happy as a lark, singing and telling Simon stories from films and operas while driving on bumpy roads through the hot and sunny Greek countryside. With gusto Simon sucked in Jeff's splendid daylong verbal and vocal entertainment.

One day they drove out to Piraeus, the squalid harbour town which had been made famous for its happy and generous prostitutes in the film *Never on a Sunday*, recently nominated for several Academy Awards. They had a nice cup of tea at four o'clock in a café in a park.

A little boy, thin, dirty, and dressed in rags, ten or eleven years old, came up to Simon.

"*File!*"[13] he said and stuck out his small tongue from his half-open mouth, showing his willingness to perform fellatio. He looked from one to the other with big, dark, and woeful eyes.

"I would fancy to see him sit between me and you in the car and masturbate both of us," Jeff said. "With suitable persuasion, I'm sure he would do a lot of things." He took out his wallet and slapped it against his thigh and nodded to the boy.

"You want this, don't you? Drachma. What's a hundred in Greek?"

"I don't know. But please, Jeff, don't do this."

The little boy grimaced with a distorted smile and stretched his dirty hand towards Jeff's wallet.

"You must dance first, sonny boy," Jeff said. "Dance for me! What the fuck is 'dance' in this impossible language?"

"Oh shit, Jeff. How can you even talk to him like this? He's

---

13 Friend!

just a child, for god's sake. And a human being."

"Yes, but he's got a sweet face, and I like the little tongue he's got. Like a huge clitoris in the middle of his pretty face. Pretty, but dirty. Poor people never seem to wash themselves properly. They have water, don't they?"

What a cruel monster sexuality could be. This vulnerable little human being was begging to be used for whatever their lust dictated so long as they pressed hard coins into his thin and dirty hand. They could rape him, use him as a toy or a tool, no matter how he was hurt and harmed. He would keep his thin little mouth shut and endure any treatment these two noble gentlemen wished to submit him to. He had experienced what desolate or cold-hearted gentlemen were willing to do to a poor little boy and he would continue with this trade for years to come. For a drachma or two now and then he eventually had his little child's arse torn apart.

"It's rare to see poverty like this nowadays," Jeff said. "A real pity. There are fewer poor people around, and they are not as poor as they were before."

"Let's go back to Athens," Simon said. "I don't want to be here." They got up and left, giving nothing to the child. The boy turned to other gentlemen; there were plenty of them. *Mein Vater, mein Vater, o siehst du Ihn nicht?*[14] Johann Wolfgang von Goethe wrote and Franz Schubert made us sing.

The little boy was the son of a young female prostitute who'd taught him the trade. Years later her son would be sentenced to life in prison. He had raped and severely harmed a girl of eight and had been previously sentenced for different incidents with children and for petty theft.

---

14 My father, my father, don't you see what he does to me?

Shortly after he was imprisoned, fellow inmates stabbed him in the back, and paralysing him. He was confined to sitting in a chair in a prison hospital cell and staring at an empty wall in front of him; they lifted him into a bed for the night. He was unable to talk or move and they fed him by a tube. He spent eighteen years in this condition.

"He got what he deserved" was the general opinion on the street. No excuses for these demons. Those soft-hearted people who claimed these monsters were victims as children, most often at home, and caught in a cycle of abuse were met with scorn. "What absolute nonsense. It's a question of right and wrong. There's no forgiveness for such dreadful deeds, no matter what childhood. We all had things to deal with as children, that's life and nothing you can escape from."

During their week in Athens, Jeff played the role of Simon's happy and devoted sugar daddy as well as his economic circumstances permitted. He drew him around in his Simca, invited him to exclusive international shows and parties, presented him to wealthy Aussie friends visiting Athens and took him to splendid dinners at the Plaka. Simon was pleased to be at the centre of Jeff's attention and servile care. See me, feel me, touch me.

With a combination of single-mindedness and a genuine desire, Jeff managed to wake sufficient lust in his bedfellow. Being touched and kissed and sucked on his throat and neck, Simon began step by step to give in to Jeff's eager courtship and unadulterated oestrus. The youngster detested having Jeff's tongue up his nostrils and pushing into his ears. But he enjoyed having the renowned Australian artist Jeffrey Smart kiss, lick, and suck his anus with the same ferocious avidity as a pig snout's clamorous rummaging through the slimy garbage from the kitchen.

"Oh, love, how wonderful you are," Jeff snuffled.

Jeff repeatedly proclaimed a great passion for the boy. However, he didn't show the tenderness or affection one could expect from a mature person with full access to his emotions and who had learned how to express them. He conveyed his amorous feelings with his dick and his tongue and his fingers into various orifices, and that was that. No fuss and no unnecessary frills. If his partner may have needed to be more than an object of pleasure that was none of Jeff's concern. When Jeff wanted him to take it in the mouth Simon put his foot down. Enough was enough.

While in Athens having sex with Simon, fractions of an elemental realisation occurred to Jeff: love demanded more than he'd ever thought and maybe more than what he was inclined to put at stake. He had to revaluate his position. Nature would never reward him with the highest carat of that ultimate gift unless he gave in completely and lost himself. He had to cast off his thoughts, his self, his reserve, and his fears, surrender to the cruel demands of existence and become just pure experience no different from that of an iguana both in his flesh and in his mind.

Tottering on a high cliff above the sea, Jeff was not prepared to make that crucial leap; the sea was too far below, and you never knew.

Then, finally, before they left and had a nice cup of morning tea, Jeff looked at Simon, who was quiet and seemed as if alone and not yet quite awake. He thought of their week together which had passed and wondered why they were together and what glued him to this boy. It wasn't sex; maybe he fooled himself.

Living in the real world in Athens rather than on a secluded island, Jeff saw in Simon's dealing with his life, with unpredictability and antisocial streaks, a clear reflection of himself and his tormented youth. This hurt him most the times he dared to see the loneliness and sadness in the young boy's eyes.

The freedom with which Simon acted out his inner conflicts and the relief he found in crying and giving words to his despair when he was drunk were not allowed when Jeff was Simon's age.

This boy, who captured him some months ago, Jeff found to be a source of pain and desperation that he had not been able to acknowledge fully until this day, in this hotel, in Athens, capital of Greece. But now it was too late. The harm was done.

When they returned to the Molos, they had a nice cup of tea with Justin and then Jeff went into his room. When they were alone, Justin gave Simon one of his Turkish cigarettes.

"When I just saw you and Mr Smart coming home from bloody Athens," Justin said, "walking on the sand along the shore, I realised you would never get into Jeffrey's cot again. Whatever happened, it is over, and I'm sure Jeffrey also realised this. I can't say I shed a tear or feel the least sorry for the poor chap. He has broken the agreement we had, to not even make a pass at you. But that's Jeffrey. If he wants something, an old agreement with a friend means nothing. Mr Smart proceeds through life with no concern for anybody else. He needs a proper punishment to wake him up, if you see what I mean."

Simon tapped his cigarette against the edge of the table. "Despite his bickering and insults, I thought you two were still dearest friends?"

"Friends? Jeffrey doesn't have friends. He doesn't know what a friend is. He surrounds himself with people who he thinks can be useful for him in some bloody way and call them friends. The person he mentioned at tea is not *his* friend, he's *my* friend. He's been my friend since Jeffrey was unknown and knew nobody. Jeffrey knows him only through me, and now he talks of him as if he is the one who knows him, and not me. If you would believe what Jeffrey says, he's got all the bloody fucking friends and I've got no friends at all.

"And the way he talks about them! Take Mic, for example, the BP president in Rome; he calls him his friend. But when he talks about him it's always about how many servants he's got, and what superb cooks he's got in his fucking kitchen, and the delicious bloody food he eats there. It's never about Mic, or what he likes about *Mic*, it's only about what Mic owns and what he may offer. It's fucking disgusting to listen to. The same with everybody he knows, it's about their country places, and the food they serve, and how many servants they have. Jeffrey is obsessed with servants. I'm sure he knows the name of every single fucking cook working for those people he calls his bloody friends. So be careful with what Jeffrey tells you. He exaggerates, and he distorts reality."

"And this is your final verdict? Jeffrey Smart has got no friends?"

"There are two people Jeffrey regards as his closest friends. I am one of them, and he pisses on and bullies and humiliates me in front of you; the other is Mic, who has served as his Maecenas over the years, and with him Jeffrey is an ingratiating arse licker."

"Poor Jeffrey," Simon said.

"How so? Poor us, I should say."

"'*Det är synd om människorna*,' Strindberg wrote. 'The human being is to be pitied' is a lousy translation but the best anybody could make. And Jeff is to be pitied as well. That's all."

"Don't feel sorry for him. Mr Smart deserves no sympathy. None. I wonder how I became part of this. Bloody stupid. I've been an idiot."

"If you don't mind, Justin, I will humbly tell you what the matter is: you, my dear old Auntie, accept any torture or humiliation because you think you would suffer more if you had to be alone with yourself. Alone with you own genuine thoughts and emotions and disturbing memories. Not to mention your guilt for failing someone you loved."

"Uff. Your words are getting too complicated for me. Have to go back to work." Justin hurried into his room, sat down in front of his easel, and lit a Turkish cigarette.

From his little collection Simon took up a book titled *The Happy Prince*. Oscar Wilde wrote this tale for his two sons when they were children. It was about a swallow's impossible love for the gold-clad Happy Prince ending with the death of both, a tragedy in prose for little children. "High above the city, on a tall column, stood the statue of the Happy Prince. He was gilded all over with thin leaves of fine gold …" it began.

In the evening Jeff came out from his room and told them he suffered from a kind of strange indigestion and would not have dinner but stay in bed.

Simon and Justin went to Kokalénia and had lovely *keftedes*—sautéed lamb meatballs bound with crumbs of piss-on-me and milk. Justin talked about life in Sydney during the ten years when he and Brian were together. On the way home, they were accompanied by a somewhat too elated and friendly young man, whom Justin led directly to his bed.

Simon took up his book by Wilde and continued to read about the fate of the besotted swallow and the statue of the golden prince who was stuffed with rubies, emeralds, and sapphires. Jeff came out to get something in the kitchen.

"Are you sitting here all alone?" he asked.

"I need to be alone sometimes," Simon said.

"Where's your Auntie?"

"She's in bed."

"Have you had anything to eat?"

"We went to Kokalénia."

"Why did she go to bed so early?"

"She's got a visitor."

"No, don't say that. What age?"

"Close to thirty, I'm sure."

"She's mad, he'll fuck her. She doesn't want that, and she'll end up with *animali piccoli*, or worse. Do you have any DDT left?"

"No, I used it all. We can buy more if necessary. Are you okay, Jeff?"

"Yes. Just needed a rest. Athens took the strength out of me, ha."

"We had a nice week, I enjoyed it. Even if it was hot without the breeze we have here on the island."

"Thank god we had the shower. It's a good little hotel. Don't you agree?"

"To shower didn't help much. After ten minutes I was still wet with sweat all over."

"For you it must be like another world. I'm more used to that kind of heat. ... Have you found anything of lasting value, you think, or has your life here been just a lot of junk?"

"I have met you and Justin, and that has been a great experience."

"You always talk as if we were Siamese twins. Always Jeff and Justin, never Jeff. Who was the great experience?"

"Both," Simon said. "Don't think I can't see you as different. But I see you as a pair. Social twins. Mental twins. But each with his own faulty heart."

"That's a serious accusation."

"No, it is not. It's a simple straight fact."

"Ha, ha, you're so funny."

"Yes, sure. I have to go to bed now."

Simon carefully opened the door to Justin's room. When he searched for the handle to his own door in the darkness, he bumped into a chair.

"For Christ's sake!" Justin shouted from his bed. "Can I have some privacy, please!"

"Sorry, Justy, I saw nothing. Are you enjoying yourself? I hope so."

"Please, please, give me some privacy!"

Simon shut the door between their rooms. Jeff was still on the terrace and heard their exchange of words. He laughed and returned into his own room.

His annoying indigestion had plagued him since he and Simon returned from Athens earlier in the day. He hoped it wasn't the beginning of an ulcer or a disguised angina. On an isolated and primitive part of the world Nature could strike him more mercilessly. If the problem hadn't passed by tomorrow morning he would go back to Athens. Staying here without proper treatment could be fatal.

Presence

Now and then, after work finished at six o'clock sharp and they had drinks, Jeff brought out paintings he was working on and leaned them against a wall. One at a time, he put a painting upside down or turned his back to it and scrutinised the painting in different mirrors, one with a smoky touch, others tinged in different colours.

Simon sat close to him and watched the artist examining his work and listened to the critical comments he made on how to deal with objects, shapes and colours, which had to be changed, discarded or in part or fully accepted.

Present while an analysing mind was working, Simon cared to understand the points the artist made and got a glimpse into Jeff's mind. Over the days and months he understood more deeply the working of this artist's mind when dealing with his work.

This time the active mind was concentrated on a painting. A similar process may take place when someone focuses on people or on other objects, even internal, as in a healing or disrupting process of remembering or reconsiderations.

In such situations, as a bystander, you are fully present, or you are not. And you share, or you don't, by experiencing the joy, the sadness, the despair or even indifference to the pain the other may not have enough internal means to deal with.

Love is manifested as sharing in this sense and by being present. Nothing needs to be said. Nothing needs to be done.

IV

Disappearing into the Darkness

The Love That Dare Not Speak Its Name

Summer lingered, but autumn approached. The sun rose a little bit later in the mornings and set a little bit earlier in the evenings and was not quite in the zenith at noon. All were aware change was in the air; that two of them would move to Rome was certain. Simon's near future was not discussed. Jeff knew the boy had vague plans, but so long as nothing was said, and nothing was decided all doors were open to the future. At least that's how the situation could be perceived.

At four o'clock Simon was in the kitchen preparing tea for himself and his patrons. "I have a crucial declaration to make," he said as he carried the teapot to the terrace table.

"I have received an appointment for an audition at the drama school." He put the teapot on the table and sat down while Jeff looked at him with some tension.

"You're leaving us now?" Justin asked.

"Yes! I am."

Jeff contemplated the almost royal blue of the sea and the azure of the sky. Had he ever painted a light-blue sky? He could not remember. Why were his skies always so dark?

"Congratulations, Simon!" Justin exclaimed. "I'm sure you'll succeed. I'm so glad."

Jeff turned his gaze to the mountains on the other side of the wide bay, where he had seen such extraordinary colours and fascinating shapes while high on mescaline. He forced a strained smile. "But actors are so stupid. You'll get bored. They care only for themselves. No attention for Little Number One, believe me. And how will you get all the long way up to that barbaric North Pole, anyway?"

"A guy will come here and then we go through Europe by boats and trains and ferries and whatever necessary," Simon said.

"Who's he?"

"He picked me up on the street one night when I was sixteen. I'm his main interest in life and his sole commitment."

"Oh, dear. What a sad existence!" Jeff said. "I thought such deplorable people were found exclusively in novels nobody cared to read."

"He loves me, I suppose. I don't even like him. I only contact him when I have a special need. Like the cost of living in Greece or to come back home to somebody who can support me while I train to turn into a famous and fabulous actor."

"You must have been irresistible," Justin said, "when you were a sweet little sixteen, and still untouched. What a dream." He looked at Simon with mournful eyes.

"If I help you to become a film star in Italy," Jeff said, "would that alter your plans?"

"Film star? In Cinecittà? You're joking, Jeffrey. No, I want to go to a genuine drama school and learn the trade and be a serious actor. I wish to play the great classics—Molière, Ibsen, Strindberg, O'Neill, and why not the old Greeks? To rely on the kindness of strangers is not a sustainable life stance."

"Oh, so we're strangers now?"

"You should know, Jeff, what I just said was a citation from *A Streetcar* and without significant meaning. Is there a problem?"

"I'll tell you what the problem is," Jeff said. "I can't even think of not seeing you every day. I will not cry, and I will not fall to pieces. But I'll have a bad time without you. That's what the problem is."

"Be a man, Jeff. Don't whimper like a toddler who's shat in his nappies."

"Oh, what a lovely, beautiful metaphor. I'm sure it didn't pop up spontaneously; it stinks of rehearsal. How can you do this to me?"

"*Courage, mon frère, courage!*" Simon said. He gathered their teacups and put them in the bottom of the sink for someone else to wash.

On the next day, one of the last hot summer days, something happened with a bang, not with a whimper. Love struck again. Simon was the target this time and he was ill prepared.

Since Simon was a toddler he had feared to be in the water and had therefore never learned to swim. His fear diminished when the water between the reef and the sandy shore by the beach behind the dunes offered him the heavenly grace of the Aegean Sea. The water in front of the reef was so salty it carried him on its surface. He could lie on his back not needing to move a single finger to keep afloat.

For months, the little beach behind the dunes had served as their private and protected reserve. But today a foreign family suddenly invaded their little pond with mum and dad and children jumping up and down and throwing toys as if they were in Saint-Tropez on the Côte d'Azur.

"Bien fait, ma chère!"

"Toi aussi, mon petit!"

They shouted and jumped around and splashed in Simon's water and paid no notice of his existence or need for privacy.

"I can't go into the water the way they jump around and splash and scream down there," Simon said.

Jeff laughed. "Oh, don't be silly." He went into the lukewarm sea and swam out to the deep water beyond the reef. On his way back, he greeted the male adult in the intruding group, and they exchanged what seemed to be polite words.

Simon stayed on the beach. His gaze was repeatedly drawn towards the intruders who disregarded him and showed no concern for his need to familiarise himself reservedly with the water.

The man looked to be about thirty-five. To Simon, he appeared to have a good education and a lot of self-confidence. There were two little girls, and an older boy, perhaps not yet in his middle teens. The mother was sitting on the beach watching her brood with a delighted smile.

The children were jumping up and down with Daddy, splashing and flopping and sloshing and shouting and screaming the way children always seemed to do. They had fun, the damn rascals. Simon's mind darkened.

There was the father. There was the son. They played with each other. They enjoyed being together. Simon's heart beat faster. He felt a pressure in his chest. He didn't find it difficult to breathe, but his whole body seemed to be affected by something. What was happening to him?

He saw a father and a son as simple as all that and nothing else. They seemed so pleased to be together. He noticed the father's joy and apparent dependability, his natural sense of presence. *When playing with my kids I am at home in life. My thoughts are here and do not wander elsewhere. I have no wish to be in any other place. I'm present, and I share. My children know I'm always there to protect them and now I am here to share their joy. When they are sad, I share their sadness. I am a father for my children.*

The son was gleaming with trust and confidence. He threw himself into the water as if he were a penguin in a zoo and had no fear. He laughed, he shouted, he was pleased and happy. Life had given him a precious gift. He wasn't yet aware of it, but he enjoyed the effect of that gift to its full extent. For a little boy, no start in life can be better than his Daddy's love. On this island, on the rubble of an ancient civilisation, he saw this "phenomenal" boy as a perfect incarnation of *der Bub an Sich*.[15] Yet Simon wasn't wise enough to understand that what he saw and contemplated was the purest form of love. The scene awoke in him, a teenager himself, a thirst and longing stronger and more overwhelming than anything he'd ever felt before. A deep infatuation captured him and took him far beyond what he could bear.

On the next day they were there again. Simon's adoring fascination had turned physical, and to his fright an ache spread throughout his teenage body, so harsh it might be dangerous, he feared.

Most affected by this pain were his testicles. The painful ache continued for many hours after their visit to the beach. On the third day the pain was so unbearable he could not walk upright.

15 The boy in his ideal form

He was distraught; something both novel and terrible had overwhelmed his mind and body.

"Why so silent, Simon? What is the matter with you?" Jeff asked when they were back on the terrace.

"It is my balls, they ache. I can hardly walk."

"Oh dear! And what has caused this misfortune, if I may ask?"

"The beautiful boy. The boy by the beach."

"Oh, him! Yes, he's extremely beautiful. A piece of art in real life. So rare," Jeff added with a grin.

"He wasn't only beautiful; his daddy loved him. It hurts so much I cannot even sit."

"You've fallen in love, my boy, that is what causes you the anguish," Jeff said with a big smile, as if he found this funny. "And your testicles encourage you with the full force of pure nature to release their content. That's the sole purpose of love: to fill the object nature chose for you with the contents of your balls in order for our species to survive. My poor sweet little thing, you've been hit by this monstrous demon. But learn to deal with it, or life will crush you mercilessly."

"Whatever you say," Simon said. "I don't want this, with balls and spunk. I only want to love him and be close to him. That's all. It's not about survival, Jeff, not now and not for me. It's pure love."

"Yes, of course," Jeff said. "I know exactly what you mean."

Simon shambled over to their neighbours with ten drachmas to get the empty bottle in his hand filled with ouzo. Within half an hour most of the fiery booze was gone but merely a little of the ache in his testicles. He sat like a knocked-out boxer in his corner of the ring, head hanging down, legs spread out, and his arms sagging from his sunken shoulders.

"Getting drunk is not good, dear boy," Jeff said. He was standing in the middle of the terrace with dirty blankets in one hand and a beach bag in the other. "You must learn to handle your confusing amorous feelings in a better way."

Jeff's tone of voice turned darker. "When you came home the first day you saw him you should have tossed off on the spot. On the next day it would have hurt you less. Toss off as often as you can to minimise your pain. No matter what, you must realize there's a hard lesson for you to learn: *you will never have him.* Do you understand? You must learn to cope with this turmoil without destroying yourself."

"Oh stop, you bore me."

"Understand, my dear boy, I'm trying to help you with advice from someone who's lived in this world a lot longer than you, and who has learned to deal with situations of this kind. Now listen to what I tell you: *almost everyone you fall in love with will not appreciate your feelings for them.* This is something you will have to learn to cope with. If not, your life will be a constant pain. Learn to deal with it and then you may survive."

"You are negative and so destructive," Simon said. "I don't believe what you say. Take Gide. He always found a way to conquer love! All his life! And the ancient inhabitants of this island they let love rule in their hearts and bodies. You know, I know, and everybody knows that you must let life wash over you, like the waves wash the beach down there! Listen to the lovely sound. Oh, I wish I were a shore and would be washed eternally by loving waves like that, over my body, soft and warm and sharing my pain with me."

"Oh, my intoxicated little hysteric! You talk as if you don't know anything. The stories you read are *fictional*! You know that. You know the difference between nature and art. Nature is cruel, ugly, sordid, dirty. In art we make it beautiful and kind. Look at what your Auntie does, she makes beauty out of torture and agony when she paints her beloved crucifixion. Every writer twists and turns his words to fabricate the story he wants. Gide chose his words so you would adopt his view. Take making love: words turn this sweaty, cumbersome activity, with blood and spunk and shit and piss right in the middle of love's corporal activities, into a sugared, creamy pastry with a pink marzipan rose on top that never smells of menstrual blood. People cherish to buy this fictional saccharine act which never ends in farts smelling like an old, rotten corpse. That's making love, my dear boy, on which our friends, the writers spray their sweetened poetry like Renaissance royalty covered their stench with powder and perfume instead of giving their bodies a proper wash with fresh and purifying water.

"Now go and toss off! Then wash yourself with pure, crystalline water! We're blessed with an abundance of it! And skip the crappy powder of your dreams and fantasies. Wake up and face reality. Forget your caressing waves! Forget the boy and go and toss off! That's life, pure and simple. And leave this sweet little boy to his sisters and his daddy and his mum. He's almost a child, for god's sake. Turn your need for passion and affection and care to a solid and mature man. Much better for you, trust my word."

"I'm also a child," Simon whimpered. "Only five, six years older, so we would fit together, this boy and me. My body wants him, Jeff! It screams for him! It kills me if I cannot kiss and cuddle with him! I want to be so close, oh dear God, oh Jeeesus help me now, and touch him and smell him and drink him. Jeff, please,

I need to be inside of him and float into him and take him in my mouth and when we mix, I will see into his eyes and I will be inside of him, and I will be like him. Oh Jeff, I can't survive! I long so much! My deep and pure feelings for him will make him happy! And he will love me! I cannot be without him! Please, please! I'll die out of despair and agony. *Je suis comme un homme iiiiiiivre!*"[16]

"Stop this!" Jeff snapped. "Your histrionic lamentations won't get you anywhere. Only time will cure you, and a sober mind, and it will still take years."

"Oh, Jeff, you're so clever, with these fine words, I don't even know what you're talking about. So, so, so ..." Simon struggled to keep his head up, but it fell down and he lost capacity to speak.

"My darling boy," Jeff said, with a rare tinge of sadness in his voice. "I'm sure you know, with your wide knowledge and excellent understanding, that since the bigots can no longer throw Wilde and his people to the lions, they search for other targets. Your love for this boy has now become the love that dare not speak its name. The love you feel for him will make it easy for the common man to take your life away from you in order to relieve himself of anguish. Whenever you fall in love like this, he would see you as a foul being who carries out its dreadful deeds. The mere mention of your love appals him, the way undesirable creatures like you always evoke disgust in common men. And he covers his vile fear with words that may resemble reason but merely are cheap excuses. In truth, he has projected onto you the feelings in himself he cannot tolerate, so he can feel that he is clean as mud and you the one who is the devil. That is the nature of the common man. He's

---

16 I am like a druuuuuunkard!

categorical and too ignorant to evaluate according to the facts and circumstances. And you, my sweetest boy, cannot evade his fear and hatred and his crude and ruthless nature, and your life will be the price to pay for his smug ignorance and incapacity to deal with his own emotions and the tension they arise in him."

"Oh Jeffrey, I've never heard you talk like this."

"You have not listened well, I fear. Take care to read behind the lines of what I've said and don't follow every sentence to the letter."

Michèl was the boy's name. He was fourteen and spoke only French. He lived in Lebanon where his father worked in a French bank. Simon dared to approach the incarnated angel and invited him, with his father's permission, to have a nice cup of tea on their terrace at four o'clock.

With intense emotions Simon, Jeff, and Justin watched Michèl glide across the beach toward the patio, shining with the peaceful love his father gave to him. The glorious boy with creamy honey skin and chestnut-brown eyes would redeem Jeff and Justin's young protégé and clean his mind of harmful memories and everything that troubled him as was expected by the normal cure of love.

And the precious son arrived and smiled, and he shone over this little congregation of Simon, Jeff, and Justin, and Riccy and young Zara, the daughter of the physicist Silvia. And they had tea together, and everybody was polite; the young incarnation was the centre of attention and all were kind. Even Jeff was so polite as he stumbled through his mediocre French. Justin smiled and beamed as he always did when there were pretty boys around, and Simon knew that Justin saw an angel on their terrace more beautiful than he had ever painted and ever would. The French boy was so delightful and lovely it seemed as if he were a visitor from a different sphere of life; maybe he was a piece of art, who by mistake, in this little moment of reality, had been placed among these ordinary people.

They took several snapshots. Simon got the boy's address on a little note, so he could send him the photographs when they had been developed in Athens or by the Arctic Circle.

The little tea party on the terrace was sober and a matter of fact. But in a parallel existence, Simon dreamt of a fulfilling meeting. With this address, his contact with the lovely Michèl would last forever. And they would meet and love each other till the end of time and far beyond eternity and be carried into the rising sun on the horizon by a golden chariot drawn by four white horses and sprinkled by petals from roses, red and pink, accompanied by the everlasting ending of Mahler's Symphony No. 3, and people would wave their banners and rejoice at what they saw was love as manifested on this earth, hallelujah, amen, hallelujah.

In the evening, Simon, Jeff, Justin, and the Wehrheim couple had dinner together at Kokalénia. From the darkness down by the shore, a boy came walking up to their table in the restaurant. It was Michèl, and he carried a little note. In French, he told Simon that his father had changed the address; Simon should send his letter with the photographs not to Michèl at their home, but to his father's office at the bank.

Michèl and Simon exchanged their address notes and the young boy smiled. He said *bonsoir* to everyone, turned, and walked down the steps to the beach and disappeared into the darkness.

"What a very pretty boy that was," Silvia said.

"He's French. I have talked to his father," Jeff said.

"I will never see him again," Simon said. "There goes my baby. His father has protected him from evil; he has protected him from my love."

"Behave yourself," Jeff said.

"Poor chap," Justin said. "He seemed such a sweet boy, your Michèl."

Back home, Simon yelled from the bottom of his wounded heart. "*Michèle, my bell, sont des mots qui vont très bien ensemble, my Michèle.*"

"It's '*ma belle*,'" Jeff corrected him. "And don't drink anymore. You have to deal with this."

"I fear for my future life, if this will be my destiny." Simon was lying on the terrace floor with a bottle of Retsina within reach.

"Don't fear, my child. You only suffered from a petty summer fling, caused by your hunger for the love you needed when you were only a tiny little boy. Our mighty fire-god up there in the light-blue sky nourishes your life with food and drink. It also equips you with an innate need for close embraces with a loving human body and it enticed you with its galactic power of seduction.

"Love doesn't always offer you the sweetness that you long for. One day you will recognise the difference when Nature offers you a bitter fruit disguised in shapes and colours that might otherwise beguile your soul. And you will say a calm farewell to that which you have learned may give a bitter taste and even hide a core of poison in its enticing flesh."

"You talk so much, my dear Jeff, you talk and talk. I only want to love. But now I want to sleep."

Simon emptied one bottle after the other until he fell asleep on the warm floor. Justin helped him to get up on his feet and carried him to his bed. He sat down beside the boy and looked at him for a while. His need for another cigarette brought him back to the terrace. He emptied a large glass of wine and stumbled into his own room and crushed down on his bed and fell asleep at once, the same as almost every other night.

The next day the family was no longer on the beach; they had left the island.

Pure Business

Ulf arrived to bring Simon back to a normal life in a well-tempered and cosy lower middle-class home in a dark and windy suburb by the Arctic Circle. He looked forward to having the boy sleeping in the bed next to his own and hoped fully for the grace that was coming to him. And why shouldn't life finally gratify him for his faithfulness and the deep feelings of true love he had for Simon?

Ulf was a pale, plain, and meek young man of twenty-six. He had not graduated. He had been raised in the countryside and after quitting school he moved into town, where he worked as a menial office clerk in a company insuring Volvo cars. He wanted life to be neat and orderly and was a dedicated admirer of Doris Day and Esther Williams. He despised drug addicts like Edith Piaf and Billie Holiday who couldn't take care of themselves and lived with brutes who used them for their money.

When he arrived at the cottage, Ulf couldn't believe that educated people with good money would freely choose to live in such primitive conditions, and for months! No water, no electricity, no radio, no telephone, no record player, no magazines, no TV, nothing! How was it possible?

"So interested is it for me to be here now," he said, when they had a nice cup of tea on the terrace. "Simon write to me many months of this house where I and you sit here. He tell me all happen in this place."

146

"How was your trip?" Jeff asked.

"Trip? If I fall?" Ulf put a packet of Benson & Hedges cigarettes on the table.

"I mean your journey from the Arctic Circle?"

"Arctic Circle? What I never hear," Ulf said, taking a long gold-plated cigarette holder out of his shirt pocket.

Jeff laughed. "That's what I call where you come from."

"I come not of Arctic Circles. I am very sad. I understand not."

Simon came to his rescue with a quick explanation and translation, despite their agreement only English should be used when any of the artists was present.

"I understand now," Ulf said and withdrew a gold-plated Dunhill lighter from the pocket of his grey gabardine trousers. He looked at it and put it on the table.

"Apologies for his bad English," Simon said. "He's nervous. The poor chap isn't well educated; that's just how things are, nor is he dazzling."

"So good you talk, Simon," Ulf said, screwing his cigarette onto the gold-plated holder.

"Can I be impertinent enough and ask you," Jeff said, "how you can afford to smoke those expensive cigarettes while you support this over-emotional scapegrace?"

"I understand not," Ulf said. "I am very sad."

"No, you're sorry," Simon said.

"I understand. It is sorry, it is not sad, is that right?" Ulf lit his cigarette.

"Yes, that's right," Simon said.

"Where can I shit?" Ulf asked. Jeff and Justin burst into laughter, and Simon hesitantly joined in. Ulf held his hands to his face.

"Sorry, an expression of pure Arctic Circle culture," Simon said. "I'm well aware you Anglo-Saxons neither piss, nor shit, nor have sex."

Simon showed Ulf the little accommodation behind the cottage. When Simon returned, Jeff shook his head. "No, Simon!" he said. "This. Is. Not. For. You! He. Is. Nothing. You deserve so much more. You deserve to be with someone much better. This fellow is nothing!" He spat it out. "Nothing!"

"Yes, I know, of course I do," Simon said. "But this will be a temporary arrangement. I won't let him come near me if that's what you think."

"Oh, I'm not even thinking about that, no, no. But you don't seem to understand: You should live with somebody with class, somebody who takes you out into the world and shows you everything worth seeing, to enlighten you and fulfil your life! Somebody with strength and initiative. This guy has nothing to offer. Not even a voice; he only whispers. And nothing worth listening to, polite little questions about nothing. He's a fucking scared little bunny. You bloody well need a roaring tiger!"

"I prefer a bunny who cares for me before a big kangaroo who would knock me down and jump away whenever I didn't please him. This little bunny supports me a hundred per cent. He'll do anything for me. Anything, I swear."

"So would I, so would I, and I swear too."

They paused and looked at each other, pondering what the other was trying to convey.

"I know you would," Simon said, "but only as long as you'd gain something. For you, Mr Jeffrey Smart, a human relationship is like a business deal. Ulf does anything for me, with no strings.

He gets down on his knees begging me, or even crawls on the floor. And I say no! But he's still there for me and does what I tell him. And he shuts up. You wouldn't do that; you would argue until you got it your way. Or you would chase me away, like a crazy Tasmanian devil. I may despise the scared little bunny, but I need him all the same, at least to feed my guts for the time being. That's the sad and sordid truth of this business."

"Oh, but that's terrible. I feel sick at the thought of you being dead and buried out in the dark and primitive wilderness, and I hate losing you. Stay! Please, stay."

"Don't talk that way," Simon said. "I must go home to care about my future. I've been lazy for too long. And it is not as wild as you think. Bjorling and Nilsson, whom you idolize, were born and reared in the wilderness you fear."

Jeff shook his head. "A cold and dark corner of the world, up by the North Pole, will offer you no future! You should live in New York, in London, or in Rome, and thrive in their glory. You need somebody who will give you all these things. The world would fall down and worship you, I swear. Up by the North Pole, nobody will know who you are, the most wonderful, beautiful, and funny person. A fabulous star on the grand stages of this world's great metropolis, that's what you ought to be. The world would be beneath you to grab. And I would help you grab it! Just promise you will stay with me and the world will be yours."

"Thank you, Jeffrey, but I am not the angel you think. When I don't get the rubies, emeralds, and sapphires you promised me, I may not be so pleasant to live with."

Jeff laughed. "I am sure I know you better than you do. I know you're an angel even when you try to act like a little devil."

When Ulf returned, he politely asked what he should do with the used lavatory paper, and where he could wash his hands.

"There's no water left," Jeff said. "The girls have forgotten again. But there's the sea, if you can see it down there? It's full of water. Simon, you deal with his used lavatory paper." Jeff returned to his room and closed the door behind him with a bang.

"Simon, have you a soap to use for me? Please, will I borrow from you a little piece and to take it down there in the sea to use it for me, please? How is this you say that, please?"

Fellini May Have Heard of You

Two days remained before Simon would leave the island. He was sitting in a comfortable balcony chair eager to continue his study of writers who expressed themselves in a foreign tongue and had come to Strindberg's *Le plaidoyer d'un fou*.

Jeff came out of his monastic cell and politely, even with a touch of humility, asked if Simon cared to go for a walk. There was something he wanted to talk about.

They left the cottage and walked inland. When they reached the outskirts of the pinewoods a young shepherd down in a valley shouted and waved at them.

"*Pou pas?*"[17]

"*Gia pefka,*"[18] Simon replied.

"*Sto kaló!*"[19] the shepherd boy shouted and smiled.

"*Evkaristó!*" Simon replied, and he and Jeff walked on.

"What was that about?" Jeff asked.

"A love call, nothing special. Just the ordinary stuff."

"Did he want you? Did you want him?"

"Jeff, please. You have lived here for over four months and you've seen the Greeks. You've seen me. You ought to be able to understand this cheeky boy and I would have arranged a meeting in the woods if you hadn't been here."

"Yeah, sure."

---

17 Where are you going?
18 To the pinewoods.
19 Have a nice trip!

"It's true," Simon said. "I like him. I love to lick his thick and wicked dick. And he kisses me like a love-hungry orphan. He loves that I want his firm round little butt, the way it pleases me to put my fingers into his hot and burning soul. He's the kind of guy I like, a normal, straight, fresh and cheeky guy who loves to be close to me. What else could I ask for? That is how I am, my dear Mr Smart. Such is the common, plain reality in this part of the world, at this particular time in history in the cradle of the European civilisation, the one you praise so heartily."

"Oh, shut up, please. What a terrible sermon, and most of what you said was false, I'm sure. Fake and false, only meant to kick me in the groin."

"If you say so, Jeff. You always know best."

They proceeded in silence. Jeff cleared his throat several times. They came to a small glade in the pinewoods and sat down on a rock. Jeff cleared his throat again and then he said, "Simon, I know I was fortunate to meet you. To live together with you has been one of the great experiences in my life."

"Jeff, please. You make me embarrassed."

"And I do *not* want to lose you. The thought you will leave, and I would never see you again, is unbearable."

"Please, Jeff, no declarations."

"Let me talk. I'm serious. I can't bear the thought of not seeing you again. I will do everything I can to make it possible for you and me to be together again, one way or other. I am prepared to make you an offer."

"Okay. Talk. I listen."

"I want you to come and live in Rome. Not like here, with your old Auntie and me. I will get you a small flat of your own. I will give you a stipend, not great, but enough to live a good life in Rome. You and I will meet at least twice a week, and more often, if that would please you. You can study Italian, go to a drama school in Rome, write your screenplay or whatever, in your voluminous spare time between our not-too-brief encounters."

"Is this it?" Simon asked.

"The main point, yes."

"Do you know what I come to think of when you say this? Your father. You copy your father who had a paid woman living in a flat he rent for her in Melbourne."

"No, no, no. That was absolutely a totally and completely different thing. She was a prostitute or had been. There is no resemblance at all!"

Jeff waved his hands in front of him as if to erase Simon's comments from the air. "And she was a woman! Christ, what silly ideas you get into your head sometimes."

"Oh, I see. Of course. Yes. I understand now that you explain so well."

"Listen. Fellini may have heard of you." Jeff paused to let his words sink in.

"So you talk to Fellini? Is that when you're intoxicated by mescaline?"

"Ha, ha, you're so funny. Listen, Justin wrote about you and me in a letter to Brian Dunlop. Brian let the letter lie around and Keith, Brian's friend, read it. Then Keith told his sister Audrey what he read about you and me. And so Audrey asked me about you in a letter. And she is the wife of my friend Jack, a film producer, and he and Audrey share their beach bungalow with Fellini and Giulietta Masina. So Audrey may have mentioned you to

Fellini. How about that? With the connections I have, I can do everything you could imagine getting you a job at the Cinecittà. There should be high demands for a blond, intelligent, and handsome young man from the Arctic Circle. Why not a male Greta Garbo or Ingrid Bergman? And I'm serious about this, more than you would know."

"You're not serious. Fellini?"

"It's true, I swear. I can show you the letter from Audrey!"

"But you plan to live in Rome with this Australian boy, who sends you, as you say, such fantastic love-letters. Eh?"

"I would scrap him. No problem. I've already written a letter and told him to cancel his voyage to Europe. I will send it by airmail as soon as you accept my proposal. He's not important; I hardly know him. He's the one who's been pushing for this. Simon, you're the one that I want. I'm prepared to sacrifice a lot for having access to your grace twice a week. Just the thought of seeing you within a day or two will inspire my painting. Don't answer now but think about it.

"Right now—" Jeff lowered his voice— "as you are aware, my finances are a bit strained, with the bloody tenant in Sydney who refuses to pay his rent and hiring lawyers and all that. But things will be different in Rome. I can eat spaghetti every day and save and scrape at first. Then I'll have exhibitions in Rome and London and in Melbourne and Sydney and sell every one of the many paintings you inspire me to create. Everything will turn to silver, I assure you, and I will give you a good life, I promise. To live in Rome and not have to worry about money, who could say no to this?"

"I could, and I will. And Jeff, what if your ... how should I call it, interest in me is pure sexual attraction or a neurotic obsession?"

"Oh, don't be bloody pompous. Christ in Heaven, is that the kind of phrases you write in your screenplays?"

"Yes, I do. To show you, as my mentor, how I can challenge and surpass Proust in terms of beauty of language, so you may cite *me* with pleasure, Jeffrey, and not him."

"You're so funny. How could I ever live without you? I simply couldn't, so something must be done. One way or other, you will be in my life forever."

"Oh, that was a nice phrase. I will use it in one of my manuscripts. I have to remember it, what was it you said? I know you will be in my bloody life for fucking ever? Was that it?"

"You're not funny when you try to be funny; only when you're not aware of it."

"Jeffrey, why did we take this trip? For you to furnish me with excellent phrases to use? 'He was funny only when he was not aware of it.' Not beautiful, but useful. I will add a special little credit to Jeffrey Smart when I use that phrase."

"Fuckface, let's go home."

"I'm not happy, Jeff. Part of me wants to stay on this island forever with you and Justin as my eternal patrons. Another part of me is a North European Lutheran, urging his grain of wheat not to be saved but to fall into earth and die and bear much fruit."

"No more phrases for today, please. Come. Let's leave, and shut up, both of us."

Two days later, in the early morning, Simon and Ulf climbed into the little bus outside the beach hotel. There were only two other couples on board. Simon grabbed the seatback in front of him with both hands. He needed something to cling to. Ulf, sitting beside him in silence, did not qualify as that necessary support, or as anything else for that matter. Just a bloody nuisance.

Jeff and Justin stood outside the bus. Jeff scraped gravel with his foot. He didn't look at the reluctant traveller. He feared to be mauled by the claws of primitive emotions and still tried to deny the reality of this departure. Instead of being present and willing to share, he tried to stay solid as a rock, *come scoglio imoto resta,* and turned numb.

They had never said goodbye properly, instead concentrating on arranging practical things—packing, washing, dressing. Their farewell by the bus was overwhelmingly emotional and badly prepared. Only Justin appeared as cool as on any other day, inhaling and puffing on a smouldering Turkish cigarette with a faint smile.

Simon looked back on his life on this primitive island in the light of his possibly fateful departure. Never had he been so appreciated by a man as by both Jeff and Justin. Leaving them behind was to lose the good life of being liked by a man. He was a different person now from when he came here.

To leave the food, the moussaka and keftedes, and the sounds of cicadas, toads, and horny donkeys, was also leaving a good life. And to leave the warmth of the sun and the sight and sounds of the sea, and the physical closeness of the many boys. Every discomfort was seen in a shimmer of reconciliation and forgiveness.

When he grabbed the seat back in front of him, his hands turned white. They lost the golden-brown colour given by that ancient sun, which once gave life to Dionysus and Apollo, to both chaos and order. Everything would soon be gone. Only memories remain. A part inside of him was crying, but he tried to smile, and swallowed repeatedly.

The engine roared, the bus shook and twisted; slowly it started to move forward. They exchanged only brief glances. There was Justin; there was Jeff. No one said anything. No waving hands. No thrown kisses. It was difficult. They were men, not sissies.

Simon was rolled away from this life. What would happen so far away? Life was behind him, in front was darkness; would he manage? He refused to acknowledge Ulf beside him. Ulf was a nobody, not worthy of a great artist's vision; he was not even worthy to lick Simon's boots, if he would have had any.

Jeff had left Simon a short note: 'The thought I may not see you again after August is so terrible, I cannot allow myself to entertain it.' The essence of every departure and every goodbye: this may be the last time we ever see each other. No matter how strong our dependence on the other.

The bus rolled away. Justin immediately turned and started for home; he had forgotten to bring enough Turkish cigarettes. Jeff stayed and watched the bus for as long as it was still visible. When the little bus disappeared behind a cliff, Jeff felt a pain in his chest, on the left side, like a pinch. It was painful, and it frightened him.

Back in the cottage, they withdrew to their rooms and began the daily work on their canvases. They kept silent for the rest of the day. At four o'clock, Justin merely said, "I've made tea." Each took his teacup and returned to his room. They had dinner at home and went to bed early.

Time Stood Still When You Left

The day after Simon's departure, Jeff observed a series of momentous events. He was convinced they were Nature's ironic comments on his plight of losing Simon.

First, Nico, their landlord and nearest neighbour, killed every single one of Lisa's new-born puppies. To watch her pathetic search, going from room to room in search of her precious babies to feed and to lavish her love on, added to Jeff's grief.

Then Jeff's watch stopped and was unstirred by a rewinding. Since Simon was no longer there, time had stopped to pass. Jeff wrote "The day you left/watch stopped ..." on the back of his painting *Athenian Suburb*, which later would be bought by an art dealer in New York. Thus, for the benefit of mankind, the effect on time of Simon's departure was forever inscribed in the history of art.

Then the big, dominant Doberman dog with an equally intimidating dong, Koudouri, who was said to own "the evil eye," lost a monstrous battle with a French poodle. Koudouri was dethroned as king of the island, dejected, its mangled face attracting huge and eager flies. Normally, Jeff did not care much for dogs. On this day, his affinity for Koudouri was boundless.

Simon's friend, the chief of police, came to visit. "Léon was a good boy," he said.

Little did he know, Jeff thought, or the chief of law enforcement had an immense open-mindedness.

"When both Léon and summer are gone, there will be no chance for me to meet English girls. So sad."

Jeff tried to figure out what the connection could be between the police, Simon, and English girls. It struck him he knew almost nothing of Simon's life beyond their terrace and the beach behind the dunes.

Justin's former boyfriend, Brian Dunlop, arrived from Rome. He and Justin indulged in private talks, left for long walks, and enjoyed private swims over by the dunes. Jeff would not admit he was ostracised. Instead he found it "uncomfortable" to be excluded from the human company he needed, even if present circumstances offered him nothing better than Justin, who was Irish, and Brian, no more exciting than a glass of water.

Jeff's sole comfort was his work. While still on the island, he finished *Piraeus I* and *Piraeus II*, both of which Simon had posed for, though he had later been erased on *Piraeus II*. He was also working on *Lecce*, with Simon in the nude, which he would later rename *San Cataldo I*.

When he left the island with Justin and Brian, Jeff feared for his well-being, leaving their primitive little cottage, now full of so many associations. He compared himself to a terrified child who'd been thrown out into the world with no protection. Fifteen years earlier, he had left another island, Ischia outside Naples, and he recognised this strange fear of treading his feet on the capricious and demanding mainland. On an island, you were in the womb, protected from outsiders and the passing of time.

Back in Rome, Jeff and Justin moved into a large four-bedroom-flat on Via di Villa Torlonia. Rome was lovely, the parasol pines and the palm trees, the pink villas, the elegance of the people and their superb food. For so many years, Jeff had dreamt of living here but he was dreadfully depressed and lonely for Simon. He tried hard to forget him. If his thoughts moved to Simon ten times every hour and ten times he fought to successfully push them away, in sleep he was defenceless, and everything poured in unstopped.

Brian visited their flat regularly. He'd travelled to Europe having been engaged by an American film company in Rome to paint the Sistine Chapel for the set in Cinecittà. The film was about Michelangelo and the Pope.

Jeff stood in the doorway to Justin's room. "Will you and Brian have lunch at home with me, or are you going out?"

"I don't know." Justin was sitting in front of his easel. "I'll ask what Brian wants when he gets here."

"There's not much in the kitchen, so if you two are having lunch here, somebody must go out and buy something for us to eat."

"We have two eggs."

"Two eggs won't be enough for lunch for three people," Jeff groused.

"We can make scrambled eggs and share." Justin continued with his work without turning to face Jeff.

"Still too little, and there's no milk."

"Didn't I see a piece of bread?"

"It's rather stale."

"We can dip it in the tea," Justin suggested.

"There is no tea."

"We can have coffee, then."

"There's only instant coffee," Jeff said.

"That's okay."

"No. I refuse to drink instant coffee."

"Then you better go out for lunch or buy coffee beans. Brian and I can make a French omelette with the two eggs, and we can dip the stale bread in instant coffee. That will be enough for us, I'm sure."

Jeff returned to the kitchen. Mic had promised to lend him money, but Jeff hadn't got it yet. There was a little pasta left, but no tomatoes. He couldn't have pasta without sauce. And there was no butter.

"I will poach an egg for *seconda colazione*," Jeff said when he returned to Justin's room. "I cannot afford to go out for lunch. I checked the coffee. There's only enough for one cup, just so you know."

"Then Brian and I will have lunch at Osteria da Umberto, no problem," Justin said.

After his second breakfast Jeff went out and bought a crisp roll of French bread, one tea bag, and one big tomato and made himself a nice plate of pasta for lunch with homemade tomato sauce. There was also Parmesan in the larder and he was pleased with the little meal he had secured for himself. In the evening he was invited to have dinner with friends.

On the brighter side of life, there was always work. One gallery, which Jeff regarded as one of the very best in all of Rome, Galleria Ottantotto, was "most enthusiastic" about his work. It was a small gallery on the basement floor of 88 Via Margutta, parallel to Via del Corso, between Piazza di Spagna and Piazza del Popolo. He was to have an exhibition there in April. He had already sold a painting but had not yet been paid for it. Since Simon had rejected the offer to be Jeff's kept boy, and seemed determined to stay by the Arctic Circle, where he had been admitted to a theatre school, Jeff had to respond rationally. His first move was to arrange for young Ethan to leave Australia and be his lover and apprentice.

Ethan was a teenage art student whom Jeff had met before he left Sydney two years ago. Ardent letters of passion and adulation from the aspiring artist convinced Jeff he could test whether a committed young partner would bring peace to his longing soul. Ethan was not Simon; he was no celestial apparition, but he heartily accepted what Simon had scorned, a life as Jeff's lover.

Still, the thought of never seeing Simon again was not possible to entertain. Jeff was of the strong conviction creating art was hard work, work and more hard work, and not more than half a per cent of so-called inspiration. Yet he was convinced he needed Simon's presence to inspire his painting. As Mozart had supposedly put it, "Love, love, love, that is the soul of genius."

Jeff looked into the cost of airfare to the Arctic Circle, just to get his batteries recharged, but it was far too costly, and what use would it be to go there, anyway? Jeff also had another idea. It was still a vague conception without words, but it grew in his mind and he was well aware that it was too precarious to clarify in detail.

V
High Society

Dirty Old Queen Elizabeth

At six o'clock in the morning on Boxing Day, the telephone rang in Jeff's room. He stumbled through the darkness to the phone by his easel.

"*Parla.*"

"Jeff, it's Mic. Can you come up to Florence?"

"Yes, of course. What's the matter? You sound strange."

"Heinz is dead. The police are here."

"My God! What happened?"

"I don't know. Bruno found him in his bed. Luigi can drive to Rome at once and you can be here in five hours."

"Of course, Mic, of course. Are you all right?"

"I manage."

"Don't do anything stupid. I'll be there by lunch."

The chief servant Bruno had eased the door open to Heinz's room, to see if *Il Signorino* was awake so he could serve him *prima colazione*. He found him naked in his bed, face down in his vomit. Bruno called the police before telling his boss, *Il Commendatore*, Mr Mic Sandford, his lifetime partner was dead.

After the call had ended, Jeff rushed into Justin's room.

"Mic just called. You won't believe it; Heinz is dead."

"Is he? And for this you wake me up? I've just fallen asleep. A little consideration, please. Is this too much to ask for?"

"Oh, Christ in Heaven."

"How can you be surprised? His death was bound to happen."

Three hours later Luigi arrived with the Bentley from Florence. Jeff nestled in the back seat. The car was soundproof, not a whiz from the motor or the traffic nor a single bump on the new *autostrada* between Rome and Florence. Jeff dozed off and as if he were floating on the salty Aegean Sea.

His semiconscious thoughts wavered from Heinz and death to a longing for life and love and young Simon. He mused on how death and copulation walked hand in hand. An insight that struck him each time when having sex after a funeral. Not a Christian cogitation perhaps, but surely Darwinian.

Heinz's death would create a painful void in Mic's life. Mourning would make him vulnerable to subtle persuasion. Perhaps not a nice thought, but such was life. You got purely what you worked hard for, and Jeff knew he was good at working hard. He had to live close to Simon; no other concern mattered. Now he would wait for the right opportunity.

Jeff regarded Alistair Wallace Sandford—Mic to those who knew him well—as his very best friend. Both came from Adelaide in South Australia and they met in London after the war, where Mic had served as a young colonel under Montgomery in North Africa. Mic studied law in England and was then stationed with British Petroleum in occupied West Germany. There he fell in love with Heinz, a young German teenager. When BP asked Mic to set up the company in Italy, he persuaded Heinz's parents to allow their son to move to Rome, provided he would take responsibility for their boy in sickness and in health, for better or for worth, until death did them part. Mic did. By the standards of the time, he was seen by his friends as brave and independent; some would even call him progressive.

Mic was the youngest president in the history of British Petroleum; he inherited great wealth when his parents died; he had the third highest income in the Italian Trade and Industry; and he spoke Italian, French, and German fluently. He lived in Rome in a palace built around A.D. 400, between the Tiber and the Forum, below the Palatine Hill where the Roman emperor used to have his home. The Queen had named him a Commander of the Most Excellent Order of the British Empire.

Heinz had no incentive to work or learn the local language and soon took to the bottle. As the years passed, the fresh and ravishing teenage boy, full of life and hope, turned into a plump and bald hysteric. He arrived blind drunk at dinners and official cocktail parties. He abused guests and made a fool of himself together with friends he picked up at his increasingly frenetic nightlife. Though skilled at dealing with international institutions and powerful politicians, Mic was helpless to address his domestic problem. There were rumours he would have received a knighthood if not for the drunken stains Heinz had left on his reputation.

Heinz's death was an affliction, but also a relief, a duality that would make coping difficult. Mic needed support. Apart from his private secretary, always reliable AnaRosa, and his young Roman servant, Angelino with his dreamy bedroom eyes, who served his master in the only way he knew, there was nobody but Jeff. They spent the following weekends together at Villa Il Bacìo, just the two of them. After dinner, they retreated to the library for coffee and drinks. A servant would enter with large silver trays weighted with crystal glasses, lemon slices, bottles of soda and tonic water, and the usual assortment of whiskeys, gins, vodkas, cognacs and Italian Campari and Strega.

"I've been asked not to leave Italy," Mic said, "but they haven't put handcuffs on me yet."

"I'm happy to see you can still see the dark humour in how they treat you," Jeff said.

"Whatever anybody may assume, I always looked forward to living with Heinz for the rest of my life." He faced Jeff as if he had asked him a question.

"Mic," Jeff said, "over the years I have seen how much you loved him, even if I realised how Heinz had become more and more difficult to deal with. And you know what?"

He paused. Mic looked at him and waited. Jeff spoke slowly, emphasising each word: "I saw that Heinz knew how much you loved him. Despite everything."

"Oh, Jeffrey, you're such a great friend," Mic said. "You're the only person I can trust, whatever the situation."

"There's always something special, not merely between you and Heinz, but with any relationship between a younger man and a mature person. Man has known this for thousands of years. *Pater et filius*, the father and the son. At the core of our religion is the relationship between them: Abraham, Isaac, and Jacob, the old and the young man as father and son."

"Yes, so true. We're stuck with that powerful father figure from birth, aren't we? And we need his love. Love me, Daddy! There's a wail heard all over the world, cried by many sons with blood-soaked tears. And if their sons can't weep because they're dead inside, they suffer manifold." After a pause, Mic added, "I never cry."

"Don't burden yourself with fruitless accusations," Jeff said. "Not everyone who cries for a daddy is doomed simply because Daddy may not deliver exactly what is expected from him. And the young ones disregard every father once was the son of a father. Do you understand me?"

"Yes, I do. Thank you, Jeffrey."

"Power is an irrefutable ingredient in every single love affair, not just those between a mature man and a youngster. Notice the language people use in their love relationships: 'I will be yours forever' and 'I will do anything for you.' To have the other person's unconditional favours at one's disposal seems like being offered an enslavement."

"Sounds terrible when you say like that. Another whiskey?"

"Yes please, but less soda this time. These modern comradely relationships between people sharing each other on an equal and reciprocal basis are a myth. Every relationship is based on power, even if that power is thoroughly disguised."

"Is this what you noticed between Heinz and me?"

"Honestly, Mic, I have no idea. Only you can know this about yourself."

"It's difficult for some of us, who others perceive as powerful, to escape the power imbalance in a relationship. One can try to get an independent partner, but then … that does not suit all of us, if any? I think of King Edward VIII, later the Duke of Windsor, whose Mrs Simpson presumably was not taken aback by her partner's sovereignty. But our own Virgin Queen didn't solve the issue when she fell in love with the young Earl of Essex."

"You think so?" Jeff asked. "I'm sure Elizabeth had a good time. By then she was in her mid-sixties and I'm sure she enjoyed the company of the young Earl more than we know for certain. Between those two there was not only a remarkable age difference but also a power difference of striking importance." Jeff snorted. "She had him executed, after all."

"Had a good time?" Mic asked. "If you're implying what I think, Elizabeth would let nobody see the English Queen exposed with her legs up in the air."

"But there were rumours, mind you," Jeff persisted. "I know there were. After everyone left the court amusements in the evening, Elizabeth and Essex, the so-called 'amorous couple,' stayed up alone playing cards and games."

"Sounds innocent," Mic said.

"Maybe, but they were alone in her room, and Essex returned to his own lodging only in the early morning hours. Tongues wagged, but who would question the Queen?"

"But Jeff, take into consideration it has been well established Elizabeth detested the pure idea of coitus. She had nasty experiences with a stepfather in her early teens. Even if this is no proof, at least it adds credibility to the idea she stayed a virgin throughout her life."

"Gosh, sometimes you sound so old-fashioned, Mic. Elizabeth was no more than just over sixty, and Essex a horny young stallion, and she was clearly infatuated. Everybody saw that. So when they spent night hours alone in her chamber, and with more than one glass of wine, it's unlikely nothing 'happened.' Every teenager with his own car knows there are so many things one can do apart from coitus.

"And if the Queen didn't take it up front, there was always the rear entry, the most common contraceptive in Catholic countries up to this day. Today, in our world, an elderly gentleman who shows some interest in a women more than twenty years younger is called 'a dirty old man.' I suggest the Queen was a 'dirty old woman' and got out of horny young Essex what she desired, plain and simple, without fuss and unnecessary frills."

Mr Sandford laughed. "Neither Elizabeth nor Essex were Catholics, for that matter, which I know you're well aware of. And I suspect you're wrong about the old sovereign's erotic habits. But let's check what Lytton Strachey says about them in *"Elizabeth and Essex."* I have his book here somewhere. I don't know exactly where."

They spent half an hour searching shelf by shelf, climbing high on the library ladder although far from sober. Bruno came in to ask whether they wanted more hot coffee and begged Mr Sandford please to come down and let him climb up instead.

"I have to arrange with a librarian to catalogue my books and put order to this disarray," Mic said when they sat down, their mission unaccomplished.

"Yes," Jeff said, "you need order not just for your books but also in your life. You can't hole yourself up and mourn and become dark and brooding. You need a close and dear friend who would help you. That's my absolute conviction. And that's what you deserve and should allow yourself."

Mic laughed. "Yes, you're right. Please, conjure such a marvellous creature out of this ice bucket on the spot, if you're my true friend."

"Don't laugh, I'm serious. You remember the young lad I've talked so much about who lived with Justin and me on our Greek island? Can I be so bold as to suggest he could be your librarian, to order your books?"

"I did not know he was a librarian?" Mic said with the benignly sceptical smile typical of well-educated people of a certain age and experience. He had learned from the Queen, who never said "You're lying" or "I don't believe you" but "Are you sure?" with the same meaning but in a dignified and non-abusive way.

"Simon is intelligent enough to make you a proper catalogue."

"I'm not in the mood for any kind of relationship with anybody."

"See it like this, he'd come here to work, and you would just get to know him. Nothing else."

"Considering my present mood, I would be a lousy host," Mic said. "Nothing here would entertain a young man."

"How can you say such a thing? You have everything anybody could want. You have an imperial palace in Rome, a wonderful villa in the most beautiful landscape in the world, with chefs, gardeners, and servants. Living here would be a pleasure for Simon and for you too. But let us not be hasty; just think about it. To make life more bearable for you, nothing else."

Mic looked down at his drink, then up at Jeff. "Your enthusiasm is contagious, Jeffrey, but I'm sceptical. I need to think, not rush into something and end up like an idiot. I don't want to be a silly Arnolphe."

"Arnolphe, ha, of course not! You can handle a situation like this. Don't underestimate yourself."

"Did you say you have photographs of him?"

Two days later the following letter was composed and at once sent to Simon at the Arctic Circle, addressed c/o Ulf:

Via di Villa Torlonia,
Rome, 8th Feb. 1965
Dear Simon,

What a bastard you are! No letter to me for months. I'm sorry if I have tortured your poor soul with too many declarations, but you must know that you are a special person for me, always. I can't shut up about that. However, I've really given up. Ethan arrives in three weeks and I can't wait to drive down to Naples to meet him.

I simply must see you again. How? Listen. And you don't need to worry, Ethan will be here to keep me quiet.

My friend Mic Sandford has possibly 4.000 books in his beautiful villa near Florence, and some in Rome. They are all un-catalogued, in a very Irish state. If you have a holiday soon from the drama school, you could come down and make some money getting the books straight. I've discussed with Mic and he seems quite keen about meeting this angel we talk about so much, Justin and I.

Your fare will be paid and when you have finished your work in Florence, you will be offered a whole month in Rome for free!!! You will receive 10,000 lire a week plus keep, i.e., about 76,000 a week with food (and servants!). And that's more than a junior doctor earns in the United Kingdom, even one with specialist training. Do you hear that? It is good pay! And for you it would be tax-free. You'll have a cook and servants!! You will have your own (luxurious) room and bathroom. There will be no one there, only the servants and a chauffeur. (NO!) But at weekends usually Mic and I and friends turn up.

Perhaps you better read a book on how a librarian works. And you'll need your typewriter. My show opens here in Rome on

April 8th, only a hundred yards from Piazza di Spagna, with all my paintings from Greece, and with you in several of them. You have to be here!

I dream of the day I meet you at Florence railway station (it will have to be a Saturday) and we drive up to the villa through the vines and olives.

Come quickly. Love, Jeffrey

In Mother Mary's Bosom

Two days later, on the tenth of February, there was a knock on the door to the flat in Villa Torlonia in Rome. Justin opened.

The visitor was a petite girl with a foreign accent. "Is this where Mr Justin O'Brien and Jeffrey Smart, Esquire, live?" Justin smiled. "Yes. I am Justin O'Brien. What can I do for you?"

"I'm from the Arctic Circle," the girl said with a smile.

"The Arctic Circle! Ha, ha, then I know. Please come in." Justin helped her with her heavy suitcase. "Jeffrey! Come! Messenger from Simon!"

"Hello, I'm Mary," she said when Jeff came running. "I arrived in Rome an hour ago. I have a message from Léon. He thought you would like to get to know me. He's talked so much about you." She put down her bags and presented an envelope. "I have a letter of introduction he wrote." She handed the envelope to Justin.

"I apologize for the cold," Jeff said. "The heater has broken down. I never expected to have to trudge around in the snow here in Rome. Please, sit down."

Jeff inspected her from head to toe with unashamed curiosity. Her chest was flat, and she'd cut her blond hair short. She wore a black T-shirt, tight black jeans, and black leather boots. She wore heavy black mascara around her eyes, and her eyelids were painted a dark blue. She resembled a boy, no doubt. Maybe a lesbian? Typical of Simon to choose a butch female friend. No sissies for him even if they were girls.

"You may be used to this kind of cold," Jeff said. "We're Aussies, so we're not. Can we offer you something to drink, tea?"

"Whisky, if there's no problem?"

"Of course there's no problem. We don't have drinks until six o'clock sharp, but Justin will get you a glass."

"Soda or water?" Justin asked.

"I prefer it straight. No ice. Room temperature, if that's available."

Justin brought her a glass and poured her a good double. They sat down, and Jeff opened her letter of introduction. "Shall I recite, or do we read it one at a time?" He turned to Mary. "Have you read it?"

"Yes. Made me so happy. What he says about me is so wonderful. I think he may exaggerate." She smiled and took a large swig of her whisky.

Jeff frowned. There was something about this visit he might not be overly enthusiastic about.

"Try one of these Italian cigarettes if you like." Justin handed her his packet. "They're very strong, just so you know."

"Perfect!" she exclaimed. "Strong cigarettes and strong drinks, that's what I cherish." She burst into a deafening laugh. Jeff gazed at her with badly hidden aversion.

"How do you know Simon?" Justin asked. "Are you also a student in the drama school?"

"Yes, that's where we met. And now we live together."

"Oh, do you?" Jeff said. "And Ulf? What happened to dear Ulf, the poor chap?"

"Léon wasn't comfortable with Ulf, so he moved out."

"You call him Léon?"

"That's how he was called in the drama school," Mary said. "I know he's Simon to you. I can use either, there's no problem."

"So he left Ulf, the dear boy," Jeff said. "One can never predict what happens with people and in life."

"That's true," Mary said. "One of the positive aspects of life. People can always change for the better."

"Or for the worse," Jeff said. His comment triggered the young woman's clamorous laughter again. He looked at her with contempt.

It turned out Mary was two years older than Simon. She was married to her former Latin teacher, a retired colonel, with whom she had two daughters, aged three and one and a half. They had recently separated, and she and Simon lived together in a small apartment in the city centre.

"My dear," Justin exclaimed. "You're a mother? I can hardly believe it."

"Yes, I am the happy mum of two lovely little girls. They live with their father now while we're getting divorced."

"How chic!" Jeff said. "Justin, isn't this charming? The father takes care of her small children. Whatever brought you to Rome of all places?"

"Both Léon and I failed to be admitted to the school at the Royal Dramatic Theatre. It was a disappointment—both Greta Garbo and Ingrid Bergman studied there, you know—but it inspired me to do something better. And that was to pursue my dream to be a writer. I needed to get away from conflicts and demands and go ahead with my writing. That's what I expect to do here in Rome."

"A writer, I'm impressed," Jeff said. "What connected you with Simon in your most delicate situation? So young and already a mother of two."

"Léon and I became friends on our way home from the drama school. We both lived with people we wanted to move away from. Then we spent Christmas together, just the two of us, getting drunk and listening to romantic music. And then one thing led to another."

Jeff frowned. "Drunk at Christmas with sentimental music. Sounds terrible."

"Not sentimental, Jeffrey, romantic: Dvorak, Billie Holiday, the Eroica, Brahms."

"Emotional, then?"

"Yes, you're right. We spent an emotional Christmas, Léon and I. Lots of gin and scotch and beautiful music and so on. We had a lovely time together. And one thing led to another. Then I got myself a simple little flat, and Léon left Ulf and moved in with me."

"So how is our boy?" Justin asked. "Is he happy? Is he doing well?"

"Yes, he's doing well. He's been on a long trip. Maybe that journey was necessary but not good for him." Her glass was empty. Justin got up and offered her a top-up, and she accepted with a nod and a cheerful smile. "But now he's finally come home where he belongs."

"That sounds reassuring," Justin said. "I'm so happy for him. It was several months since I got his last letter, so I've wondered."

"And what home is that?" Jeff asked.

Again the same voluminous laughter, which Jeff deemed to be out of proportion and indeed as inappropriate as a fart when you shake hands with the Queen.

"A woman's body," she said. "That's where our darling boy

at last found his proper home in life." She closed her eyes and smiled.

An ominous silence descended over the icy parlour.

Jeff forced a smile. "Oh, is that so?"

"We've lived together for over two months." And she whispered as if telling a secret to a child, "And we've been fucking like rabbits."

"Yes, I understand, of course, but in polite society it may not be quite appropriate to disclose such intimate details."

"I haven't hurt you, I hope?" Mary took the cigarette out of her mouth with a sweeping, grandiose gesture.

"So I was right all the time!" Justin exclaimed. "I told you Simon was straight, but you laughed at me. You don't laugh at me now, do you?"

"Dear Justy, keep to all the available and simple facts, and don't jump to immature conclusions without thinking first."

"Sorry, Jeffrey."

Mary turned to Justin with a sympathetic smile and slowly shook her head. Justin smile back.

"You probably don't know Simon has been offered a serious job here in Italy, to catalogue the books of one of my dearest friends, who has a large library in his villa outside Florence."

"Catalogue books? Why? Léon doesn't know anything about cataloguing. Why should he do this?"

"I see your whiskey is finished. A top up?"

She nodded.

"Justy, the young woman's glass is empty. To be completely honest with you, dear Mary, when my friend and I discovered that he needed to have his library catalogued, at once I thought of

Simon as somebody who would benefit from living in a rich atmosphere of literature and music and art. Where could he do that if not in Italy, in Rome and Florence? So I wrote him a letter and told him about this opportunity. He may not have received it yet. But when you tell me both he and you were unsuccessful in your early careers, I realize he's free to leave and come here."

"He has a job as a dresser in one of our greatest theatres."

"I still think Simon's place is in one of the great artist centres of the world, in Rome or London or New York."

"He is just a simple boy with a lot of problems," Mary said.

"Problems?"

"You know what I talk about, Jeffrey."

"Wouldn't you be happy to see him here, Mary?"

"Would you?"

"Not as you think. I will live with a young Australian friend who will be arriving in Naples from Sydney in only a couple of weeks."

"We'll see. *Que sera, sera*." She emptied what was left in her glass.

Would Mary's entrance on the scene scupper Jeff's marvellous plan? He needed to investigate and have his say. He offered Mary an assorted entertainment for the evening, which she was glad to accept. First, he took her to the opening of an art exhibition. Then they met Jeff's friend Jack, the film producer, who was a friend of Fellini and his wife, which Jeff did not forget to mention—twice, actually.

Their inaugural evening together ended at Pier Luigi's. Mary had her fifth double whiskey on a more or less empty stomach since she had arrived in Rome in the early afternoon. Jeff noticed there was no sign in her behaviour that she might have had too much to drink.

"Are you familiar with the sexual development of young men?" Jeff sprinkled an extra pinch of Parmesan onto his plate of steaming hot lasagne. "Particularly that of boys who experienced disturbances at a young age?"

Mary exploded into ear-piercing laughter, causing several diners to turn their heads toward the source of this obnoxious noise.

"I'm familiar with the sexual behaviour of ordinary men," Mary said. "And it's not impressive. They're shy, insecure, and see the act as a performance test. Afterwards they need to be assured I've given them the highest grades." She let the cigarette hang from her lower lip the way Belmondo did in films by Godard. "Léon differs from most men I've had the dubious pleasure of meeting. He's not shy or insecure and doesn't claim grades since he doesn't make a performance test. He simply enjoys himself. His experience of being an object of conventional male sexual behaviour might have taught him something."

"A valid observation, I'm sure," Jeff said. "Being lovers to mature men should be a kind of conscription for the lads, like in old Greece. You also know, I am sure, that young males often go through phases in the development of their sexual orientation, as they call it. Unwittingly, boys experiment with different activities and with different partners. Young boys may fancy men for a time and those who love men may fancy a woman for a short while."

"Just a lot of crap, isn't it? Who knows these things? Nobody." Mary finished her double whiskey and reached for the wine bottle.

"We know *something*. About Simon we know he had a hostile and rejecting father and an obsessively devoted mother, to put it mildly. I make the qualified guess this coloured his sexuality and not least his emotional attachments. He will *always* try to find the loving father's loving touch. As much as he enjoys your company, Mary, which I am sure he does, he will never get that fatherly love from you."

"I suppose he didn't get that fatherly love from you either, Jeffrey. Or else he would have stayed with you. But he didn't, did he? He came to me instead."

Jeff stared into her eyes. There he did not see a human look, just two black pupils, and beyond them nothing but nerves and brain tissues.

"Yes, but he doesn't live with you now, does he? For some reason you have left him, whatever that demonstrates."

They were silent. The steaming lasagne had cooled, and they concentrated on their meal.

"I am frightfully sorry to have to say this to you, Mary, but you take a great risk attaching yourself to Simon. I only want to inform you of the reality of things, of simple straight facts, so you can make a sober choice for your own life."

"Your kind concern warms my heart, dear Jeffrey, but I think your arguments use little pieces from old theories supporting how you want things to be."

"No. Absolutely not. I have no particular wish in this. I let things be the way they are. But whatever you think or may want, Simon is a typical confused young man. One day he goes to Greece looking for love among peasant boys, a dead project from the start. Next day he finds a mother to get cosy with, a young married woman. After this … what should I call it, joyful detour, isn't that what your relationship has been for him? Sooner or later he will turn elsewhere. I'm certain he may soon be the lover of a mature businessman."

"That's not his thing," Mary laughed. "I guess this is the man with the large library. To be honest, I get the impression you don't know Léon as he is. Men of good positions have invited him to live with them; you're not the only one. Still, he lives with me and he makes love with me, not with them or with you."

"Ha! Great. Let me wish you good luck, dear Mary, and suggest we bury the hatchet."

"That's okay with me."

"Let's divide the bill equally," Jeff suggested.

"No. I've had more to drink. Let me see the bill."

Jeff handed it over to her.

"I'll pay three quarters," Mary said. "And leave to you to decide how much you want to tip *il cameriere*. I didn't like how he tried to flirt with me. He should just do his job, nothing else. You can take that into account."

Jeff did, and the waiter lost his tip.

"Now, I will show you to a little *Pensione* which we recommend to visiting friends. It's a good place and not expensive."

"You're so kind, Jeff."

"As Simon's friend, you are my friend as well."

Back home, Jeff wrote to Simon:

Mary has just arrived. We think we love her already (but this is after only one whiskey). How strange she was on her way down here at the same time as my letter to you was going in the opposite direction.

Now, think!

Do not just rush away and come here. That would be wrong!

Still, I know I will see you soon. It must be on a Saturday.

Love, Jeffrey

Mimosas in Bloom

On the last Saturday of February, the morning sun was shining in Florence. In the sudden warmth of early spring, people dressed in light clothes for the first time since last summer. The migratory songbirds had just arrived on their way from wintering in Africa to summering in Scandinavia. Their coquettish love songs thawed every icy heart. Sunlight, bird-song and warmth made glorious entries into the minds and hearts of young and old and love was in the air.

Mr Alistair W. Sandford, CBE, and Jeffrey Smart, Esq., had changed their weekend routine. Usually they left Rome early on Saturday morning. This weekend they had left Rome late on Friday afternoon to receive the young man who was going to work as Mr Sandford's librarian. He was due in a Wagon Lits train going from Copenhagen to Rome, which would arrive in Florence at 9:47 A.M.

Jeff was excited, close to frantic, having waited for this moment for half a year. He had feared he would never see his celestial vision again, who captured his heart a year ago and hadn't left his mind for a single day or night.

A small dark cloud tainted the sunny blue sky—a woman. Jeff was convinced Simon's infatuation was no more than an inevitable aberration in the life of a sexually active young man who did not restrain himself as did many young men in their own Anglo-Saxon culture. Simon would live in a villa in the countryside

182

outside Florence, and the woman would remain in the *Pensione* in Rome where she was writing a book for children. Surely it would be easy to keep them separated. Jeff was hopeful, even confident, Simon and his dear friend Mic would click.

The cast-iron hand on the huge clock hanging from the roof over the railway platform slowly moved toward the thirteenth minute to ten. If the train was not late and if the clock showed correct time, Simon should arrive in only a minute or two, provided he was on the train. Jeff closed his eyes and breathed in the heady air of early Italian spring. He was excited, and his cheeks burned like he was a teenager again. Love was in the air, oh dear.

"He will be here in two minutes. Hopefully." Jeff said.

And now they viewed the locomotive slowly approaching. It arrived into the Florentine station as gently as the waves caressed the sandy shore on their Greek island on a day with no wind and stopped with a light shake. A harsh voice announced on the loudspeaker that the train would soon leave for Rome, its next and final stop.

A few passengers descended. He would see him soon.

And there he was! And in a suit, and a white shirt! And a tie, so sharply dressed ... Oh, wasn't he a vision, his most gorgeous, wonderful, lovable dear boy—

"Bloody hell, what's this?" Jeff hissed. "My God, this can't be true." Behind Simon, climbing down the stairs, was that fucking woman. In her bloody black boots, and her fucking black jeans, and her black shirt and those fucking painted eyes, like two black holes in the skull of a skeleton. How the bloody hell could she be on that train from Copenhagen when he saw her in Rome yesterday evening?

Thank God Jeff had informed Mic of her existence, since he had more than suggested Simon could be Mic's prospective life partner. Whenever Jeff planned a change that would suit his life's composition Nature always cheated him. What the hell was she doing here, destroying this moment he had dreamed of for months and planned so meticulously?

Mary had gotten up early in the morning in Rome, caught a train to Milan, and waited on the platform for Simon's overnight train to arrive from Copenhagen via Paris and Zürich. Simon was not informed of her plans, so he was indeed *very* surprised to see her waving at him outside his window.

Mary climbed up into the first-class coach and they walked slowly toward one another in the empty corridor. For the first times in weeks they could embrace and kiss. They assured each other of their commitment, now and for the future, in spite of recent events in Rome and their reiterated impending separation.

"I want to be with only you, my Piglet," she said.

"And I want to be with you, my Pussy-Puss," he replied.

They went to the dining car and had a continental breakfast.

On their trip together down from Milan to Florence, Mary brought Simon every available piece of information about the "librarian project" that she had obtained from Justin, who gladly gave her all the information he had available of how Jeff and Mr Sandford planned to snare the young man.

When Mary had arrived in Rome, Justin realised she was a pearl in his constant skirmish with Jeffrey. She was a sty in Jeffrey's eye and Justin could use her to get a horn into that pompous bully Mr Smart. Her mere presence in Rome and her frank and fearless attitude bore promise she could scupper this "sordid and egoistic project" Justin thought his old friend Jeffrey Smart had concocted together with Mic Sandford.

So when Simon walked along the platform with Mary by his side and observed Jeff and Mr Sandford slowly pacing toward them, he was well informed of their plans and expectations. Simon was not surprised. By now he knew that Jeff was scheming to get all the right objects in the places he wanted them to be on his life canvas. Now Mic and Simon should be moved closer to each other, one in scarlet red, the other in rosebud pink. And Simon would be available for Jeff every weekend to meet at Villa il Bacìo, a stimulation he thought he needed to produce great art. As for the woman, he wished he could scrape her off, obliterate, delete and annihilate her from his life canvas or somehow arrange for this unwanted being to evaporate into nothingness.

Both Jeffrey Smart and the Commander of the Most Excellent Order of the British Empire had been properly brought up to behave as expected from a gentleman. They greeted the woman by kissing her on both cheeks.

"I would be glad," Mr Sandford said to Mary, "if you accept my invitation to share lunch with us today."

She turned to Simon. "What do you think, my piglet?"

"Yes, but of course, my sweetheart! And you will see where I will live and work! How kind of you, Mr Sandford."

There was space enough in the Bentley. Mic in front beside *il fattore*, who served as the driver today. Jeff squeezed himself in between Simon and Mary in the backseat. Sitting with their fresh young bodies pressed against his own, Jeff thought of a possible threesome. He would love to see his angel fuck a woman and fuck him at the same time. Jeff could feel the beginning of an erection. Thank God, Ethan would arrive in Naples by boat from Sydney in a couple of days to ease Jeff's heart-provoking tension.

When arriving by car from Florence one could see Villa il Bacìo from a distance. The mansion rested in a light tawny-coloured dressing with emerald-green ornaments around doors and windows. Surrounded by splendid vegetation in the sunshine on top of a hill the villa sparkled like a fairy-tale princess.

"Look, Simon!" Jeff exclaimed. "Isn't this the most wonderful landscape you've ever seen? And up there, throning on a glorious hill, your new home! The most beautiful villa I have ever seen."

"Yes, I see," Simon said.

"And look around you, the vineyards and the olive groves. Can you think of anything more wonderful to rest your eyes on?"

"No," Simon said.

"Everything you see is Mic's private property. The vineyard produces the most superb Chianti, Vino del Bacìo."

A long avenue lined by cypress and mimosa trees led up from the road to the villa's main entrance. The mimosas were in bloom. An abundant splendour of soft little yellow balls on light-green branches greeted Simon when he entered into the hall of his future home and possible reign.

Alerted by the chauffeur's signal, Bruno and Graziella hurried out with the other servants and stood in a line on the raked gravel yard beneath the round double staircase up to the main gate. King and Caesar jumped up and down while Graziella tried to calm them. Old Pippo was asleep in the kitchen, too deaf to hear the commotion on the yard.

To celebrate the weekly arrival of *il Commendatore*, fresh flowers from the garden had been arranged by the eldest daughter of Bruno and Graziella and placed on tables made of the finest Italian marble. Expensive Belgian chocolates from Marcolini, the size of apricots, filled three large crystal bowls in the grand salon.

Everything had been dusted, cleaned, and polished. In particular, the collection of old silver teapots, which Mr Sandford inspected every weekend with the eye of an eagle. Occasionally he added a newly acquired object to his highly rated collection of the things he valued most among his many precious belongings.

After lunch Mary and Simon were shown around in the garden, and then were taken to admire the sight of the vineyards and the olive trees on the many hills below the great mansion. Mr Sandford then kindly arranged with his chauffeur to take Mary down to the railway station in the Bentley, to give her proper time to get back to her *pensione* in Rome before nightfall. Though he assured Mary that making her acquaintance had been a great pleasure he didn't say she was welcome back. Mary never visited Villa il Bacìo again.

Was Baba the Turk a He or a She?

Mr Sandford put his hand on Simon's shoulder as they walked up the semi-circular stone staircase and went in through the huge main gate and into the grand salon. Jeff and an assortment of weekend guests were discussing whether an opera protagonist called Baba the Turk should be sung by a man or a woman and was Baba a he or a she. The libretto gave no conclusive answer, which annoyed their American guest.

Simon was now in Florence and Mary had been shipped off to Rome. Was Simon bothered? Why was he there? For Mary? For Jeff? For a life with Mic? His major reason was not Mic, nor to see Jeff, and not to be with Mary.

After she arrived in Rome Mary had sent letters home to Simon every day. She informed him the young son of the owner of her little *Pensione* was courting her. The son was an attractive young man in his late teens, excited by the young blond woman sleeping in one of their rooms, maybe even naked between the bed-sheets he picked up every third day to get washed. The normal twice a day frequency with which the boy relieved himself doubled after Mary's arrival.

She welcomed the young man's ardent courtship and soon invited him to be her "bed warmer," in Mary's words, in the cold Roman early February winter. The young man's daily releases now took place deep inside Mary's shivering body to his and her mind-blowing pleasure.

Nausea and dizziness beset Simon, worsened by every letter. Losing his breath out of sudden anxiety, he pictured their two young bodies making love in Rome without him. He strived to calm himself with cigarettes, whiskey, wine, and Polish sausages he chewed on even while he smoked and knocked back whatever was in the mug. And he drank, and he drank, and he drank once again.

But as a saviour from a gracious heaven the letter from Jeff arrived. "Oh Lord, I'm on my way, I'm on my way, to a heavenly land," he sang as he limped around like a Porgy deprived of his goat cart. He would go to Rome and show Mary who should warm her bed!

Was he jealous? He was actually more envious than jealous. This insight appeared for him in short flashes. He tried to drown them into oblivion with one bottle after the other of cheap Portuguese wine from Estremadura.

He wanted Mary, for sure. But more than that, he wanted to be in Mary's place and be courted by a young son of the owner of a Roman *Pensione*. Above all, he was envious of her natural lust to be fucked, to be *masi* with these guys, which Simon almost never could enjoy.

And the boy in Rome was making love with Simon's girlfriend in a way that Simon never could. With Mary he was only partially engaged, while this Roman boy's whole mind and body urged to be with a woman and Mary fulfilled every part of his entire desire.

Simon would never experience this full and complete love-making that these two were engaged in. With a woman Simon's emotional engagement would be airy and had to set aside a lot of interfering emotions. With a boy or a man he was not connected physically with total and complete togetherness, as Mary was with this boy and he with her. Whatever practical adjustment Simon made with others of his sex, there was no mutual connection with equal gratification for both parties as for a pussy and a dick, only a second-rate attempt which never reached the fulfilling glory of the original act of love.

This release of painful truth flashed for milliseconds in his young mind with total clearness—and disappeared with haste and was at once as dead as any blue Norwegian parrot.

Sobering up, Simon decided to temporary shelve his ambition to become an actor. Instead he would engage with the bookshelves at Palazzo Gangi in Roma, *la città più bella del mondo*, and in Villa Il Bacìo in Firenze.

Early in the evening back in her *Pensione*, Mary called her husband on the telephone. The line was weak and crammed; they hardly heard each other and had to shout. She begged him to let her talk to their little children. He demurred with vague excuses and begged her to come home at once and promised her that all would be forgiven. Three sad people needed her! She longed with anguish for her little daughters crying in the background. Her maternal love cut like daggers into her chest, the only love she thought should count when things were seen in their right perspective.

Soon afterward a careful knocking on her door, not challenging, more like a humble question, asked if she would welcome him to come into her room. A young and eager little gentleman who wanted to admire her, aroused and filled by a devotion to be as near to her as he could be to no one else. She had no reason to reject his plea.

The knocking was repeated; he knew that she was there. He

was hard and strong in his determination to share himself entirely with this girl, who gracefully had let him be with her as nobody before. He had a gift that he would give without regret, just pour his present over her like drops of summer rain to fill her up with, gratefully and joyously.

She did not hesitate for long; her need for love and for another person close to her had been rejected earlier in the day. With delight she welcomed the smell of his body and his heavy breathing and the beating of his eager heart. She would accept this gift of simple love and let him bury himself warm and hard inside of her. She opened herself to let him come in to leave his drops of summer rain, with a groan of both pleasure and strain, in the magical parts of her body where life could be made.

She wept. He kissed away her tears. She smiled at him and kissed his face. Then he got up and left, shutting the door behind him as carefully as he had opened it when entering an hour ago— or was it two?

The friends in the little congregation in the grand Salon at Villa il Bacìo agreed that Baba the Turk ideally should be sung by a castrated Russian transsexual with a busty woman's hairy chest, well décolleté. Then they went upstairs and dispersed into their bedrooms, alone or in pairs.

Simon and Mr Sandford went upstairs together. "I will see you later, I hope," Mr Sandford whispered and gave Simon a short embrace, the kind that dressed-up gentlemen would always give. They smiled at one another and they nodded with their heads.

"I am so curious to see you in those light-blue fleecy cotton pyjamas you told us about."

"Yes, sir," Simon said. "They're nothing special, but if you want me to…"

"Let me tell you this, my dear boy," Mr Sandford said. "I think Jeffrey has done a superb job for both of us, bringing you to my home. I never thought the boy Jeffrey talked about with such ardent fervour would be so pleasant."

Simon smiled. "I don't know what to say, sir."

"We're friends now. I'm Mic, not sir." Mr Sandford put his index finger under Simon's chin and lifted his face till their eyes met. Simon turned his gaze away first.

"Yes, sir, sorry. Mic, I mean."

Mr Sandford showed Simon to his bedroom door. "Here, my boy, you can open our little trapdoor, so we will get into contact with ease."

Alone in his room with a glass of gin on his bedside table, Simon lit a cigarette and began to undress.

"Simon?" Jeff stuck out his head from the door between their two bedrooms. "How's it going?"

"How's what going?"

"Are you going to bed now?"

"What are you doing here?"

"Is Mic asleep?"

"How would I know? He's not here."

"Have you said good night to each other?"

"No, we haven't."

"Are you going to?"

"Oh, Jeff," Simon sighed.

"And you undress first, I see."

"I'm putting on my pyjamas."

"Oh, is that what you're doing?"

"Yes."

"Good night then."

"Good night Jeff, and sleep well, and dream of your Aussie boy who's coming all the way to Europe to make you happy. I'm curious to find out how he is, the young chap."

"Are you? Let me give you a piece of advice before you go to sleep or whatever. Don't rush into things, Simon. You may not be able to weather the storm if you make your life too tempestuous."

"Thank you for your kind advice, Jeff. But now leave me alone. I will take off my underwear, and will be indecent, so if you don't mind."

Jeff said nothing and shut the door. Simon returned into Mr Sandford's bedroom in his new light-blue fleecy cotton pyjamas his mother bought him a week ago.

Mr Sandford was in bed reading documents. Simon stood waiting by the bedside, struggling to stand straight.

"You look appetising in that outfit, my dear boy," Mic said." Let me see what is beneath it. You don't mind, do you?"

"No, sir. Sorry—no Mic, not at all."

Simon pulled down his pyjama trousers and left them on the floor. His half-erection protruded under the pyjama shirt and came slowly creeping out of its foreskin.

"Let me look at you from behind. You are such a splendid boy and a pleasure for the eye."

"Thank you, Mic." Simon turned around.

"Pull up your shirt so I can enjoy more of you, my boy."

Simon did as he was told and waited for next request. Nothing was said. An icy hand stroked the inside of his right buttock and soon the other hand pushed his back, so he stumbled forward. To keep his balance he moved his feet apart. Mr Sandford eagerly stroked his anus and pressed hard against the sensitive sphincter. A shaky finger penetrated the muscular barrier and Simon shivered with both arousal and the thrill of submission.

"Come." Mr Sandford lifted his blanket and patted on the bed beside him. "We don't need this shirt now, do we?"

Simon took off his shirt and slid himself stark naked on the cool sheets of silver-coloured satin on Mr Sandford's spacious bed.

"Let's get to know each other a little more, my boy. Now that we will spend every weekend together here." Mr Sandford stroked Simon's smooth-skinned and firm chest and stomach. "That girl you brought here today—is she living in Italy, or did she come here with you?" Without waiting for an answer he added, "I will just tell you I did not like her." He fondled Simon's half-erection. "To be a hundred per cent honest with you, my boy, she looked a little like a cheap tart. I hope you don't mind my saying so?"

"She's special," Simon said, "and she's well-educated. She teaches ancient Greek and Latin." The thought of Mary increased his erection.

"Take this advice, my boy," Mr Sandford said with a wobbly voice. "Be careful with what you do. I take it you don't want to live under the knife-sharp heel of a woman. You want to be a free man, don't you? I notice that. Independent, yes?"

"I like her very much," Simon said.

"Fine, it's good when people like each other. And I like *you* very much, my boy. I hope you and I will be the best of friends. To tell you the truth, I already feel we are on our way to a beautiful friendship." Mr Sandford tried to put his wet and spongy tongue, browned by heavy smoking, into Simon's mouth. Simon turned his face away. Mr Sandford grabbed him by the neck with a strong hand and turned Simon's head so he could force his tongue into the boy's mouth.

"Open your mouth so I can suck your tongue."

Simon opened his mouth wide and stuck out his tongue to be sucked and chewed upon. Mr Sandford turned Simon over, spread his legs, and put lubricant in his anus. He rubbed it in firmly and deeply with two hard and eager fingers.

When his preparations were accomplished, Mr Sandford put himself on top of the boy and inserted his short and thin but hard dick with forceful thrusts. Mr Sandford's penetration and rapid pelvis movements were effective and performed without fuss or unnecessary frills.

When he had finished, he sighed, farted and fell asleep. Mr Sandford's habit of rapidly going to sleep after coitus gave Simon the freedom to slunk back into his own bedroom, light a cigarette, drink more gin, toss off, and go to sleep.

Later in the night, Jeff made a tour of Simon's room. He stood looking at him for a while before he returned into his own luxurious bed in his luxurious bedroom.

Gorgonzola for Breakfast

On Sunday afternoons, when Mic and his weekend guests left Bacio to return to Rome, Mic more and more often asked Simon to join them. Simon would accept without hesitation. Life in the Eternal City offered a greater variety of events than his solitary existence in the huge villa in Tuscany. In Rome there were cocktail parties, invitations to drinks at six and to dinners at eight in the homes of friends. He would enjoy the company of both Jeff and Justin, and not least of the newly arrived young Ethan from Australia.

When Mic had business luncheons or dinner parties at home for politicians and international bankers or for British MPs on short visits from London, Simon was always present and introduced as Mic's Scandinavian librarian.

"He's from the Arctic Circle," Mic joked, "and he eats gorgonzola for breakfast." His guests would respond with ingratiating smiles. They were well enough brought up to accept whatever their host chose to say about the handsome rye-blond young man who was seen in the company of the BP president more and more frequently.

When the president had an official cocktail party for BP at home, ambassadors and cardinals were invited. Rules demanded special armed security for such prominent guests representing foreign powers. A solid railing was put in front of the salon's large tapestry, which was said to have been painted by Raphael and insured for more than the rent BP paid for the large apartment in the palace.

Mic introduced Simon to everyone who was important. There were the prince and princess Granit and Xhaka of Albania. There was also the Widow Duchess of Mantua and her young, handsome, and well-endowed protégé Badú Jáo from the Volta District on the British Gold Coast, who spoke only Ewe. Simon was captivated by the unbridled and savage aura radiating from the young African. His staring at the handsome boy was so unashamed the Duchess began to giggle. Mic grabbed him by the arm, and they walked away to meet many other people to shake hands with and smile at.

"Naaw zat yoo aare in society," the German-born countess of Rodborough told Simon with a challenging and defiant countenance, "you muscht cut your hairr and not appeer like zose Beetlez, or vateverr zey are called." She turned to Mic with a suggestive and malicious smile. "Get some propa *orrderrr* into ze boy, and ziz time zings may turn out vell for yoo."

"Dear Brünhilde," Mic said, "I think you are so right. We will certainly have a sincere review of his hairstyle, most definitely." Simon kept his half-long rye-blond hair.

A petty incident occurred when the Duke and Duchess of Sicily invited Simon and Mic to drinks at 6 P.M. in their home at the top of Via Veneto. They wanted Mic's advice on their sons' education in England.

"Has today's very sad news reached you?" the Duchess asked Simon when they arrived. "Your Queen died today."

"Oh, did she? No, I haven't heard this."

"My sincere condolences. She was such a humble and charming person, even if she had a fierce temperament, at least when she was young. Did you know her?"

Queen Louise, born Princess Louise of Battenberg, sister of Lord Mountbatten, First Earl of Burma, and sister to the mother of Prince Philip, the Duke of Edinburgh, and a second cousin to Queen Elizabeth's father, King George VI, and great-granddaughter of Victoria and Albert, had died that day at seventy-five.

"I know who she was ... she was the Queen," Simon stammered. "But ... eh ... we were not acquainted personally, if I can say so, not at all."

This little exchange of information showed the Duchess was not a close friend of Mic, who never picked his young male partners from high-class people or friends of royalty, only from the opposite end of the social hierarchy.

Simon soon learned to appreciate Mic's excellence in making seating assignments when they had guests for dinner. He always seemed to understand each person's special assets and deficiencies and arranged them accordingly. One could get the impression Mic acted at the spur of the moment and never had given the matter a thought before the party went into the dining room. But Simon was always impressed to see how each participant always was given the most suitable table partner.

To sit at the right side of the host was a special honour. At one occasion Simon earned that privilege. He beamed like a child whose father was showing to the world how much he loved and cherished his only begotten son. Mic's displayed appreciation of his librarian made the unavoidable hardships Simon had to suffer with his employer easier to endure. At those moments he closed his eyes and thought of England's Three Lions Team.

One evening Mic had invited business colleagues at BP and their wives to dinner. Simon was struggling with his tie when a servant came into his bedroom carrying a telephone. *"Signorino, scusi. Il Commendatore è al telefono e vuole parlare con voi, scusi."* Mic had been delayed at the Ministry of the Interior and could not leave. He asked Simon to be host for the evening; he could even be so late they would have to start with the dinner without him.

Simon entertained the four couples with proper beverages and a conversation about suitable subjects. Mic arrived an hour late and required a hot bath and an undiluted gin on the rocks before joining the party. He asked Simon to stay with him and chat about the guests while he lay in the steaming bathtub enjoying his cold drink.

As always, Mic's chef had prepared a most exquisite dinner. *Filet de Renne à la Sauce Marsala aux Champignons* and *Pommes de Terre Duchess* was the main course. Mic's chef preferred to pour the sauce over the potatoes despite Mic's objections, which were weaker than his chef's tenacity.

Mic sat as *capotavola* with Simon on the opposite end of the table, the wife's position in a conventional household. To sit on his right side this evening, Mic had invited the old, ugly, and boring wife of his most senior colleague. Mic told Simon this colleague had led a conspiracy to persuade BP not to make Mic president of BP Italiana because of his intimate relationship with young Heinz. Now Mic gave his secret enemy the greatest honour in his own home. Magnanimous in victory, Mic gained his librarian's admiration.

Simon maintained his belief that Mic had arranged his own nonattendance to test whether Simon had the capacity to host a meeting with expectant and critical guests. Due to the insufficient transparency of the Italian government Simon failed when inquiring who were present at last night's meeting at the Ministry of Interior if there even were such a meeting.

Simon sparkled and let himself enjoy his success as a host. Mic told his staff in Rome and in Florence to refer to Simon as *Signorino*, or Little Master. Simon grew comfortable with his position in the household, in the fabulous Palazzo Gangi, as their dear friend Mr Jeffrey Smart would say. Sometimes Mic and Simon laughed at Jeff when they talked about his love for anything "grand."

Sweet Love of Youth

Since Simon worked in Rome increasingly often, and since Mary had left Rome and hired a room in a Tuscan village a half-hour's walk from Villa il Bacìo, he and Mary met more seldom. To conciliate his elemental human needs he arranged a brief encounter with his girlfriend.

Like a hormone-driven stallion led to a mare in heat, he expected to recoup delights he had missed. And more importantly, after having finished the beautiful, sweet lovemaking of youth they would plunge into the consolation of kissing and cuddling, always the icing on the cake, that indispensable and necessary cake of making love.

Mary had made friends in Florence. They gave her the key to a *stanza da ragazzo*[20] in central Florence to let her use for the night. After a solitary dinner at home, Simon told Bruno to take him in the silver Bentley and pick up Mary at the outskirts of her village and drive them into the centre of glorious Florence. The apartment was close to Piazza della Signoria but was not a room with a view; there wasn't even a window. As soon as they had closed the door to the apartment, they ripped off only so much of their clothes as necessary to perform the required act.

"Oh, Piglet," Mary moaned, "what big dick you have!"

"All the better to fuck you with, my dear," And scarcely had he said this, than with one bound he was on top of her and bit her neck.

---

20 Boys' room

Mary yelled like a sow on a slaughter bench; Simon, more subdued, grunted like a stuck boar.

"Oh, Christ, I want you so much!" he groaned.

"And Jesus, I want you too!" she moaned.

They spoke their native tongue and used its typical words to express deep or strong emotions: Jesus, God, heaven, hell, and the devil instead of the everyday Anglo-Saxon words fuck, screw, shit, ass, dick, cunt, sod, and bugger.

After only a few quick thrusts the mission was accomplished. They exchanged tame kisses, and Simon soon fell asleep.

Mary wiped his sperm from her thighs with the bed-sheet, got up, lit a cigarette, and poured herself a large notched teacup full of lukewarm scotch. There was no window, the ventilation had broken down, they were both heavy smokers, and Simon had the habit of farting for a considerable time after a good fuck. Still, after her fifth cigarette she put her pen and manuscript sheets back in her briefcase and returned to Simon snoring in bed. AMOR OMNIA VINCIT[21] she wrote in text hand on the last page of her manuscript. After not too long she fell asleep.

In the middle of the night a sudden strong urge to urinate woke Simon up. Mary was asleep or half asleep, he didn't bother to find out. He managed to put his cock into her most available hole. No need to move in and out; he let open the gates and let it flow out of him and into her. The pleasure shot up from under his feet, through his spinal cord and neck and made his head explode. In his half-sleep, he dreamt he was pissing into the sky like a Roman fountain with titans and giants and minor deities. He was entertained by the gods in an ancient heaven, for sure, and being there was fucking

21 Love conquers everything.

great. He farted and felt even more relaxed.

Then more lovemaking, for the third time, early in the morning, before they got up. Mary was now awake to enjoy her lover's wild percussion drill. He moved his family jewels with ease and constant pleasure in and out, "in mummy's stomach," as Mary's oldest child, the three-year-old Lisa, used to call the intimate coming together between her mother and this boy when she reported to her grandmother.

This time Simon had to work just a little bit harder to reach *la grande finale*. He took her from behind and grabbed one of her tits with one hand and fingered her wet pussy with the other. His fingers join with his Great Master in her hole.

He thrust with a strong force. And so all came out well and bestowed him with the final reward for seizing this opportunity available to him, to squeeze her pink inner lips with his fingers. Like when you crush a moth between your thumb and your index finger or snatch an expensive Belgian chocolate brought to you by a young, handsome servant with a posterior out of this world on a silver plate. And then press the delicious apricot-size chocolate between your tongue and your pallet. This gave the right feeling in his dick and arse and all the body parts involved in offering him the greatest pleasure of this meeting, the ultimate gift from the Heavenly Powers.

Oh gosh, give it to me. More. More! More! The pleasure that only wants more and more. Oh pleasure, wonderful, heavenly bliss, a God's most graceful gift to a praising mankind. *God, thank you*, he thought when he had a last violent squeeze of her flabby breast and pink and slippery pussy-parts. The pleasure! The pleasure!

After Simon's final hard-worked depletion Mary wiped the spunk still pouring out of her onto her thighs. After two parturitions her vagina was not enough supple to keep his spunk inside so most of it poured out of her, messy and sticky.

Simon rested, pleased and relaxed. Mary took a snapshot of her darling boy stretched out on the bed, temporarily without tension or built-up frustration. He had needed this relaxation and heavenly pleasure for weeks.

"You look so cosy, Piglet," she said and stroked his cheek.

"Oh, what a night, it really was such a night," he said.

"Good. I love my Piglet so much, my own little cuddle cushion."

On the next day a young, newly employed servant came up to Simon's bedroom with a letter on a silver tray and bowed. Simon's eyes followed the young servant as he left. That bum looked delicious. Something to put his tongue into and lick and suck. As for the letter, a pompously large and colourful Italian stamp covered most of the envelope, but there was a small surface left for his name and address.

My sweetest little piglet. We may have been so pissed when we woke up in the morning, we didn't notice the bed was drenched in urine. My friends want me to buy a new mattress! Can you help me with at least 10,000 lire? I am not sure you owe this, but surely you can get if from Mic. You need not tell him what it's for. Invent something. Mille basiorum from your own pussy-puss who loves her piglet so much.

I will see what I can do, Simon wrote back. *I get 6,000 from Mic each weekend, but as you know, most of my fee is in kind. I refuse to even mention money with him, but to save 10,000 would take time. I am sure your friends will understand. Are you sure we*

made this mess? Suggest someone else may have done this and see if you can lower the price. I think 10,000 sounds like far too much. Kisses, your piglet.

He never heard about the mattress again and forgot all about it. Hopefully Mary properly resolved this unfortunate incident with her local friends. She was superb at getting people to accept what she wanted. A strong and independent woman with real balls, that's what she was, almost like a man. And she was there for him when he needed her.

Arse and Art in the Uffizi –
Advice to a Young Man

Jeff came to Florence to study originals by Piero della Francesca. The central part of Florence was a museum in itself but works in Pitti Palace and the Uffizi Galleries by Botticelli, Titian, and Raphael also attracted his special interest.

As they passed through the Uffizi, Jeff took Simon to the little room with the statue of nude wrestlers by Philippe Magnier, a Roman copy of a lost Greek original. He led Simon to the backsides of the wrestlers, stood behind him and grabbed him by the shoulders. "Look!" he said. "What you see here is beauty in its ultimate manifestation. There's nothing more beautiful in the world than the well-shaped behinds on these two young men. The proportions are divine."

"Is this what centuries of artwork offers you, Jeff? Male buttocks? Arses, in the plain language of the common people?"

"You're so funny," Jeff laughed. "But listen to what I want to say when we look at these two naked young men. Beauty is awaiting your discovery in *everything*. You can see beauty in everything if you open your eyes and let it pour in and hear the sounds of beauty in your ears. You can taste what is beautiful for your tongue and palate and smell it with your nose. Not least you can *feel* beauty with your skin and with the palms of your hands. To openly receive all those gifts, my beautiful young boy, is to fully enjoy the beauty of our world, and that is to enjoy life … and to make it a good life." He turned Simon around, still holding him by his shoulders, and looked into his eyes. "I want to lead a good life," he said. "I don't want to dwell in misery like you Strindberg- and Bergman-people up there in your icy cold. No wonder so many of you try to commit suicide, with such idols. But I tell you this: once I decided not to. I wanted to live. And to live a good life."

"There's beauty also in thoughts," Simon argued, "and in human efforts to cope, mind you, not only in young men's arses."

"You're so funny! What would you prefer—a night with these two lovely boys in their splendid nakedness, or watching a dreadful play with disturbed people by Strindberg or a depressed and suicidal priest filmed by Bergman? And be honest!"

"I'd take the boys for one night, and then Bergman and Strindberg for the next ten … well, maybe five."

"I would want the boys for every five nights, Jeff said, "and then perhaps I could tolerate Bergman or Strindberg for one."

"Are you sure? On the island, you took T. S. Eliot to bed for over twenty weeks and a boy for only one single night."

"Ah, but that was because of you. In Athens I had only you for a whole week, and no Eliot. I would gladly have abstained from Eliot to receive your ferociously wanted grace; don't you understand this?"

"You're hopeless, Jeff. Please, no declarations. Let's continue and go and find Caravaggio if they have him here?"

"There, you see! Now you're exposed! Why do you want to see Caravaggio? Because your flesh is always willing. You want to see the naked flesh of Caravaggio's cheeky and probably delinquent boys. Strindberg is a detour, a route you take when you find nothing more inspiring to do to illuminate and satisfy your senses!"

"You seem to be well acquainted with lust, Jeffrey, even if you call it to enjoy beauty. How about your own painting, is this a detour or a pleasure?"

"Hmm, my painting is neither. More like breathing. A compulsion. No pleasure. No pain. Must do it. To live, to survive."

"I don't believe you. Where's the pleasure for you? There has to be. Be honest."

Jeff was quiet. They walked down a long corridor. Then Jeff stopped and turned to Simon.

"The appreciation by those few who may understand."

"So far I like what I've seen of your paintings—does that matter?"

"Yes, it does. But in this you're an amateur. The real pleasure comes from acknowledgement by serious art dealers or editors of respectable magazines and from museums in England or America if that would ever be the case."

"And the money?"

"The money only serves to make it possible to keep painting."

After several hours in the Uffizi, they found an outdoor café in Piazza di Santo Stefano, close to Ponte Vecchio. They each had a large cup of cappuccino and a creamy cannoli from Mongibello. The setting sun spread a warm ochre-coloured light on the Renaissance buildings surrounding them in the small square.

"You know, Simon, as an aspiring actor, writer, artist, or whatever, you must understand to practice any of the arts requires free time. But free time is expensive and can only be purchased with money. That's why I slaved for twelve years in nasty Australia, teaching, writing articles, broadcasting on the radio, and finally doing television. Not because I liked doing it, and not because I wished to be rich. I wanted to buy time because the only thing I wanted was to be an artist and spend my time painting."

"You're lucky, Jeff." Simon licked the ricotta off his lips. "Lucky because you knew what you wanted, and lucky because you knew you had the talent."

"I was determined. There was no luck. I always admired those writers, musicians, and painters who had to do terrible things to even get a part-time job so they could pursue their work as artists. When I think of noble Brahms playing the piano in a brothel in Hamburg, or Anthony Trollope working in the postal department, or Renoir painting horrid designs on cups and plates, my heart is stirred. Gauguin at the stock exchange. The horror!"

"Don't you like your cannolo?"

"What?"

"You haven't even touched it."

"Oh, I was thinking of important things to say to you. Do you want it?"

"I thought of what you told me in the Uffizi, enjoying life through your senses. I enjoy this cannolo both with my eyes, my nose, and my palate. They have made it with Marsala wine, don't you feel that? If you still want to have yours, I order one more for myself."

"Oh, you can have it, I'm pleased with the cappuccino," Jeff said. "Yes, senses. But that's what I'm still talking about, the time and effort it takes as an artist, a writer, or even an actor to express in art what you experience through your senses. To be more than a dilettante demands effort and time, and to get that free time, you must have the money."

"So I may have to do 'horrible' things, as you called it, to get free time for creative work. Is this your message?"

"Well, horrible for an artist, not for a common man."

"You know what Mic says about art and money? When bankers and business executives meet at a dinner or a cocktail party, they talk about opera, concerts, and ballets they have enjoyed. When artists meet, they only talk about investments, interest rates, and the most recent value of company shares."

Jeff laughed. "Yes, that's probably a correct observation. Mic has a hawk's eye for people's realities. You can't fool him, you know."

"Why do you say that? I never intended to fool him! I'm honest with him. But he doesn't appreciate my honesty since what I say doesn't suit what he wants."

"Accept my simple advice in this, Simon: Leave. That. Woman. You must find out where you want to be. What makes you believe this poor Sheila will accept that you keep running after boys? And what man will want to be with you if he knows you regularly dip your dong in that dreaded dungeon. To keep oneself to only one is an old, respectable habit. Your obsessive change of bed-mates—"

"I'm always with only one at a time. Now Mic, mainly. Then Mary, mainly. I've told Mic I'm going back to live with her when I leave him."

"This was straight information. I didn't know your future plan included Mary. Rethink, dear boy. Your future would turn much brighter with Mic. This I'm very sure of."

"Tell me, Jeff, how would I earn the money to get time to create great art? If I had been a gold-digger, which you know I'm not, you would have been poor as a church mouse by now." They both laughed, Simon a bit louder.

"In practice, getting enough money is simple," Jeff said. "But it demands tenacity. For years I was silly and didn't save money. I discovered, human nature being what it is, that I had to ask my firm to put part of my salary into a separate account that I had no regular access to. When I did so, my freedom began."

"I'll get myself a separate bank account when I come home," Simon said. "Another cannolo?"

"You've had two! No, let's go home. And now you know how to become a great artist."

"Yes, by whoring."

"Oh, please, don't use such nasty words. You modern kids."

"You said I had to do terrible things to buy time. Did I misunderstand? Mic told me you hinted that if he bought me this car, which the Saint drives in his TV series, I might stay with him in Rome."

"I know, I know," Jeff said. "I know you don't even think in those terms. That's one reason you're so unique—you're no Felix Krull and not a gold-digger. It's difficult to believe how honest you are."

"If I'm so honest, how can you suggest I should cheat your best friend to get favours?"

"It's not cheating, my sweet little thing, only a matter of using one's potential. Look at women—most of them have no talent, and they're withered before they're thirty. But they can be successful and powerful when they use what they have: their hole. Nobody would ever call them cheaters or suggest they're dishonest. It's commonly accepted they use their most valuable asset. Well handled, this fissure between their legs may take them all the way from a slimy gutter to a golden throne. Take Eva Perón. Men praise such canny women; their sisters despise them."

"And that's what I'm supposed to do as well? Suck up to Mic?"

"Simon, I only advise you to think rationally about your future. All of us must suck up to somebody or something, be it a company president in Italy or a radio and TV company in Australia. Freedom always comes with a cost, and few are prepared to pay the high price for real freedom. But always be aware of what decisions you make. If you play your cards damn well, there could be more impressive profits waiting for you than what you can imagine. Stay here and live with me and Mic and I will be eternally grateful."

"I will choose to have another cannolo."

"If you make that choice, I'll leave without you. It's getting chilly."

"So weak is your love for me, Jeff? It has gone with the wind and you don't give a damn. Poor Simon, nobody loves him. Everybody fucks him. Except Mr Smart, nowadays, who's got his own inflatable Aussie arse at home."

Jeff laughed. "I wish all three of us could be together. That would be sublime. We've already fucked each other, so why not a beautiful threesome? I'd love that. Please, Simon, don't spoil this for me. For old friendship's sake. You, me, and Ethan, that's what I want."

"I told you what I will do. You or Mic can do nothing to change my mind. I will go home and be with Mary."

"Do you really love that woman?"

"Love? What is love?" Simon asked. "I do not know."

"That slippery hole beats everything. It's preposterous. I never thought I would see you, sweet little thing, become one of its victims."

The sun was setting, and the Tuscan air was getting chilly. They got up and walked over to the Bentley parked on Via Guicciardini on the other side of Ponte Vecchio. The driver, who was asleep behind the wheel, woke up and drove them out of Florence up to Villa il Bacìo.

Wild Strawberries Are Frightfully Exclusive

Jeff made plans for Simon's impending birthday. He wanted the celebration of the boy to be grandiose. And he had a special surprise to deliver.

"His birthday isn't for weeks and you're already busy planning," Mic said. "No spectacle, Jeffrey, please. Simple and dignified, as the Queen says."

"She's so right, Mic, the dear Queen. Will his suit be ready in time?"

"We've had a first visit with my tailor; three more are scheduled. The suit will be ready the day before. We've chosen fabric and design, and the first testing will be tomorrow. He didn't know the prices of the various fabrics, but it turned out he chose the most expensive, so my tailor was pleased."

"He's got a good taste, the dear boy," Jeff said

Mic frowned. "Jeffrey, tell me, how would it be proper for us to behave towards that woman? Does she still live in the little Tuscan village?"

"Yes, she went back home to the Arctic Circle and returned with her mother and her two children."

"You're joking! She brought her children? What's she up to? Starting a family here?"

"What can we do? Ignore her, what else? To have her at the dinner would spoil the whole evening."

"Wouldn't that sour what should be a happy occasion for the

dear boy? He seems a bit fond of her, after all."

"I will be honest with you, Mic. I'm confident that plates with golden decoration, silver cutlery, crystal glasses, candlelight, the fragrance of cut flowers and the most exquisite champagne will silence any thought of womanhood in the dear boy. You and I should treat that woman with respect when necessary but keep our clear opinion in the secrecy of our minds. I'm sure you know what I mean, and that we can agree on this."

"Is Mary not invited?" Simon asked when told about his birthday dinner.

"We thought it would be too complicated for her to get to Rome," Jeff said, "responsible as she is to care for her old mother and two small children. She would probably not have appreciated an invitation anyway, we thought."

Simon met Mary outside Florence before his birthday. "Would you have wanted to be invited?" he asked.

"Jeff can't stand me, and I think he's a piece of pure crap. All the same, I have a little present for you." She handed him a small parcel.

"Oh, what is this?"

"Don't open it until your birthday, and open it at the party, and let them see I'm still alive and kicking, if they hope for anything else."

The guests were asked to arrive for drinks at seven o'clock and have dinner at eight. Simon wore the elegant suit Mic's tailor had sewn. The dark-blue pinstriped suit was paired with monogramed golden cufflinks, a present from Ulf on the day Simon graduated, and a newly bought yellow and blue silk tie from Brioni.

The young servant Angelino beat on the gong to announce

dinner. The dining room was lit up only by candlelight in silver candelabras that cast a warm and welcoming glow. An arrangement of yellow daffodils and blue irises at the centre of the table added both a rural and a national touch to the evening.

Simon had not been able to decide about the first entry, black Kaluga caviar or foie gras de Strasbourg. Fatigued by considering every pro and con, he ultimately came to the conclusion he should not overburden himself with carrying out key decisions of matters that were not crucial and would only deepen his fatigue. So he chose both, first Kaluga caviar and then foie gras de Strasbourg served around half a grilled lobster tail. A cold glass or two of Krug Brut was served with the entries. Simon was almost slightly embarrassed to ask for this luxury, but since this shamefully expensive champagne was not for only himself but for all the dear guests, he took for granted Mic would foot the expense on this great day, which he did, dear Mic. At times he showed a truly accommodating side.

Mic had called in an extra servant, an attractive young man of partly West African descent, indeed offbeat at the time. Those, who so desired, could rest their eyes upon this magnificent specimen of a man while they let the black Kaluga caviar rest on their tongues and fill their mouths with seldom-experienced pleasures. Not to mention the firm, white asparagus, thick and succulent. The guests should be pleased with this feast for their palate and for their eyes. Simon was pleased. *À chacun son gout*!

To honour the birthday boy, Mic let Simon sit as *capotavola*, and Mic took Simon's place at the opposite end of the table. The servants were struck by confusion when they entered the dining room with their plates and pots and saw this strange arrangement.

Who was *capotavola* now, *il Commendatore* or *il Signorino*? So where should they begin to serve? Before they could infuriate, or even worse, humiliate *il Signorino*, Mic made a discreet gesture that they should serve *il Signorino* first.

For the main course, Simon delighted his guests with *Coeur de Filet Boeuf d'Avignon avec d'Asperges Blanches et Sauce Cognac* and *Pommes de Terre Hasselback*, the beef so tender it was like cutting with the knife into soft butter. Mic insisted on serving homemade wine from Bacìo. Simon would have chosen something more exclusive. It's exclusive, in a sense, if you can serve your own homemade wine, but he would have preferred a more celebrated label. Sometimes there were irritating limits imposed on one's freedom to choose, Simon concluded with a deep sigh and was immensely fatigued.

For dessert there were *Fraises Sauvage avec Crème Naturelle*, which Simon thought would be proper for a son of the Arctic Circle to serve to his guests. The wild strawberries were transported by express-air from southern Scandinavia. Wild strawberries were frightfully expensive since they could not be cultivated and grew only in a few spots under certain trees and with a unique soil and a special relation to the sun and the wind, etc. Exclusive and highly enjoyed preferably on a small plate with fresh cold cream.

The mild but exquisite taste of wild strawberries made you feel as if you were lying among wildflowers on a summer meadow in southern Scandinavia under the light-green leaves of young weeping birches. And small birds were singing their appetising love-songs in the surrounding shrubberies.

When the wild strawberries had been enjoyed to everybody's expressed delight, *espresso doppio* with *cognac* or *liqueur* was

served in the library. Now was the time for the dear boy's birthday presents.

Simon stood up. "This little box is from Mary, my own sweetheart, who sends the warmest greetings to every one of you. She
regrets she could not enjoy your illustrious company today for
family reasons. She sends a kiss to each and every one of you,
which I know you will all appreciate." He unwrapped Mary's little
parcel and opened the box.

"Oh, look, isn't this sweet?" He held up a round golden plate
dangling on a thin gold necklace. "Gold, it's gold. I just love gold."

"Did I see an engraving?" Jeff asked.

"Yes. How sweet of her. She loves me so much, look at this."

"What does it say? Read it."

"It's so simple, but on the spot. It simply says Léon. Isn't this
lovely of her?"

"Why Léon? Why not Simon? Or Lennart?"

"We were two with the same name at the drama school, so I
asked to be called Léon, and that is how Mary knows me."

"I see. Different names for different apparitions. Practical.
Maybe confusing for those around you?"

"Nah. No problem, I'm sure."

Simon put Mary's token around his neck. He unbuttoned his
shirt and loosened his Brioni tie so that everybody could see the
little medallion during the rest of the evening.

When they had finished listening to Callas singing "Suicidio"
by Ponchielli at Simon's request, Jeff stood up and turned off the
record player.

"Commander Sandford, dear Mic," Jeff began. "My vision
from the monastery church on Easter Saturday, our dear birthday

boy Simon." He made a pause. "And dear friends. On this very special day when our beautiful, intelligent, kind, and wise friend, the lovely Simon, is celebrating his twenty-first birthday in our company, let me remind you of the little story we all know so well. Many times I've told you about Simon's 'little nightly adventure' in the goat cave."

"Oh, please Jeff, not again," Simon said. "Everybody here knows everything."

"No, they don't. But the unknown shall be revealed today. There's still one little secret I've kept for myself. As you all know, when I saw that huge hedonic hickey on Simon's face, I was so excited. I went into my room, locked the door, pulled down my pants, and released a load that shot diagonally across the floor from one corner to the opposite. I could swear the batch landed at least three, maybe even four yards, from where I stood."

"For Christ's sake!" Justin exclaimed. "Are we going to hear this again? Your great interest in your own ejaculations is not shared, Jeffrey. I'm so sorry to have to inform you of this very straight fact."

"You think you know, but you don't. Because I have told nobody the great and magnificent end of this story. A few of us have even seen the proper cave: Simon of course, and I myself, but also others, with whom I have made an historic excursion to show the scene of this special event. The goat cave and Simon together have a reputation, albeit limited to a close group of dear friends. But first I will hand over this commemorative birthday present to our own Simon, my dear little thing."

Jeff picked up a parcel from behind the sofa and handed it over to Simon, who got up and unwrapped the flat, thin and rectangular parcel. It contained a gouache painting of a big peaked rock with a little cave. In front of the cave was a pair of black sunglasses, painted with a felt pen.

It turned out to be an old gouache painted on Ischia about fifteen years earlier. The cave was in the lava formation typical of Ischia, and he had named the painting *Spiaggia di Maronti* and signed it "Jeffrey Smart 44." There seemed to have been some underlying text he had erased. In front of the cave he had drawn a pair of dark sunglasses with a marker pen and written in the left corner of the painting *For Lennart 21 April 1965.*

In 1944 there had been full war in this area between German and fascist Italian troops on one side and Allied troops on the other. Jeff moved here five years later, and that is when he painted this gouache. He added his signature and the sunglasses in 1965, changing the year from 1949 to 1944, when Simon was born.

"Later on that infamous day," Jeff continued, "I secretly followed you when you went searching for your lost sunglasses. After you found them, I hurried up the little hill. There I was confronted—and I must use this sharp word—with that sordid place full of fresh and old, stale dung. There you had been so brutally used for the sexual pleasure of two young, strong, and sweaty peasant boys who filled your arse with their warm and sticky spunk."

"Please, Jeff." Simon waved his hands. "In polite society we don't use those words."

"Hah, you're so funny. But let me go on. That cave served for keeping goats and was covered in their raw and filthy shit—pardon me, dear. To witness this scene was the pinnacle of this whole adventure—the rawness, misery and poverty oozing out of the place where these brutes savoured our little Simon boy and raped him so violently made a profound impression. I hurried home, locked the door, and tossed off again. I can assure you all, this time I shot at least one whole yard further than in the morning."

Jeff lifted the gouache. "As I have shared this 'adventure' with you, in a certain sense, I wanted to commemorate our mutual pleasure in an artistic form and elevate the lowest squalor to the highest aesthetic level. Congratulation, birthday boy!"

Everybody laughed but Simon, who was not amused. A simple gouache was a bit cheap. Jeff should have given him at least an oil instead of an old painting from fucking ancient times. And the shape of the cave was wrong.

They stared at him. What did they want? That he should thank them for their gifts? He wasn't up for speeches. He sat down and grabbed a glass and gulped all its contents at once; too late he found he had drunk a whole glass of a cognac he could not tolerate. His head whizzed. He tried to stand, but that was not a good idea, so he fell back into the sofa and began to sob.

"What's the matter?" Mic said. "Take it easy, boy."

Simon's cries of anguish turned to choking. He waved his arms in terror, fighting to catch his breath. Mic ran out of the room and returned with a bottle of pills.

"Give me a glass of water, quick, or some wine."

"Oh dear, what happened?" Jeff asked. "Was it something with his throat?"

"Open his mouth, Ethan, he has to swallow at once."

The first pill came up in a mouthful of vomit mixing with tears and snot on his chin and collar. Simon slid down to the floor waving his arms and fighting to catch his breath.

"Get his clothes off!" Mic shouted. "The shirt, his tie. But quick. Get me the pills, the bottle there." He pressed two heavy tranquillisers down Simon's throat and clamped his mouth shut. Simon coughed but swallowed the pills.

"They work quickly," Mic said. "Help me get him to his bedroom."

Simon half-stumbled on weak legs, carried by Mic, Jeff and Ethan. Before they reached his bedroom he was off.

"He's asleep in his bed," Mic said when he returned. "So typical that evenings beginning with glamour ends in tears and outbursts. Why always me?"

"He's so emotional," Jeff said. "He often cries when he's had a lot to drink, poor little thing. We listened to his histrionic lamentations on the island many, many times."

"I think I'll leave now," Justin said. "It's been very nice, so thank you, Mic, for your kind invitation."

When Simon woke up in the late afternoon the next day, his bed was messy and stinking. He had urinated, and God forbid, also defecated. He needed help from someone. The sheets had to be saved, and what about the mattress? A mattress again. How had his life come to this?

He took a quick shower and went to the kitchen to talk to the head servant about his misfortune. He was not there, only the cook preparing dinner. There would be three guests in a few hours. Simon had to get rid of the piss and the shit before then and disinfect the room. The stench was beginning to spread.

"*Quando arriva Ricardo, voglio parlargli súbito,*"[22] Simon said to the cook.

---

22 When Ricardo arrives, I want to talk to him right away.

"Si, Signorino, glielo dirò non appena sarà tornato."[23]

The embarrassment of having to ask Ricardo to take care of the mess, Simon couldn't think of it. Gosh, he felt ashamed, what happened? He remembered nothing.

He took a walk up behind the Quirinal Palace and passed the Forum and strolled down Imperiali to the Colosseum. Only tourists there in the afternoon. The flesh market wouldn't open until the sun had set. He ambled home along the Circus Maximus. Not a single guy there to rest his eyes on.

When he came home there was a spotless bed in his room. Ricardo had even folded the sheets and quilt in the usual way. Hopefully Ricardo wouldn't tell Mic what happened.

Mic wasn't home yet. The guests were due in less than an hour. Simon sat down and stared at Jeff's gouache resting against the wall. He decided to keep the painting, despite his dislike of it. A gouache by Jeffrey Smart could come in handy on a rainy day. Not that it would compensate for the suffering his arse had been forced to tolerate. And the rest of him as well, for that matter. It was time for life to start paying him back with interest.

---

23 Yes, Little Master, I will tell him as soon as he returns.

VI
Arrivederci, Roma

I'm Sitting Here
Writing a Letter to My Sister

Two weeks later on a Sunday afternoon, Simon planned to go for a walk and enjoy the fresh Tuscan air and be alone with only himself in nature while the others had their customary after-lunch nap.

No part of nature was as cultivated as Tuscany, but he could still hear the sounds of the countryside—birdsong, chickens cackling, and the occasional low of a cow. And the intoxicating scent of horse dung on the fields brought him back to the all-forgiving warmth of his childhood summers spent in the countryside.

When he came down to the great hall and passed the library, Mic was bent over his writing desk. He looked up, put down his Cartier pen, and waved to Simon.

"You're still up?" Simon took a reluctant step into the room. Mic patted his desk and waved for Simon to come closer.

"I want to tell you something," Mic said. "It's Sunday, and it's half past two in the afternoon." He paused. Simon shuffled his feet and waited. Why was Mic telling him what time it was? "I am sober, I didn't even have wine at lunch. And I'm sitting here writing a letter to my sister." He paused. Were there tears in Mic's eyes? "And I don't want to go to bed with you," Mic continued. "But this is not what I want to tell you."

He looked up at Simon, who kept his eyes on Mic's writing desk. "I want to tell you …" Simon wished for a cigarette but understood vaguely this was not the moment. "That I love you." He looked up at Simon and added, "my dearest boy."

A long silence descended over the exquisite library, so extensive that the ticking of their watches was heard.

"Oh, do you? Eh, I see, yes … well. What shall I say?" Simon tried not to look away from those tearful eyes staring at him. Mic looked ugly at that moment, with his big, ill-shaped nose with a jack in the middle, and that loose flesh hanging under his eyes, and those tears, cried for no one.

"You needn't say anything, my boy. I only hope you're well, and everything is fine with you. That's all."

"I planned to go for a walk …"

"Do that, my boy. Do that and feel well and be happy. I wish you all the best in the world. All the very best life can offer you."

"See you later." Simon got up from the desk on shaky legs. If Mic expected an embrace Simon did not deliver. He did not want to, and he couldn't. He wasn't sure what Mic had said was honest, and he had no sympathy for the man, anyway. The simple truth was that Mic disgusted him. So what the fuck was he doing here? On his way out, he stumbled on the threshold.

Mic dried his eyes and polished the condensation off his glasses. He waited for a while, then took up his pen. He reread the last lines he had written in the letter to his sister. He put back the pen in its casing, went upstairs and lay down on his bed. He did not fall asleep, but stayed immobile on his bed for more than an hour.

Later in the afternoon, at six o'clock sharp, Mic and his weekend guests had drinks out by the swimming pool. Simon was leaning on the balustrade with a bitter Campari on the rocks, his favourite for this time of day. He was looking at the olives and the grapevines and feeling bored when Mic came up to him.

"What are your plans when your two months as a librarian have passed? I find it perfectly suitable if you decide to stay. You can live here or in Rome as it would please you."

"As I've told you before, Mic, I'll go back home and live with Mary. She's the most important person in my life, and I want to be with her. I'm grateful for your kind offer, but it's nothing I even need to consider."

"So why did you come to Italy to live with me in the first place?"

"You invited me, I suppose, with our mutual friend Jeffrey Smart as the benevolent middleman. I never heard a word from you before I came here, but I trust Jeff was writing to me on your behalf?"

"It never occurred to you there could be a conflict of interest if you were living with a woman and intended to continue to live with her?"

"No. She is broad-minded. And so am I, I believe? Jeff was informed I lived with a girl. Mary informed him in person, and he told you, so you knew that as well. You still invited me."

"Broad-minded?" Mic said. "There are those who would call you inconsiderate. At your age, you ought to know better. It's a serious business to play with other people's feelings, don't you understand this?"

"I'm sorry, Mic. I didn't mean to hurt anyone. I didn't know anything like feelings would be involved in the work I accepted."

Mic wheezed and took up the inhaler with his asthma medication, which he always kept in the right pocket of his jacket. He shook his head, left Simon, and joined Jeff and his weekend guests.

Simon looked for Ethan and found him in the music room, immersed in some dreary Wagner opera. When absorbed by Wagner, Ethan lost contact with reality and Simon's attraction was small compared to that of Wotan or Isolde.

Simon poured himself a large gin and tonic and went upstairs and lay down on his bed, waiting for the time to pass so he would get food and then go to bed. He would not be available for Mic this night.

On the day Simon left Italy, Mic skipped work and walked around with the inhaler in his hand. He could hardly talk without getting an attack; best to leave him alone. Simon gave him a short hug and said nothing; no hard feelings toward the poor old BP president. Simon hoped Mic would enjoy his impending early retirement with all the time in the world to pursue his old dreams of regularly visiting Covent Garden in London and writing sonnets in the style of William Shakespeare.

Mic was standing in the open gateway with the inhaler in his mouth. The chauffeur carried Simon's suitcase to the Bentley. Then he drew the car slowly out of the little park outside the gate to the Palazzo Gangi. He continued down to Via del Teatro di Marcello and up to the Piazza Venezia, passing the small balcony where Benito Mussolini bellowed his fiery speeches that his father had adored listening to ten years before Simon was born, and then further out of Rome to the airport Leonardo da Vinci.

Now that Simon had been elevated to be Signorino, there was no Wagon Lits train back to the Arctic Circle. AnaRosa had bought him a first-class air-ticket that took him first to Geneva and then to Hamburg, where he had to change flight again to get home. He would not have chosen this route if he had ordered the ticket himself, but what the hell, the ticket was free, wasn't it?

While in the terminal in Geneva he sat face to face with Birgit Nilsson, who seemed lonely. She didn't look up; her entire attention was held by something she was reading. Rehearsing *Elektra*? Or *Turandot*? With Ulf he had seen her sing *Aida* at the Royal Opera House. People had stood up and applauded and shouted and stamped with their feet in the floor when she entered the stage. She was the kind of person you would meet when you could afford first class.

Mary, back on home soil, was waiting at the Arctic Circle airport with her three-year-old daughter and Simon's dazed mother. He spotted them up on the balcony in the arrivals building when he came down the stairs from the airplane. He was wearing his elegant dark-blue birthday suit with black stripes, the sight of which made his mother gasp. Around his neck he wore a small gold medal with his name on it. He had left a group of men and was now welcomed home by three women. He would have easily disposed with two of them.

In his suitcase he had the gouache painting by Jeffrey Smart. He showed it to nobody; they would not have understood. He kept the bloody birthday gift in a cupboard for many years.

Taut as a Bow, Her Body
Was About to Burst

Back home in their one-room flat by the Arctic Circle, the relationship between Simon and Mary showed signs of deterioration. Both had vital interests that conflicted with their relationship. She wanted to be with her daughters, who lived with their father in a large villa outside town. Simon lacked the stimulating presence of close male company.

Mary gave private lessons in Latin to wealthy female students. Simon wrote short stories for cheap pornographic magazines. With the aid of many bottles of wine, he invoked the muses of the literary art while the young women in the other corner of the room struggled to find the proper vocative to use when calling for a muse in Latin.

Jeff and Ethan planned to spend the summer on the island of Mallorca. Simon wrote and asked if he could come and live with them. Ethan answered in a note:

At the moment Jeff and I are on our way back to Barcelona after a fabulous week in Madrid, visiting the Prado. Mic was with us for a week and we all had a wonderful time. As we are leaving for Majorca, I feel I should answer your question about joining us. I feel we would all have wonderful times together. I feel, and Jeff especially feels, that we are going there mainly to work for those months and he feels that you may be a distracting influence, and as you know it is most important that Jeff has no distractions—es-

pecially at a time like this when we feel his paintings must be good and sell! I hope you don't feel we don't want you to come because we don't like you because you know that this isn't true. We are still friends and shall always be so. You are much more sensitive and easily hurt than one might imagine you to be, Simon, and I really mean it when I say I don't mean to hurt you or pass you off as just another acquaintance.

Simon bought cheap consolation bottles of wine from Estremadura. He asked Mary if she would like to go to Costa del Azahar in Spain, which was only a short boat ride from Mallorca, and she accepted.

During their summer holiday in Peñiscola Simon hankered for the Spanish boys they met on the beach, especially for luscious Paco with the behind of a pagan divinity and dark, dreamy eyes. But Paco lusted for Mary, and she had picked up a stinking vaginal infection that hampered central aspects of her life with Simon.

When they returned to the Arctic Circle in the autumn, they agreed that Simon should spend more time abroad and return home when he had "sown his wild oats sufficiently," as Mary put it. When Simon was away, she could live with her daughters and write her book.

Simon had two standing invitations from men he met during the last years. One was from Count Francesco Guicciardini. He lived in his family home, Palazzo Guicciardini on Via Guicciardini between Ponte Vecchio and the Pitti Palace in Florence. A friend of Mic whom Simon had met in Mic's company. A letter of invitation from the count offered Simon to spend the summer with him in his palatial retreat in Tuscany.

The writer and surgeon Albert Danly in Dublin, whom Simon

had met on the Greek island with his wife, provided the other invitation. Dr Danly sent long letters to Simon with extensive excerpts from a novel he was writing. He was most anxious that Simon should come and live with him and his wife in Dublin whenever this suited Simon and would gladly support him with both food and lodging for as long as Simon wanted.

Count Francesco's expectations for Simon were more advanced than anything Simon was able to deliver so he left Italy and tried his luck in Dublin. In theory, wife and husband agreed on how to live together. In practice, Simon's presence taxed the middle-aged couple's fragile cohabitation. Living with their young guest became unsustainable when Simon began to fancy their youngest son, the seventeen-year-old and slightly mentally disabled Cormack, and repeatedly tried to seduce the boy, eventually with a degree of success.

Simon had no intension of satisfying what turned out to be the most extraordinary sexual demands by the meek surgeon. Life in the Irish medical household became unbearable. Should he return to Mary and make the best of his relationship with her, or if not, where else should he live?

His funds were emptied. Mary sent him money for an expensive plane ticket. She met him at the airport on a cold and rainy November evening. Rain covered the inky asphalt and glittered as in a film noir. People crouched like hunchbacks under black umbrellas as they trudged along the dark buildings. The torrential rain pattered on their taxi's roof and slammed against the windows.

"Where are we going?" Simon asked, noticing they were not headed toward their home in the town's centre.

"After a lot of thinking and agony, I have concluded you and

232

I, my Piglet, should live apart for some more time. I live with the girls now. I need them so much and they need their mummy. We've been away from each other for far too long."

"Sure, I'm sure. Very important, no doubt. I fully recognise this. But don't forget there's someone else who needs you too."

"I know, Piggy love, I know."

"So where am I being deported, eh?"

"Take it easy, sweetheart, I have arranged something good for you."

He was sure nothing good awaited. He looked at her, crouched in the corner of the back seat, wearing a black Persian fur coat, popular among menopausal women. How miserable. A slightly faded, ageing woman was not what he wanted in his life. He'd had enough of that, thank you.

"Marianne has agreed to let you live with her for a while," Mary said. "Until we find a good solution for everybody." Marianne was Mary's divorced mother, a former restaurant director now working as an assistant in a suburban bookshop. Once she had been married to Mary's father, a successful building constructor and a bully with a fierce temperament. She lived alone in a large four-room apartment on the seventh floor in a newly constructed sterile suburb. The evenings she spent alone in front of the TV sipping a glass of either dry Jerez or sweet Oporto, depending on her mood.

Simon's heart grew cold. He had no positive feelings for the woman in the black Persian fur coat. He didn't need to look at her to find her vulgar and inconsiderate. She was no longer his Pussy-Puss. This woman, sitting there beside him in the car, he had known since early childhood. She had imprisoned his mind and scared the shit out of him when he was an anxiety-ridden child. She was the evil mother of sweet little lovely Snow White. Now he saw her long, sharp claws and her crooked nose. Her true nature finally appeared to him, crouched and humiliated in this bloody, fucking taxi.

When they made love in her mother's spare room later that night, his anger and loathing, mixed with a pinch of despair, gave him a hard-on of solid Arctic steel. Simon fucked her silly as if wearing a pneumatic drill between his legs. She got a first orgasm and screamed as if hit and mistreated. He slapped her tits. And she began to weep. She wept, she yelled, she cried his name. Ah he, what could he do? The more she yelled the harder and more mercilessly he drilled into her flesh, desperate and loathing. She had one orgasm after the other and with every new ecstatic height her screeching grew even ghastlier and more uninhibited. The atmosphere was more of a slaughterhouse for huge sows than of a small suburban bedroom in a flat on the seventh floor of a calm and sober suburban building in a typical Arctic middle middle-class neighbourhood.

Simon filled her up with three weeks of warm spunk. When the load shot out from his hard member inside her she was on the verge of fainting, maybe she did. Her body was taut as a bow about to burst.

Simon gave her a final kiss.

He got up and went to the loo to rid himself of piss, sweat, spunk, spit, and shit.

His dick was soaked in dark red blood; she may just have gotten her period.

Her old mother, unable to fall asleep in the adjoining bedroom,

234

received an illuminating glimpse of the nature of her daughter's relationship. If she hadn't understood her daughter's affection for this young man before, she now had something to reflect upon.

Simon stayed with Mary's mother. Mary soon came to stay there a night or two with her daughters; they shared the bed and were soon back to the life they had created for each other. No intimacy or tenderness left, only a wild and insatiable urge to rub their genitals against each other for an occasional sexual relief, whatever that was worth.

On one afternoon they were sitting on wooden chairs about two yards apart from each other and looking out the window on the seventh floor at an overcast and wintry sky.

"Do you love me?" she asked.

He was silent; he needed to be honest without causing an end to their relationship. But he could not allow himself to be silent for too long.

"I need you," he said.

She got up from her chair. For a while, she stood looking down at him.

"I won't return this afternoon." She was tranquil and composed and spoke slowly. "Perhaps it would be better if you found a more permanent place to live in. Your stay here was never meant to be more than a temporary solution. I'm sure you understand. Take care of yourself." She left the room and went out. He stood up and drew the curtains.

In the promising and lovely warmth of spring, the next month saw a more unmistakable end to their relationship. Mary returned to Italy and embarked on a second marriage. The day before she wed, she telephoned Simon's mother to tell her she would love nobody as much as she had loved her son.

Simon was now homeless, loveless, and jobless; he didn't know what to do or where to stay. His life passed by with little events here and there and people who came and left and nothing turned into anything. At present, finding a place to live where food was cheap was more urgent than thinking about a possible career. He sang with Marlene: *"Ich bin von Kopf bis Fuß auf Liebe eingestellt, denn das ist meine Welt, und sonst gar nichts."*[24]

There was something solid about Jeff. Would he still … where else could he go?

He decided to return to Rome. Perhaps one or two of his Roman acquaintances would have mercy for his soul or raw lust for his body. And let him stay with them until living together inevitably became unbearable or not to their liking. The same process as so many times.

---

24 From head to toe I'm set for love, and that's my world,
   and nothing otherwise.

Adjusted to a Small Enclosure

"I know, I know." Jeff shook his head. "I feel so sorry for you, but this was inevitable even if I'm sure Mary had a lot to offer. But you were never a woman's man. Nature presents us with inevitable circumstances that cannot be fought against. We can do nothing but surrender."

"Surrender? You? I thought being solid as a rock meant you would never surrender to your nature?"

"Ha, ha, you're still so funny, Simon. Of course I have to surrender, like every sensible person. But never without stating my terms when I make the necessary concessions. There's a lot for you to learn about how to master your inclinations. But let's set aside the trivial issues of love. I have something wonderful and special to show you. I don't believe in miracles but finding this gem of a home was indeed a wonder. It's still difficult for me to believe we actually live here. Above all, I will let you enjoy our shining jewel, our terrace. Come. We'll have a drink up there."

The little apartment Jeff and Ethan had found was on Via dei Riari in Trastevere, halfway between St. Peter's and the Basilica di Santa Maria. From the roof of the three-story building was a view of the Orto Botanico behind the Palazzo Corsini.

After abdicating her throne and converting to Catholicism, Queen Kristina of Sweden had lived in the Corsini Palace for twenty-five years and died there in 1689. For Jeff, the Queen's former presence in the vicinity was a significant feature of his new home as the movie where Greta Garbo played the queen was always fresh in his mind. Jeff felt a special affinity with these two icons, one of Hollywood in the 1930s, the other of papal Rome at the height of the Baroque period. If the Pope was the Emperor of the Vatican state, Kristina was the Empress of the Catholic Church but regarded as an apostate by the Protestant world. She had abandoned her poor Lutheran kingdom by the Arctic Circle after her father, King Gustavus II Adolphus, died on the battlefield in Germany fighting for the Lutheran faith against the troops of the Catholic Holy Roman Empire.

Living close to Queen Kristina's famous home put Jeff into the centre of both history and the world, since Rome was still the centre of the superior part of Western civilisation in an otherwise bleak world. Papal Rome, Greta Garbo, Jeffrey Smart, the Roman Empire and Queen Kristina. Great and fabulous.

"The most beautiful flat in Rome," Jeff said.

"Yes, it's nice," Simon agreed.

"Nice? No, it's not nice, it's extraordinary, and so are its surroundings. This street is one of the most fantastic in Rome. It's original, it's well kept, and it's not expensive to live here. It's a wonder in its own right."

They climbed a narrow, steep, and uncomfortable flight of stairs that ascended outside of their apartment and so were shared with the other tenants of the building. In the corner of the roof four large pots with bushy plants delineated the space that Jeff had claimed as his personal terrace. A cast-iron table was surrounded by a set of six stackable metal chairs. A little birdcage sat on a small end table.

"Isn't this a wonderful terrace?" Jeff exclaimed. "Look here, behind the wall on the other side of the street you see the Corsini Garden with its tropical birds and unique trees. I could never in my wildest fantasies imagined I would live in this, the most beautiful and illustrious town in the whole world. And with the most gorgeous lover. Sometimes life appears so generous, even to an old sinner like me. And have you seen the floor?"

"Marble, I suppose?"

Jeff burst out laughing. "No, no! You're joking. They don't put marble on the floor of a household terrace. I think you're joking with me, Simon. No, these are original Italian tiles, handmade, no less. No factories. The Italians make art out of everything they touch, so every single tile here is unique. Can you imagine?"

"I'm not a tile expert, Jeff. But when I'm drunk and don't manage to get all into the porcelain throne, I piss on tiles like this."

"Ha, ha, you're so funny. But I talk too much. You have to tell me what you think."

"It's nice. It's very nice."

"No, Simon, you can better. Let me hear what you honestly think. Don't tease me."

"Very nice pots, these pots. But I'm no gardener, so I can't compare with anything."

"If you don't know about tiles, you know about Queen Kristina, anyway. And she lived here as you probably know."

"On this terrace?"

"Oh, you're so funny, Simon, but please, don't joke with me."

"Are you sure it wasn't Greta Garbo?" Simon did his best not to laugh. "At times, you seem to get them mixed up. Greta Garbo was never a Swedish queen, maybe you didn't know?"

"The truth is," Jeff said, "I've known only one Swedish queen, and it wasn't Greta Garbo."

"Yeah, sure. Very funny."

Ethan emerged from the tiny door. It was six o'clock sharp and today's work had finished. Jeff poured him a drink.

"Quitty, quitty, how do you feel today, my little sweetheart?" Ethan talked to the bird in the small birdcage. "Quitty, quitty." The bird was not the kind you normally saw in a small cage. It turned out to be a crow. "I found this poor little thing in the gutter and took it home," he explained. "The poor creature seemed to have been rather brutally wounded, you know. After a couple of days in my care the poor little thing seemed to be all right. Now the darling has adjusted to this little enclosure and to stay here with us. This sweet little crow has become a good companion. There's a real affinity between us."

Ethan's long silence begged for a reaction.

"I see," Simon managed to say.

"Don't you fancy birds, Simon?"

"I don't dislike them—why should I? I love the starling's song in spring and small birds like blue tits and wagtails. At least when they're free. I never like to see a wild animal encaged and not able to fly."

"I fear you take your freedom too seriously, Simon dear," Jeff said. "At times one must adjust oneself to what is possible and give up one's ambitions to fly. If you're too fearful to commit yourself to anybody or anything you may end up being all alone in a hostile cage. I am too fond of you to want you to pursue such a route."

"Thank you, Jeffrey. Your words—and even more, the thoughts

behind them—have touched my heart. I'm sure you're right when you imply that truth and freedom are but constructs to reflect upon like time eternal and space without a limit. So welcome me to the beloved brotherhood of human bondage and of the lies that comfort our poor minds."

"What ghastly gibberish, Simon. Calm down," Jeff said. "Have one more gin and be a normal person with me and Ethan, your old bed-buddies."

After a tense silence they resumed their normal chat. Jeff gossiped about people Simon knew or had never met. Jeff referred to this type of chat as 'latest news,' and was now his favourite topic of conversation.

Ethan invited Simon to an outing in Trastevere, to show him what life was like in their new neighbourhood. He regarded an outing as a practical and concrete way to show his feelings of affinity for Simon.

The first station on their outing was a large indoor urinal. It was made of the same white Italian marble as the copy of Michelangelo's David in Florence's Piazza della Signoria.

"What're we doing here?" Simon asked.

"I usually go to this place when I go out. I like it here. What d'you think?"

"It stinks of piss and disinfectant. And these men are old, over thirty."

"When I see these men urinating, I feel a great affinity with people. Can you understand this?"

"Affinity? I may get horny watching a young straight bloke pissing, is that affinity?"

"Not really. I don't think so. We can go to another place, somewhere outdoors where it doesn't stink, if this disturbs you. But I kind of like this fragrance, so basic, so true, so realistically human, don't you think? There's some pure realism here."

"Oh, shit. Do you need so many words to excuse whatever you like here? Of course it's realistic, what else could it be? You like it, and that's perfectly all right and enough, as I see it. No need to ideologise or give it an abstract perfume. Sorry I'm being so critical."

"That's okay. If you were, I didn't notice."

"Fine. But the blokes here are old, and that puts me off. Poor Ethan, you like them old, I guess, or you wouldn't live with ancient Mr Smart, would you?"

They crossed the Ponte Mazzini over the Tiber and walked along the Lungotevere to a round outdoor municipality toilet. Two pieces of bent sheet metal forming a circle comprised the commode. One could stand half-hidden in relative seclusion carrying out one's errand, shielded by the rusty metal from one's knees up to one's shoulders. The space was suitable for two if they were there only to take a leak. Three or four could squeeze together if they were not too fastidious about their privacy.

Male Roman citizens were buzzing like bees around a rosehip bush. If there was enough liking between at least two, they could cuddle up in the narrow space and touch or look at the private parts of the others. The men outside the urinal could also have a sneak peek at what was going on inside. If they were lucky and brazened enough to stand close and peek over the rusty metal sheet, they could get a glimpse of various juicy activities.

Two fathers dressed in their clergy uniforms fluttered around like bats, not together but each on his own mission. Ethan was courted by one participant, after all he was considerable younger than the others and attracted a special clientele, the same as warm cow dung attracted huge buzzing flies carrying around bacteria.

Simon needed to pee, but this place was too sleazy. Closer to the river there was a shrub that offered him some privacy while he could look down on the Tiber. *Tiberis, Flumen Tiberis*. Now he was living there, in Trastevere, *Transtiberim!*[25] In Rome you were part of history. SPQR was stamped on the rusty sheet metal making up the urinal. SENATVS POPVLVSQVE ROMANVS, the Senate and the People of Rome. So great. Imposing. The oldest badge in the world, the same as over two thousand years ago.

Simon shook it off, returned to the urinal, and waited for Ethan to come back from his recent visit to the pastures of plenty. When he appeared, he looked the same as before, disengaged. No smile, no indication he had experienced anything uplifting.

When they returned to Via dei Riari, Jeff told Simon about his birthday gift to Ethan. One of those typical Jeffrey Smart "stories" that formed part of his renowned talent for entertaining, which some of his friends appreciated while others abhorred them in deep silence.

Jeff had arranged for two elderly gentlemen to be at the flashy indoor urinal. He invited Ethan to stand by the piss trough with one old man on each side of him. By grabbing their dicks, Ethan's old dream was fulfilled—to masturbate two old gentlemen, one on each side of him. Then hold their dicks when they pissed after ejaculating. Jeff didn't disclose his whereabouts while the scene unfolded, whether he was up close to watch the proceedings in

25 On the other side of the Tiber

detail or held himself at a more modest remove. The couple saw this birthday gift as a victory for realism and for love. Whatever love meant.

On one of the last times Simon visited Via dei Riari, Jeff asked him to come up with him to the terrace; he wanted to say something not meant for Ethan's ears.

"I want to thank you for having been so kind and considerate," he began.

"What?"

"For having said nothing to Ethan about my proposal to you."

"Proposal? What proposal is that?"

"No, Simon, you haven't forgotten! Don't make me believe that!"

"You mean what you talked about on the island, keeping me in Rome the way your father had kept a mistress in Melbourne? Hah ha."

"Any homosexual I have known in all my life would immediately have run to Ethan and told him I had preferred him before Ethan. He would also have given Ethan all the details of what I offered you while Ethan was constantly writing me love letters and preparing to come to Europe to live with me. If you had done this you could have changed Ethan's life and done a lot of harm to his and my relationship, but you didn't."

"But why would I have done that? I don't understand."

"And so more remarkable, considering the close relationship you and Ethan had when you were living with Mic. Even in bed with him you didn't say anything."

"I never thought about it. Why should I have told him? I don't understand."

"You see," Jeff said, "it's because you are basically a kind person. You are so kind you don't even have to decide not to do harm because doing harm never occurs to you. What an extraordinary person you are, Simon. As I have always known. But I bet you will never receive any benefit from being an angel. The world will always destroy sweet and kind people like you. They cannot stand plain simple human kindness and harmlessness; they have to take advantage or destroy. One way or other, subtly or brutally, doesn't matter. Evolution has always and will always continue to favour predators. The meek will survive only as long as they serve as food or slaves. No text in any manifesto or lofty verbosity from all the destructive idiots who cherish to march singing to the gallows can ever change this. Nature will win in the long run."

"Gosh, you're getting serious, Jeff! Give me another gin. One ice cube and only a tiny drop of tonic, I'm starving!"

With the cordial help from his dear friend Jeffrey Smart, Simon had a roof over his head every night he lived in Rome. Short of means, he could no longer pay for a hotel room, and for the rest of his stay in Rome he had to rely on the kindness of strangers. Kindest of all was Jeff.

First he found Simon a former lover, Bryan Westwood, an Aussie who had recently arrived in Rome, hoping to become a prosperous portrait painter in the centre of the Catholic world. This man turned out to have severe problems with his sexuality, so he asked Simon to move out after fewer than ten days and nights.

Two dreadful English queens, Jeff's friends, living in a large apartment by Santa Maria Maggiore, let him a room. After a night of entertaining a young, hairy and not quite clean Sicilian boy, they were confronted by the maidservant when she brought Simon his breakfast in the morning. Later that day the dreadful English queens asked Simon to move out.

Jeff was also a good friend of an Australian conductor visiting Rome for a special performance at the Accademia Nazionale di Santa Cecilia. He owned a large flat in Rome and had a room free to let. Jeff accompanied Simon, who was chain-smoking with an extra bad hangover. They were greeted by the conductor's PA, a young man who caught Simon's interest. The PA noticed Simon's interest and brought him an ashtray after his cigarette dropped ashes on the hallway floor.

Tonight's symphony was howling out of loudspeakers in every corner of the flat, even in the hall. After a while the conductor appeared with the baton in his hand. He looked at Simon from head to toe and smiled.

"Jeffrey, dear, I understand how urgent this may be for you. However, I am awfully sorry, but just now life is very stressful, and I need calm and peace at home. So I have decided not to let strange people live in my home for the time being. Maybe later. I am so sorry."

"Not at all, not at all," Jeff said. "I understand perfectly well. Best of luck with the concert tonight. I'm sure every Australian in Italy regards it as a great honour to have an Australian in Rome to lead an Italian symphony orchestra. Who would have thought this possible only ten years ago?"

But Jeff did not give up. He helped Simon to get a cheap room in the home of his old friend Eleonora Arrighi. After a week Mrs Arrighi asked Simon to move out. Only God and Mrs Arrighi knew why.

Sounds of Happiness by Stazione Termini

When the lodging situation looked miserable, Simon's dear old Auntie opened his heart and took Simon in. Justin was living alone in a small apartment just off the Stazione Termini near Via Principe Amedeo. Jeff called this area, similar to any nineteen-century block of flats in any major European city centre, "the only ugly part of Rome." To Jeff, choosing to live in the ugliest part of Rome was part and parcel of Justin's deplorable Irish nature.

When Simon arrived in Justin's home with his typewriter and a heavy suitcase, they gave each other a short Anglo-Saxon embrace. They smiled at one another and they nodded.

"I was so glad when they first invited me," Simon said, "but staying there has become an ordeal. They're so sweet and give me pasta to fill my empty stomach with, but they have become strange. Jeff acts as if his ordinary, simple flat were a palace. This ludicrous mismatch makes me question Jeff's evaluation and description of things in his life, and, *nota bene*, not only his evaluation of *things*?"

"Isn't Jeffrey's flowery verbosity a sign of ordinary happiness to be sharing a home?" Justin asked. "A normal exaggeration by people who love each other and love the home they found for each other?"

"If so, why the need to persuade all and sundry to join the choir? You're not left in peace to feel comfortable there. You're constantly being alerted to one or other mundane little detail you failed to give praise to. So you must take the floor and again bear witness how extraordinarily wonderful is also this little detail."

"Perfect, Simon," Justin said, lighting a cigarette. "Like on a new-born kitten, your eyes have begun to open. May take time before you see the world properly."

"Yes, he babbles about all the fabulous and grand things around him in his life. When you get to know Jeff's 'fabulous visions' they're just ordinary. When I realised this, my own place as a vision on Mr Smart's inflated life painting was suddenly challenged. His fantastic celestial vision from the monastery church on our Greek island, discovered on Christianity's holiest day of the year, became transformed into something ordinary. What was I now? And what had I been on the island that year? I shivered and dwindled. Please, Justin, I need more gin, having suddenly become no more than a withered vision. Thank you. I always found it worthwhile for others to pay for their clear sight—long live the truth! I'm less enthusiastic to pay the price for my own unpleasant personal insight."

"Poor child. Have one of my strong Italian cigarettes, I love them, they're even better than the Turkish ones, if you remember? You'll recover. Time is a beautiful healer, not always and not for everybody, but most of the time for most of us. Believe me, I know."

Brian Dunlop was an almost daily visitor in Justin's home. He and Justin were still close friends, but never again as close as Justin had once wanted. There were also regular visits by a young Roman. Maurizio was a boy of fifteen who was at first employed as a model for Justin's drawing practices, the same as Georgios on the island. Jeff had recommended him, after recommendations by Mic, who knew him from a clandestine locality in Rome with young boys that Mic regularly frequented. As a matchmaker, Jeff would not have a young boy come and pose for Justin if he didn't find it plausible that the boy would become Justin's "close little friend."

Professionally familiar with men fond of young boys, Maurizio recognised at once that Justin was such a man. The first time he posed he got a prominent erection within a minute after lying down on Justin's bed to be drawn in the nude. A long-lasting relationship between them began that morning, so close that Justin would later become the godfather of the boy's two daughters. They also made at least one visit together to the little cottage by the Aegean Sea on the now less isolated Greek island.

The young boy was upfront about how he lived and what he did and didn't like. Justin wasn't used to having sexual relationships with boys who courted girls at the same time. He simply assumed a person was born with a particular sexual orientation.

"I like him so much," Justin said. "He is so cute and nice and lovely to be with. But I'm puzzled, since he goes out with girls. Isn't this strange?"

"You ask *me* if it's strange? It's normal, proper nature."

"But he likes to be with me—how can he do that if he's straight?"

"Oh, Justin dear, things are not that uncomplicated. Straight or not are just simplified clichés made by simple people. Nobody 'is' anything, we do this or that more or less often with different commitments, and people perceive each other to act in a particular way and give it a name. The name 'straight' is just a construct."

"Is it? Then I am one of those unschooled people you talk about. But to be more specific, let me ask you a simple straight question, since I'm puzzled by what he says. Yesterday he told me he was going to the beach with his girlfriend, so he wouldn't be here until later today. Girlfriend! What do you think about that? Is that true? Or does he say this only to test me? Maybe to make me jealous, if you see what I mean? He's so sweet. I don't want to lose him."

"Why shouldn't it be true?"

"But he likes when we have sex, very much so. When he gets a visit from Farther Up, he is pleased and comes at once, scuisssssssh! He splashes all over, and it's not a little! And then he laughs and gets cuddly, he's so sweet."

"Ha, ha, but of course, why shouldn't he like it? To have his little butt well treated by a loving man. Who wouldn't love that?"

"What a strange place the world has developed into. In Australia straight boys didn't behave like this. But then he says *lasciami*[26] as soon as I touch him, when we walk around in the kitchen. *Lasciami!* But very cuddly in bed, he's so sweet."

Lasciami had become a favourite expression Justin repeated many times during the day—while sitting alone in front of the easel or cooking by the stove, and not without affection. *Lasciami!* Saying one of the few Italian words Justin knew summoned Maurizio's presence in Justin's heart and mind.

There was a knock on the door, and Justin came back with a sparkling Roman boy. Maurizio and Simon had met before, and they nodded to each other, both accepting the other's presence in Justin's home, no threat to either. It was soon mealtime and Justin

---

26 Leave me alone

and Maurizio went into the kitchen. Brian was expected to join them for dinner.

Simon was reading the daily news. Amorous voices and sweet chit-chats came from the kitchen. He knew they were lovers. From the sounds they could have been a father and a son. The murmuring caused distress in Simon's lonely heart. He had no reason to be jealous, but he was envious of both. The sound of love and happiness emerging from the kitchen was truly unmistaken.

A Friendly Chat About Jeffrey Smart

"When you left the island, Jeffrey and I stopped talking to each other. We may have lived together in silence the whole summer if you hadn't come to live with us. More peaceful but less lively, if you see what I mean." Justin paused and looked at Simon and lit another cigarette with the one he was smoking.

"Not for a second do I regret you came to live with us. But your presence changed Jeffrey's and my relationship. I don't blame you, not the least. Bloody hell, this is difficult to talk about."

They were silent. Simon smiled and chuckled. Justin fumbled with his cigarettes.

"Why do you think Jeffrey treated me so badly?" Justin asked.

"If you want, I can tell you what I think."

"Yes, please do that. But wait, I'll get a glass of wine." Justin returned with a bottle and two glasses.

Simon shook his head. "No. Not for me. I'll be serious. You ready?" Justin nodded, lit another cigarette, swallowed half a glass and sat up straight on his chair.

"Fear!" Simon began, "determines how Jeff deals with life and people. Not love or curiosity or anything else, but fear. First, he fears his life would be so bad he no longer wants to live."

"Oh Christ, not Jeffrey."

"Yes, Jeff once wilfully rejected to commit suicide after a period of depression. Then to keep the dark forces at bay he decided to 'force himself to enjoy life,' in his own words. Today he describes his life comprising only enjoyment, success, beauty, and appreciating friends. He never says a word about the unavoidable experiences forming part of a normal everyday life—sadness as well as happiness, lack as well as fulfilment, etcetera. For reasons we don't know Jeff fears he cannot handle adversity, so he blinds himself to difficult parts of life and lives in a world where everything is grand and beautifully coloured or despicable: our Greek island was a garbage dump, you are worthless being Irish. Thus, he leaves out from his perception large parts of life's grey realities.

"But more than anything, our dear friend Jeffrey Smart fears to commit himself and be close to someone. To keep the destructive forces of love at bay he has developed what he calls a 'security device, a mechanism of bells, red lights, buzzers and safety valves' with the purpose to warn him when he is confronted with a person who may threaten him with demands for a close and committed relationship.

"But with this device effective, Jeff would be empty and lonely. So to mitigate these unwanted effects Jeff's mind found him a coping strategy: to experience *vicariously*, through the experience of others

"For this strategy to work, Jeff needs people around him who risk the perils of love. People whose lifestyles strike him as exciting yet repulsive since they submit themselves to the risk of a life in chaos and disarray so typical of people 'sickly' obsessed by their love relationships, like you and Brian. Your love for Brian is important to him, which he is not aware of and would never admit. He experiences love 'vicariously' through your love for Brian.

"But he needs to confirm for himself how worthless such people are. So he belittles them, as he did Brian by calling him a glass of water or calling me a 'little thing' or to bully you for being Irish and God knows what.

"As for me, in the church on Easter Saturday his defence devices went into red alert. Did a god offer him love together with that boy? To cut his fear, Jeff decided to listen only to nature, and nature made him horny. A typical defence reaction Jeff has learned over the years. Dick, not heart. Less dangerous and less demanding. He never tried to make me his lover. Instead he gleaned vicarious pleasure by enjoying my relationships with other people. He needed me to be there, but at an emotionally secure distance—no commitment, no closeness, no love. Vicariously he experienced a destructive passion shown by the peasant boys who raped me in the cave; he has made abundantly clear what effect that experience had on him. Then he wanted me as a kept boy installed in an apartment in Rome, like a dildo in a drawer in his bedside table. With the flair worthy of a Rossini overture, he then handed me over to Mic as a human offering. Close but not too close.

"Jeff's friendship with Mic is characterized by a similar vicariousness. By spending every weekend with Mic at Bacìo, he vicariously experiences life as a wealthy person and the splendour of having a magnificent villa in Tuscany loaded with servants. Jeff doesn't need to be rich. Mic is rich for him. He doesn't need to love. You experience love for him. He didn't need the trouble of making me his lover. He let others fuck me in his place and made me the lover of his best friend. Perfect solutions to experience wealth, love, and sex without having to risk a devastating loss."

Justin refilled his glass of wine and had a good swig.

"Harsh, Simon. You don't suppose Mr Smart loves anybody?

Ethan? He may love that jerk one way or other?"

"Ethan serves the same purpose as a figure in a Jeffrey Smart painting, put there as a piece of shape and colour to make the composition look good. Young teenager Brian made you love and live, Ethan makes Jeff ejaculate and feel in control."

"You undress him. It's scary to watch Jeffrey naked. I can't say I like it."

"Ironically, Jeff's vapid and detached use of Ethan's arse as a device for Jeff to masturbate in receives social praise and is legal. Your loving involvement with Brian when he was a young teenager and now with the fifteen-year-old Maurizio is reproached and may even be illicit."

"Hm… don't say that…" Justin whined.

"Jeff has found an arena in life where he is the only creator, Jeff as a god and nature. Here he has total power over what to include or leave out, what to enhance and what to belittle. He uses the same strategies as in his life. Order is imposed by geometric rules keeping everything in control, no sudden disturbance may introduce something he has not reflected upon beforehand. The few people in his paintings are not living individuals but spots of proper shapes and colours. Chance and impulse have no impact on his brush strokes. This approach takes its toll. His strict coping strategies lead him to produce paintings of a world where you find no love, only a vast and well-organized emptiness. The imposing structure and the colourful beauty of Jeff's paintings underline and enhance their lack of life. He presents a refined but sterile hell, frightening to watch; solitude and emptiness, painted with a meticulous lack of pity and compassion. He projects his inner solitude and cramping control of anxiety and the lack of love in his life and in his heart."

"Oh, bleeding hell! What you say is terrible to listen to," Justin whispered as if careful that nobody should overhear. "Perhaps his painting is what he loves in life?"

"No, I don't think so. He may love the praise and the recognition he gets from the mighty men with money, whom he adores. And from the owners of galleries and editors of renowned art magazines? Should we call that love? They give the praise and recognitions that little boy Jeff didn't get from his stern daddy, didn't he? Mummy's little polite and obedient friend, not his daddy's plucky boy."

"Perhaps Jeffrey loves only his mum?" Justin suggested.

"The horror! The horror!"

"Simon, you talk as if we never leave our parents. As if our whole lives are repetitions of our childhood."

"Yes, that's how we automatically function. Our minds make their attempts to mend what was broken. I guess most people manage fairly well enough. Some of us don't. The shards are too many, too sharp, and they create new wounds."

"Poor Jeffrey! I never imagined I would feel sorry for him. You talk about him as if he were a scared little boy fighting for his life. I could have been better off without him, not been so bloody oppressed by this pompous bully, if you see what I mean?"

"It's hard to be alone, Justin. You know that. We need other people, and sometimes we must pay a ruthless price. When you hear shrieks of agony resounding in your skull from someone that you loved and left behind who walked astray in life, then you need at least the presence of another human to ease your pain even if he only offers chatter about nonsense."

"How can you say such things? How do you know? Whom

did you leave in life, whom did you love, my friend?"

"We need not suffer everything first hand. We learn to understand by listening when others laugh or scream or tell you their sufferings and joys in art and music and in texts and if a single person cries and tells you from his naked mind."

"But Jeffrey is always pompous, he never tells you anything but stories you can laugh at or how well he always manages where others fail."

"Jeff cares to be your friend in life," Simon said. "To be bullied is the price you must pay for being his friend. Nothing comes without a price to pay. He taught us this and he earns a certain merit, doesn't he?"

"Sure. But there's no bloody reason to be so nasty, and make me feel so bad about myself, is there?"

"I've just explained. For him, there are all the reasons in the world."

"How can you know so much, Simon, and understand all this about him?"

"Look at yourself beneath the surface and recognise how similar we are. By understanding ourselves we get the chance to understand the other one as well."

"Have you just told me you can understand the way that Jeffrey functions by looking at yourself?"

"Yes, I have."

"But if you're right we're all the same?"

"No. We're all different, very different, but all the same as well. The crux is to realise when we're different and when we're all the same. It's not an arbitrary matter."

"My God. What's happened to you since we met on a sunny

day on our beloved little island?" Justin swallowed his glass of wine and sucked on his Italian cigarette. He put down his glass and filled it back up. He searched for the pack of cigarettes in his pocket and put it in front of him. Sweat was pouring down his wrinkled and unshaven cheeks.

"This is far beyond me, Simon. I have a boy to love. Is that not good enough?"

"Oh yes, it's good all right. But many evil people will want to grab him from your good embrace and put you in a jail. Let's hope that this won't happen and let's imagine all's well that ends well."

Last Letter from Italy

Six years later, a letter reached Simon up at the Arctic Circle. It had been sent from Via dei Riari on 21 January 1971.

Dear Simon,

I feel that I am writing into outer-outer space. I wonder if this old address will find you? If so, please answer! This letter brings you very sad news, Mic had been very ill last year with asthma, and underwent a heavy treatment of cortisone. On Sunday the third of January his heart gave out, and he died. It seems hardly possible that someone with such vitality is no longer alive. Most unfortunately Ethan and I were out to Australia to paint a mural and spend Christmas with our families. We came home slowly—a week in India, a week in Persia. No one could contact us, and when we arrived poor Mic was already buried in the little chapel at Bacìo.

While we were in Sydney, we met Mr Bryan Westwood again; he asked us to his place for dinner! Unfortunately, I see him very differently these days, and cannot say I feel the old warm friendship again.

Ethan and I often mention how you said, just after you left his flat, that your "mind was poisoned." We both hope whatever he said has not curdled our friendship. We are often worried that we don't hear from you. So whatever he put in your mind about us, wash it out, and receive our assurances of our continuing affection, and our hopes to see you again.

We are all well if sad. Thank Heavens, Justin is well, still with the same Italian friend, Maurizio, I think you met him? My painting goes well, had a very successful London exhibition last year. Let us have your news—how you are, where you are, what you are doing.

Yours as ever, Jeffrey

VII
Via della Conciliazione Leads the Faithful to the Holy Father

On an Easter week tourist trip from the Arctic Circle, Simon visited Rome with two friends, a couple. The guy was a medical student who captained the local rugby team; his girlfriend was seventh months pregnant. Simon got drunk every evening, desperately in need for his mate who had no love to share with him.

Simon was in decline, with a long greasy hair unwashed for weeks and an overgrown beard. His dirty and stinking body bore witness of strong nicotine dependence and habitual intake of large quantities of cheap alcohol.

Exactly ten years had passed since he stood alone as a fresh and confused teenager in a small monastery church on top of a huge cliff on a Greek island and Jeffrey Smart saw him as a celestial vision.

This Easter afternoon in Rome, he was walking on a narrow street parallel to Via della Conciliazione, between Piazza San Pietro and the second-century Castel Sant'Angelo, where the Roman chief of police, Scarpia, imprisoned and executed the painter Cavaradossi in the opera *Tosca* by Puccini. When Tosca, the painter's beloved, learned about his death, she threw herself from the roof of the fortress and met her death on the hard stones below.

A light rain was pouring from a grey sky as Simon walked toward the fortress by the Tiber. On the same pavement, but heading in the opposite direction toward the Vatican, came a thin little man taking short, quick steps. Ten years earlier, Simon used to carry this fragile creature when he was drunk and vomited over Simon's chest. Now Justin was on his way to the heart of the Catholic world to listen to Il Papa deliver his Urbi et Orbi for the tens of thousands of faithful believers assembled outside St. Peter's.

Simon continued his walk along the pavement. Maybe Justin didn't recognise him, this flabby bearded chap with long greasy hair who approached him on the narrow sidewalk in the rain. Ten years of boozing, chain-smoking, and fornicating with strangers in the early morning hours had taken their toll. Nobody could see him as a vision. Justin, in a simple trench coat, bent his head to shield his wrinkled face from the pouring rain.

With a faint smile on his lips, Justin hastened straight ahead, and so did Simon, and in the drizzle, they passed by each other like any two strangers.

Postscript

All people still living as of 2019 were given fictional names.

Brian Dunlop: Born 1938; died 2009 at 71
Had a daughter
1980: won the Sulman Prize
1984: painted a portrait of Queen Elizabeth II
1990: Lynne, Strahan, *Brian Dunlop*,
Craftsman House, Sydney
2004: finalist for the Archibald Prize

Gosse Lane   Born 1890
Not available on Google; nothing known
about him
"Dear old Gosse" was not mentioned in
Jeffrey Smart's memoirs which contained an
Index with hundreds of names of friends and
an occasional lover.

Ethan   Born 1945
Parted with Jeffrey in the 1970s

Mary   Born 1942
Had several children
Lived a shattering life, mostly in the public eye
Published more than twenty books,
one translated to several languages

Simon	Born 1944
	Worked with scientific research and teaching
	1982: published his PhD thesis
	1999: retired as docent

Mic Sandford	Born 1916; died 1971 at 55
	1948: awarded United States' Medal of Freedom
	1968: appointed CBE by Queen Elizabeth II
	His name cannot be found on Google in connection with BP or British Petroleum Italiana

Simon
: Born 1944
Worked with scientific research and teaching
1982: published his PhD thesis
1999: retired as docent

Mic Sandford
: Born 1916; died 1971 at 55
1948: awarded United States' Medal of Freedom
1968: appointed CBE by Queen Elizabeth II
His name cannot be found on Google in connection with BP or British Petroleum Italiana

Justin O'Brien
: Born 1917; died 1996 at 79
His painting *The Raising of Lazarus* was bought by the Vatican
1997: France, Christine, *Justin O'Brien: Image and Icon*, Craftsman House, Sydney

Jeffrey Smart
: Born 1921; died 2013 at 91
Several books about his paintings have been published
1989: *Not Quite Straight*, Jeff's memoirs, dedicated to Justin O'Brian and Mic Sandford
2001: appointed officer of the Order of Australia
2011: received an honorary doctorate from the University of South Australia
2014: A building at the University of South Australia was named the "Jeffrey Smart Building"